Her fragile heart couldn't chance acceptance despite the sincerity—maybe even the truth—she saw in his eyes. She swallowed past the knot in her throat. "In Normandy, when we first met face-to-face, you said you'd stay out of my life if that's what I desired, isn't that right?" The words came out in a pitiful sort of whisper.

William dropped his hands and took a half-step back. He shook his head. "Don't do this, Katie. Please for the love of Heaven, don't do this to us."

His pain tore at her soul. Despite the agony, she couldn't give him what he wanted. She couldn't. "I need...I need you to...to go away. I can't. Please understand...and don't come back."

He dropped his gaze for a moment. His agony, his suffering, shot like a blazing arrow through her heart.

As he lifted his head and gazed into her eyes, she saw both acceptance and resignation mingled with his pain. "So be it."

Katie opened her mouth to take back her words. Somehow she must take away the anguish and the sorrow she inflicted.

But she was too late. Far too late. William had already disappeared.

I0607381

Love Letters from Heaven

by

Debbie Peterson

This is a work of fiction. Names, characters, places, and incidents are either the product of the author's imagination or are used fictitiously, and any resemblance to actual persons living or dead, business establishments, events, or locales, is entirely coincidental.

Love Letters from Heaven

COPYRIGHT © 2018 by Debbie Peterson

Cover Art by *Debbie Taylor*

The Wild Rose Press, Inc.
PO Box 708
Adams Basin, NY 14410-0708
Visit us at www.thewildrosepress.com

Publishing History
First Fantasy Rose Edition, 2018
Print ISBN 978-1-5092-1888-2
Digital ISBN 978-1-5092-1889-9

Published in the United States of America

Dedication

For Phyllis.
Thank you for the incredible adventure.

Chapter One

The Double D Diamond Ranch, Torrance County, New Mexico

Katie Adelton snatched the keys from off her antique sideboard and stepped outside. As she headed for her car, the low rumble of thunder drew her gaze toward the sound. Dark, ominous clouds covered the sky from horizon to horizon. Before she could unlock the car door, those clouds released a torrent of rain that came down in buckets. She didn't care. The weather's mood matched hers and somehow she found that fitting.

The short drive to the home of her parents Diane and Andrew didn't allow a final rehearsal for what she would say once she arrived. She had made the decision to divorce Chad. How would they take the news of that announcement? After all, they loved him like a son. Would they support her choice or would they suggest she reconsider? Maybe they'd tell her she and Chad needed a cooling off period or worse yet, a marriage counselor. The thought made her gag.

No thank you. She'd gone well beyond all of that and there would be no turning back now.

She turned onto the dirt road leading up to her childhood home. All the while Katie's heart hammered inside her chest and climbed up her throat. The pace of it doubled as she spied her mom and dad sitting on the old oak swing to the right of the front door. The covered porch gave them shelter from the rain as well as a comfortable place to enjoy the stormy weather.

Over to the left her Uncle Jake—strong as an ox and twice as tall—stood just inside the hay barn with his cell phone glued to his ear. With that silly smirk on his face she had no doubt he spoke with one of the many women vying for his attention. Well, she wished whoever he spoke with the best of luck with that one.

She caught sight of Toby. Her younger brother sat in the cab of his pickup truck with the door wide open. The moment he turned his gaze toward her, he gave her an enthusiastic wave. She returned it—minus the enthusiasm she just didn't have.

Once she parked her Jeep Cherokee, she sucked in a deep breath, and exited the car. As Katie ambled toward the house, her mom gave her a welcoming smile. All the while lightning lit up the sky while booming thunder rolled across it. The smell of rain and damp earth acted as a much needed balm to her soul.

"Hello, Katie! You're just in time," Diane sang out.

"Time for what?" she asked as she climbed up the porch steps.

"This morning Toby and his friends made a CD of the songs they've been working on for the big dance. He wants us to hear it," Diane said.

Her dad chuckled. "Says it will make them famous."

Katie grinned. "I bet."

"They're all original," Toby hollered out. "Well, except for the final track, but that's nothing. Wait 'til you hear it."

"Okay, so why are we outside for said activity? I

mean, you all know it's pouring rain, right?" she asked.

"Because," Toby said as he stepped out of the truck. "For one, there's no better sound system than the one I have right here. Two, we should enjoy the lovely cool temperatures while they last. Heaven knows it's been hotter than a firecracker this month. Besides, since when did a little rain from the monsoon season bother you, huh? Hey, Jake, you coming or what?"

Jake shoved the phone in his pocket. "I'm ready. Let 'er roll."

Toby leaned into the truck and tapped the button on his stereo. In a flash he jumped up into the bed of the pickup and shook the rain from his dark blond hair. As the first song began, he bobbed his head. His foot began a slow rock as he snapped his fingers to the beat of the music. All the while heavy rain flooded the ground like nobody's business. Pools of water gathered in every low spot possible. Once filled to the brim, the water overran the boundaries and crept toward the house, just like it did every year.

While the rain fell, Toby played the fool and made like a rock star. Despite her mood, Katie laughed as he played his air guitar and danced back and forth across the bed. The first song ended to the sound of the praise and applause he so obviously expected.

Before the second one began, her brother wiped the relentless rain from his face and turned his gaze toward her. "Hey, Katie, could you come here and put it on track four for me real quick? Listen close, Jake, this one's for you."

The moment Katie stepped off the porch, a flaming bolt of lightning blended with an earsplitting roar of thunder. The enormous bolt hit the big mesquite tree out front and it shuddered. The gnarled bark belched out fiery shards that flew across the water. Katie turned her face away from the blinding light. In that same instant, a shock of electricity assaulted her. The jolt rattled her from the top of her head and all the way down to her feet. She couldn't move. She couldn't breathe. Darkness that both suffocated and frightened her followed the attack.

Even though she fought her way out of the gloomy shadows, some sort of strange sensation had overtaken her. She blinked several times before she could focus on anything. As her vision cleared, confusion beset her. Some woman—whose face she couldn't see—had fallen limp as a ragdoll onto the muddy, rain-soaked earth. Where on earth did she come from? She hadn't been there a moment ago, had she? Regardless of how she arrived, the woman needed help. Now!

Yet, no matter how hard she tried, she couldn't move from the spot upon which she stood. She'd never felt so helpless or bewildered. She looked first at her parents and then at Jake. Why didn't someone help the poor thing? Had some kind of fog gripped all of them at the same time? Once again she gazed at each person in turn—and that's when she noticed the oddity.

Everything moved in slow motion. The world around her moved so slowly in fact, she could count the raindrops as they fell. Right now she didn't understand the strange phenomena, nor could she explain it.

"Jake!" she screamed out. Surely her big, strong uncle could pick the woman up and take her into the house. "The woman needs help!"

She drew her brows together. Did he not hear her? If he did, he ignored her completely. Perhaps a feeling of helplessness had possessed him as well. Though his lips quivered, the wide-eyed man couldn't utter a single word. If the situation hadn't been so serious, the family might've laughed over the fear that—for the first time in his life—had rendered him speechless.

Toby bounded out of the truck. At a snail's pace that seemed surreal and defied all sense of logic, he shot past her. All the color had drained from his face. He knelt beside the woman and moved the disheveled hair away from her face. His eyes all but bulged out of his head as he sucked in a breath. "Dad! I think lightning hit Katie…and…and she's not breathing!"

She shook her head. "Don't be ridiculous, Toby. I'm standing right here. I'm fine."

No one acknowledged what she said. They didn't even look in her direction. What was the matter with everyone?

At once her mother stood up. She had a white-knuckled grip on the swing's massive chain as she stared at the girl. "Oh, Katie, no! Andy, quick! Do something!"

Her father hurtled over the steps and rushed toward the fallen woman. "Diane, call 911," Andrew shouted. "Tell them to hurry!" He dropped to his knees and turned the woman over as her mom ran into the house to make the call.

Horror overcame Katie as she stared at the lifeless figure on the ground. The woman wore the same clothes she had on. The layered, shoulder length, auburn hair matched hers to perfection. Dull blue eyes that didn't blink stared up at the sky. But no…surely that couldn't possibly be her lying there. Not when she stood right here. Katie's hands trembled as she covered her mouth. They felt dry…

"Katie." At once the calm, husky voice compelled her full attention. "Don't be afraid."

She turned around. A broad-shouldered man dressed in the army fatigues of World War II stood within a rainbow of luminous light. She knew him well. No doubt about that. In fact, he'd been with her the entire week without once leaving her side. As always, he had come when she needed him. Her most cherished friend—and from the earliest memories of her childhood—opened his arms wide in invitation. Until this moment, she had never glimpsed his face. Somehow that never mattered. The companionship, comfort, and support he gave without question, regardless of circumstance, seemed enough.

She gazed first into the handsome man's captivating steel-gray eyes. Within those eyes she perceived an inner strength that invited one to share their burdens both great and small. Yet at the same time they were gentle and warm. She also detected a touch of humor lurking just beneath the surface. His face was a little more square than oval, and the short, army-cut style of russet colored hair emphasized it. His lips, just shy of full, were turned up at one corner. That crooked grin revealed a dimple as he beckoned her.

Katie didn't fear him. Far from it. Nonetheless, she declined his invitation with a simple shake of her head. She feared what the invitation might mean.

He took a single step toward her, extended his arm, and offered her his hand. "I can see you're a bit bewildered. You needn't be. I promise you, everything will sort itself out. You see, I've been through this myself. All things considered, the experience is a beautiful one. You just have to let go of the fear."

"I...I don't know what you mean."

The smile he gave her all but turned her into a thick puddle of pudding. "You will. Just give yourself a moment. When you're ready to ask them, I'll answer all of your questions, all right?"

She backed away. "Who are you? What I mean to say is...I don't even know your name, or...or anything else about—"

The enchanting grin returned. "I think you know who I am, don't you? As far as my name goes though, it's William. William Malloy Griffin."

"Katie! Don't do this, baby girl," her dad whispered. "Come back...breathe, Katie, breathe! Please...please don't leave us."

She turned away from her soldier. Her father's desperation and sorrow tugged on her heart. With each breath he took, he willed her to live. She could feel it with every fiber of her being. He pressed on her heart in a rhythmic fashion and then blew air into her mouth. Again and again he repeated the action. As he gazed at her body, anguish filled his eyes.

"Toby," he hollered out as he bent over her body. "Go get me a pitcher of ice water. Hurry!"

Toby leaped to his feet and raced to the house. He returned with a bucket of ice water, filled to the brim. Her father grabbed hold of it and splashed the entire contents over Katie's face.

****

William dropped his arm to his side. The ice water did the trick. Without a backward glance, Katie left him standing there alone. In the instant her heart resumed its intended function, she returned to her body in one fluid, graceful motion. Her eyelashes fluttered a bit before they closed.

"Katie," her father called out. "Open your eyes, Katie, and look at me."

She did as he asked. For a moment she gazed at her father. A split second later she fell into a state of unconsciousness. Her father scooped her up as if she was the most fragile glass, carried her into the house, and over to the sofa. Her worried family gathered around her as they awaited the arrival of the paramedics. William supposed he should shout out a hallelujah that Katie's life hadn't been cut way shorter than the time decreed by destiny. However, the selfish part of him that wanted her at his side here and now didn't see the need for it.

He heard the sirens and saw the flashing red lights well before her family did. Once the emergency vehicle turned down the muddy drive, Toby rushed just outside the door. He frantically waved the paramedics toward the house.

The first man out of the vehicle didn't waste any time getting inside. He dropped to a knee beside Katie. At once he opened his bag and got to work as his partner extracted a gurney from the back of the truck and then joined him inside the small living room.

"You say she quit breathing after the lightning struck her?" he asked.

Her mom dabbed at her tears and sniffed. "Yes."

He wrapped a blood pressure cuff around her arm. "For how long?"

"I don't know," wailed Diane. "It seemed like forever."

"I'd say about four, maybe five minutes. Might be

less." Andrew dropped an arm around his wife and tugged her close to his chest as she wept. He shook his head and swallowed past the obvious knot in his throat.

William had never seen Katie's dad this shaken before. He couldn't blame Andrew though. If Katie had been his daughter, he would probably react the same way.

The paramedic glanced at Andrew. "Are you the one that brought her around?"

"Yes. I tried mouth-to-mouth and CPR as best I could without any real training as to the way it's done. When that didn't work, I doused her with ice water," Andy murmured. "I didn't know what else to do."

The man, whose nametag identified him as Hal, nodded as he pulled a radio out of his jacket. At once he called in his observations, readings, and preliminary treatment. After several exchanges with the staff at the hospital, Hal gave them an estimated time of arrival.

"Is she going to be all right?" Diane ventured.

Despite the worry William could see in Hal's eyes, the man gave her a smile. "We'll do our best to make that happen, ma'am. Now, do any of you know if she has any allergies?"

Once the men finished their administrations, they loaded Katie into the back of the van. Her mom insisted on riding with the emergency team. William waited until Diane chose her seat before he climbed in and hunkered down on the opposite side of the gurney.

The moment the engine, lights, and siren roared to life, Jake jumped in his pickup. Toby and Andrew climbed in beside him as Jake revved up the engine. All the way to the hospital, William held Katie's hand. In that moment he knew she had already buried the brief moment they had just shared deep inside her subconscious. Unless some kind of miracle occurred, she wouldn't remember it once she woke up. In fact, the memory probably wouldn't surface until her mortality ended.

He accompanied her into the emergency room cubicle while her family waited in the lobby. William paid attention to everything the medical staff said and did. She had arrived in grave condition. They worried over the fact she hadn't regained consciousness despite all their efforts to rouse her. That worried him as well.

Of course, they had said, that could be due to the internal damage she had suffered when the lightning struck her. Damage that needed immediate repair. Once all tests were complete, they prepped her for emergency surgery. All throughout the delicate procedure, William remained at her side. He never once turned loose of her hand. Through that vital connection, he offered her his strength and for the first time, he offered her his heart. Did she truly understand what that meant? The surgery took the greater portion of three hours.

"Okay, that's it," the surgeon said, as at long last he stepped away from the table. "Let's close her up. While you're doing that, I'll go talk to her family and let them know how she's doing."

"Tell them the effects of the anesthesia I used should wear off in an hour or so. Once she comes around, they can visit her in recovery," the anesthesiologist said.

"Will do."

William gave Katie's hand a gentle press. "Looks like they're just about done in here, my love. In case you didn't hear them, they think you'll wake up while you're in the recovery room. That should bring both joy and some relief to your family, don't you think? After all, you gave them quite a scare."

She didn't respond, nor did he expect it. He accompanied her from the operating room into the small recovery cubicle. Soon her family would gather round her. Once they did, her need for comfort would turn away from him. Instead, she would get it from her family. That's as it should be, he supposed.

Minutes ticked off the clock as he waited for her to awaken. All the while he recalled countless memories from the years that made up her life. He'd witnessed all of her moods—been aware of the moments that filled her with joy, as well as those that brought her down to the deepest depths of sorrow. Although he'd been there whenever she needed him, he never once told her—

He leaned down and kissed her on the forehead. "Before everyone comes in here and steals you away from me, there are a few things I'd like to say. Things I have always wanted you to know. I've never said them aloud before because it's difficult to find the words of the heart. At least it's difficult for me. Always was, and unfortunately the death of my mortal body didn't change that flaw. I'll probably mess it up and stumble all the way through it. Nonetheless, here goes—

"Know that I love you Katie Simone Adelton—and far deeper than what you can possibly comprehend or understand in your mortal state. There isn't a soul, past, present, or future that could compare with the magnificent woman you are. I cannot express enough gratitude for the day I finally found you. I'm grateful, because I didn't think such a day would ever come. You know, there for awhile, I truly thought I'd wander eternity alone. Now we have forever ahead of us and that's an amazing feeling. Though you won't join me now, I know one day you will."

He paused as he recalled the joyous moment her soul had called out and irrevocably connected to his. To this day she remained oblivious of the incredible event. After all, she couldn't have been more than three or four years of age at the time. Even if she had felt something, she wouldn't have understood it. Nonetheless, almost from that day to this, she had sensed his presence whenever he visited her. He knew without doubt she sensed it even now.

Of a certainty, she wouldn't remember her brief encounter with death. He, on the other hand, would never forget it. He conjured a sigh. "I can't help but wonder where we'd be right now, if only you'd walked into my arms and chosen to stay."

Chapter Two

William appeared inside Katie's hospital room with a single rose in his hand. He slipped it into the vase on the nightstand and approached the bed. From all appearances, his sleeping beauty hadn't moved a muscle since he left her yesterday. He had never seen Katie so still for so long a period of time and it troubled him.

Coma was the word doctors used weeks ago for her condition. A condition that had gone on far longer than any of them thought it would. They didn't share that knowledge with her family though. Instead, they told her parents they couldn't predict how long it would take for her to awaken. The doctors said by all reports, the time varied for those struck by lightning. Some victims would regain consciousness very quickly. Others needed far more time to heal. They reminded them that Katie had taken a more violent hit than most.

Yeah.

That was their way of saying they didn't know anything more now than they did the day they rushed her to the hospital. They didn't have a clue as to why she didn't wake up. If they all wanted him to, he could sum up the reason in just two words. Chad McCrae.

To the accompaniment of the rhythmic beep, beep, beep of her monitor, William combed his fingers through the locks of her lovely auburn hair. The light from the window played with the golden highlights created by the kiss of summer sun. Those highlights framed her face in a way that made him smile despite the gravity of the situation. Now, if she would open those gorgeous baby blues of hers, he'd be content. He hadn't seen them in awhile and he sorely missed getting lost in them.

He took hold of her hand and placed a gentle kiss against her full, luscious lips. "You need to wake up, sleeping beauty. Come on now. You either need to wake up or let go. I'll accept your choice whatever it is, but you just can't stay in this limbo. I know better than anyone else how badly he hurt you. But you can't let him rob you of—"

He halted mid-sentence. The voices right outside her hospital door demanded it. The first belonged to Carol, her morning nurse. The second?

Speak of the devil and he'll walk in every single time.

Chad strode into the room with Carol not more than a step behind him. He stopped at the foot of Katie's bed and waited as Carol changed her IV bag and took her vitals. After she finished her tasks, she gave the man a smile. He didn't deserve it.

"Everything looks good this morning," she said.

Chad gave her a wink alongside a nod. "That's good. Do you think maybe she'll wake up today?"

"There's a good chance she might." She smoothed the wrinkles away from Katie's blankets and stepped away from the bed. "After all, your wife is getting the best of care and from what we can see, she's doing quite well physically."

Wife.

The word filled William with disgust. When had Chad ever treated his precious Katie like a wife? Indeed, he treated her more like the lowest member of a sultan's harem. A thing she suspected throughout most of their marriage, but finally witnessed for herself. The undeniable sight shattered her heart and left her crying like a wounded animal. In that moment he could quite literally feel the intensity of her pain. He could do nothing more than hold her as she sorted through the broken pieces of her life.

If not for the support she needed from her family, she would never have gone out to the ranch. The lightning never would have touched her. The worst thing about it all? Katie didn't have the chance to confide in her mother. She didn't get a chance to tell her about the hell Chad had put her through—or the decision she had made because of the last and final straw.

Once Carol left the room, William sidled up next to McCrae and leaned in close to his ear. "Are you worried that when she wakes up, she'll tell everyone about all the women you've dallied with since you married her? Tell them what kind of scumbag you are beneath that charming smile of yours? That'll change everybody's opinion of you right quick and in a hurry, won't it now. Perhaps you hope she'll sleep long enough she'll forget what she saw, hmm? Then again, maybe your greatest wish is that the lightning destroyed the memory altogether."

While the man fidgeted, William moved to his other side. "I hate to burst your bubble, but that won't happen. Oh, and by the way? She doesn't need or want you here. You make her sick. So why don't you just skedaddle on out of this room and keep on going. If you have even a shred of decency about you, you won't come back. Not even for the sake of appearance. What you should do instead is find a dark hole somewhere, crawl inside it, and stay there. You know why? Because you're a lousy excuse for a human being. That's why."

Chad shoved his hands inside his pockets. As he jingled his keys, the second hand of the clock on the pale green wall cycled twice. All the while that tic in his jaw got a hefty workout. Then, in what William considered an act of mercy from Heaven itself, Chad's cell phone went off. At once he made an abrupt about face and exited the room.

Good riddance to the worst of rubbish. William turned his gaze toward Katie. Ever in tune with her spirit, he could see the effect McCrae's visit had on her soul. In response to Chad's voice, she had withdrawn even further inside that small haven of protection she'd created deep within herself, a haven wherein she still felt a little self-worth. If she advanced much further into that shell, she might not come back. Perhaps he could do something that would change the tide? An idea he had considered once before and dismissed might have merit after all.

At that moment, Katie's mother entered the room. He moved out of her way as Diane approached the side of the bed.

She took hold of her daughter's hand and gave it a squeeze. "Good morning, sweetheart. How are you feeling today? I see you have another fresh rose. Smells heavenly, doesn't it? Now if we could only discover who your secret admirer is, I could ask where he gets them. I think a full bouquet on the kitchen table would be a perfect centerpiece, don't you?"

William saw the hope in Diane's eyes. The same hope she had carried with her every single day since Katie entered the hospital. Her mama couldn't know it, but from the way Katie responded, he knew she took a great deal of comfort in her presence.

"Daddy will be up later. So will Jake and some of the boys. That ought to be a hoot, don't you think? Let's just hope they don't kick us out of here once they get going. You know how they are when they're all together. Anyway, I thought a little bit of sprucing up would be in order. Would you like that?" She took the brush from off the side table and put her bag in its place. "I also brought up some of your favorite perfume. I'll dab a little of that behind your ears after I help you with a bath and get the tangles out of your hair. That'll make you feel better, won't it? Oh, and instead of that hideous mustard yellow gown, the nurse brought you in a white one with bouquets of pink flowers printed all over it. You'll look smashing."

William grinned. Perhaps the family visit she mentioned might give Katie a much needed laugh. At the same time, it would give him the opportunity he needed. With the sure knowledge he left her in the best of care, he passed through the portal from her realm and into his. As he headed for home, he ran into Private Richard Barnett. A big, infectious smile lit up the kid's face. He couldn't help but return it.

"Hey, Sarge! How's Katie?"

He shrugged. "About the same."

"Aw, that's a shame. I take it she still doesn't know you're hovering over her like an old mother hen?"

"No more so than usual. Katie knows I'm with her.

She takes comfort in my presence just as she always has, but nothing more than that, I'm afraid."

"Well, if anyone can think of a way to change that, it'll be you, sir."

"Thanks for the confidence, Rich. I have an idea that just might work this time. At least I hope it will. I guess we'll see."

"Well then I'll let you get right to it. You've got to let me know how it goes though. We're all pulling for you." Rich gave him a casual salute and moved off to the side so he could pass.

"You'll be the first to know if anything changes. I promise."

As he continued his journey homeward, William turned his gaze toward the incredible beauty of the verdant meadows. Within those meadows, the most beautiful horses ever created freely grazed. Magnificent trees, the likes of which no one on earth had ever seen, encompassed the entire area. He never tired of looking at the leaves that glistened like silver dewdrops under a morning sun.

Far more glorious than anything he had ever envisioned during mortality, he had chosen to establish his residence here on the outskirts, instead of farther inside Golden City. No doubt in his mind but that Katie would love it here as much as he did. She would especially adore the flowers that were everywhere present. They were more vivid and rich in color than what even her wildest imagination could ever imagine. Likewise the fragrance they offered those that passed them by. One fine day he would take great pleasure in showing all of this to her.

One fine day.

Upon arrival, he ambled up the burnished amber walkway that led to his home. The brilliant white marble facade surrounded a multitude of square-paned windows. They allowed an abundance of radiant light to fill each room. He entered through the large double doors framed by the same white pillars that supported the second story veranda.

Once inside, he headed straight for the desk inside his cozy library decorated from floor to ceiling in various hues of gray, burgundy, and blue. He sat down and opened the top left-hand drawer of his highly polished desk. With the greatest of care he withdrew the journal nestled inside. His great-grandfather had urged him to keep the diary right after he found his Katie. He had taken his advice. After all, if not for Isaiah Griffin, he would never have known she existed.

He and Isaiah had a bond that went well beyond the one of kinship. Isaiah too, had left his mortality behind on the field of battle. For his great-grandfather, that field had been Murfreesboro in Tennessee during America's Civil War. However, unlike himself, Isaiah had left behind a beloved wife and three small children. At the time, the little ones were all under the age of five.

William recalled with absolute clarity the grin on Isaiah's face the instant he bemoaned his lonely, solitary state. They were out by the sparkling river that ran behind his home. Lush vegetation and flowers in every shape and hue gave them privacy. From the boughs of the trees, the sweet song of birds serenaded them.

"Do you think you're alone in that, son? All you choose to see are cheerful couples, living their happily ever after. Open your eyes, boy. Take another good look around you. Not everyone here has a soul mate at their side, at least not yet."

"Easy for you to say, you've got Florence."

He nodded. "That's right, I do have Florence. I won't apologize for that. Nevertheless, I'm here to tell you that through the good Lord's fairness and love, there's a special someone out there for everyone. Heaven wouldn't be Heaven if it weren't so. Wouldn't be fair to the millions of men and women in the same circumstance as you, would it now. I mean, think of all of the single people in the history of the earth who died from disease, accidents, plagues, and wars. Don't you think they should have the same opportunity as everyone else?"

"I suppose so. But if all that's true, where is she?"

"That I couldn't tell you. Could be she's right here somewhere, bellyaching over her solitary state as well. On the other hand, she might be living out her mortality right now. There's also a possibility she hasn't been born yet. Nonetheless, she's out there. You just have to find her."

He picked up a pebble and with a bit of force, flung it across the clear blue water. "Well isn't that just dandy. Talk about looking for a marble-sized snowball in a howling blizzard. Do you have any idea how long it would take to search out every single woman here, as well as those in their mortal state?"

Isaiah chuckled. "Do you know how much longer it will take if you don't get started now?"

William rolled his eyes. "How would I even recognize her amidst the sea of faces?"

A thoughtful look had entered Isaiah's eyes even as

the grin faded away. "You'll know her when you find her, William. You'll know."

He looked down at the journal he held in his hands, opened the cover, and flipped through the pages. Almost all of the white sheets in the book were filled now with words penned in golden ink. Every line had something to do with Katie in one way or another. Rather than a diary, they were more like letters. All written for and to the woman he loved and had loved from the dawn of time. Perhaps if he read them to her in her unconscious state, she would respond. If she understood just how much he loved her—if she knew forever and always she was his as he was hers—her heart would heal.

****

The bath and fresh gown made Katie feel better. So did the time her mom spent brushing her hair. The gentle strokes carried her off on an ocean wave of contentment. So much so, she almost looked forward to the promised visit by her family. Almost. In truth, she didn't know if she wanted them here right now. More often than not, a part of her wished everyone would just stay away and leave her alone. Other times, only family could give her what she needed. Only they could bring a bit of peace and comfort to her tattered soul.

No, wait. She did have someone else.

The secret companion she'd never told anyone about could comfort her better than anyone. Katie never told anyone about him because—well, because he was hers and hers alone. She didn't have a name for her beloved companion. Yet without any doubt whatsoever, a male presence had become part of her life and for as far back as she could recall. His kind, gentle essence never failed to appear when she needed him most. She didn't know or even understand the why of it. Even so, he provided unconditional love and acceptance regardless of any wrong or foolish choice she made. Like marrying Chad, for instance.

Bile rose to her throat. *Please, for the love of Heaven, don't think about him—*

In response to the pain, she focused again on her unknown companion. Could he be her guardian angel? A ghost who'd lost his way perhaps? She didn't know. As long as he appeared when she needed him, it didn't matter.

As she contemplated her friend, a host of boisterous voices tumbled into her consciousness. Her mother did her best to shush them. They weren't having any of it. *No surprise there.*

"Hey, Katie!" said her Uncle Jake. "Look who's here!"

Someone took hold of her hand, leaned down, and kissed her on the forehead. "What? I've come all this way and you're not going to open your eyes? Really? Well, you could at least mumble out some kind of hello, can't you?"

The voice belonged to her cousin Justin. If she could, she'd smile. She just couldn't muster the strength. He tsked. In all likelihood he rolled his eyes as well. "That's kind of rude if you want my opinion, Katie."

Yes, probably. Sorry.

"You know what I think? I think she'll wake up for me. She always did like me best, after all." Jared, Justin's twin brother, grabbed her other hand. "How about it, Katie? If nothing else, you could belch out some kind of gut-busting insult for your favorite cousin. I mean, it's the least you can do since we had the most abominable time you can imagine getting here."

Jake guffawed. "That's putting it mildly. Wait until you hear this! You're not gonna believe it."

"Believe what?" her dad asked as he entered the room, minutes behind the rest. He dropped a kiss on her cheek, just as he did every time he visited her.

"Every rotten piece of luck we went through to get here, Uncle Andy," Justin said. "Why don't you grab a seat and I'll tell you all about it. Pay attention, Katie. We suffered through the awful ordeal just for you."

"Keep in mind, if for anyone else, we would've hightailed it for home at the first sign of trouble," Jared said.

"You bet your sweet bottom we would have," said Justin. "First off, it took us forever to find a flight leaving this afternoon. We had to call every airport in the book. Once we found one with empty seats, we had to drive like crazy to get to that tiny podunk town on time. Wouldn't you know it? We had a flat tire along the way. Jared didn't care. He said if we stopped, we wouldn't make it. So we bumped along the highway with hope upon hope the tire wouldn't fall apart before we got there. You should've seen everyone staring at us like we were a couple of morons—or worse. They honked, hollered, pointed, and waved. We just smiled and waved back. By the time we got to the airport we were riding on a bent up rim."

Diane gasped. "Oh, you did not."

"Oh, yes we did," Justin insisted.

No, they didn't. Not even close. If she could find the strength, she'd roll *her* eyes.

Jared laughed. "Hey, we made it here, didn't we? Now getting home will be something altogether different. Anyway, on with the story. We rushed up to the ticket counter without a second to spare and rang this stupid little bell. Who the heck uses those anymore? Anyway, some old geezer moseyed out from the back room and sold us our tickets. Once we had them in hand, he looked at his watch and shook his head. After scolding us for being late, he told us we better get ourselves to gate one or we'd be left behind. So off we went."

"Of course, once we arrived at said gate—one of only two gates I might add—we found ourselves staring at this old wreck of a plane. A leftover from World War II at best. I swear nothing but twine held the right wing together. Jared and I looked at each other and shrugged off our concerns. We felt the sacrifice a small one to pay if we could just get here and see you all cob-webby and comatose. Your inability to spout off any of your sass added icing to the cake. I mean that's a once in a lifetime opportunity if you ask me," said Justin.

"No way were we going to miss it, either." Jared snickered. "Oh, and you should've seen the inside of that plane, Katie. The seats looked like something out of an old, beat up pickup truck—a Ford, I think. There were some wooden cargo boxes to the rear and a bunch of junk piled everywhere else. Despite the dangers to life and limb, we climbed in. Much to our surprise, the same guy at the ticket counter showed up at the gate and took our tickets. He leaned in the doorway and told us to strap on our seatbelts. The captain would be with us shortly, he said. The only trouble with that? The seatbelts—what there were of them—didn't work. Are you listening, Katie? This is good stuff here."

Her mother giggled. "You guys are making this up."

Of course they were. It's what they did best. Katie wandered away from the voices as she traveled back to her childhood. In those days, she, Justin, and Jared made up a wild threesome no one could keep up with, least of all their parents. They kept most of their foolhardy shenanigans under wraps until well after they were grown. At that point, they were far away from the trouble they would've gotten themselves into when they were young. A host of memories engulfed her. Sweet memories from a far simpler time and place.

"Not even a smile, Katie? I mean, you should be in stitches by now. Everyone else is."

Justin's words called her back and at once she focused on the here and now. The boys went on about how the man at the ticket counter, by nothing more than a change of coat and hat, acted as flight steward and then their captain. Ridiculous story, but she expected no less from her favorite cousins.

Justin cleared his throat in an exaggerated manner. "You know me. Before I could shut my big fat mouth, I asked our doddering pilot if he actually thought we'd make it to our destination in one piece—"

"For the raging storm that filled the man's eyes, I could see trouble brewing on the horizon," Jared cut in. "To save my brother's life, I made up something about Justin being terrified to fly. In turn, he said, 'Son, I've made so many trips from Texas to New Mexico that I can't even begin to count them all. As you can plainly see, I'm still here and so is my plane. Don't you worry, I'll get you to where you're going.' At that point I could only gulp back the tears, smile, and nod."

Their wild tale continued. They said something about the turbulence and being bounced from off their seats and onto the floor with holes so big, they could stick a leg through it. Somewhere along the way, their absurd stories as well as their voices again faded away as she slipped into the peace darkness provided.

Nonetheless, a part of her knew when they all got up and left. The solitude and shadows that surrounded her made her privy to that. Her otherworldly companion hadn't returned from wherever he had gone off to either. No matter. She didn't really need him right now anyway. At that moment a lazy billowy cloud picked her up and lulled her toward sleep. She didn't fight the sweet contentment it offered, she welcomed it.

"Katie?"

"Hmm?" The voice nudged her back toward the pain of awareness. In the same instant she knew her ethereal companion had returned. He'd also brought her another flower. She could smell the distinctive fragrance. Katie loved the heady scent even if right now, she didn't have any idea what the rose looked like.

Wait a minute.

Did he just call her by name? He'd never spoken to her before, had he?

"I need you to listen to me and in the place you are right now. You'll do that for me, won't you?"

She concentrated on the location of his voice. If not mistaken, he stood just off to her right and near the head of her bed. Something in his tone compelled her full attention as well as her cooperation. For the life of her, she couldn't say why. She took in a deep breath and gave it a slow release.

"Yes."

She could sense his joy over the uttered word. Why? Did she say it aloud or could he somehow just hear it?

"I know you've been aware of my existence for quite some time now. In fact, you sensed my presence when you were just a little girl. Do you remember the day? Miss Scot bucked you off after she got bit by a horsefly. You fell into that old barbed wire fence before you tumbled to the ground. I think your pride took a worse hit than your backside did."

Now that he mentioned it, she did remember. He helped her to her feet, brushed her off, and wiped away her tears. *He was so sweet.*

"You weren't afraid. In fact, you've never been afraid of me."

True, Katie mused. She had never feared him. Should she have?

"What you don't know—what you couldn't know—is just how long it took me to find you, or even the reason I needed to find you. Nonetheless, the moment I saw you for the very first time, you turned my whole world upside down. You did it in the most incredible way you could possibly imagine. So I thought maybe I'd talk a little bit about the journey and why I took it in the first place. Would you care to tag along?"

Chapter Three

To Katie's great disappointment, the dream faded away before she could capture even the most meager part of it. Even so, she knew without question, the dream—or perhaps a series of incredible and wonderful dreams—had kept her company all throughout the night. Perhaps that's why she felt so tired. She didn't have a clue as to what the dreams were about now. Nonetheless, she did know they filled her with an unbelievable sense of joy such as she had never known before. How she wished she could remember the reason for that. Better yet, she wished she could bottle the bliss and use it as needed.

She winced as she turned over onto her side. The strange soreness that somehow invaded her body during the night took her by surprise. From head to toe, every muscle ached. Why on earth would she feel like she'd been run over by a Mack truck? Why the abominable thirst? She worked at swallowing past the rough dryness in her throat. The tip of her tongue explored the length of her bottom lip and found it as dry as the inside of her mouth. She should get up and get a drink of water. Maybe some crushed ice might be good as well. Despite the desire, her body protested the thought. In the end, exhaustion overrode the thirst. Perhaps she'd sleep a while longer and then get up and get some water. She snuggled deeper into her covers and once again drifted toward the pleasure of slumber. Perhaps she'd have that enchanting dream again. If so, she'd hold on to it this time.

"Code blue. ER room 32, code blue. ER room 32."

Katie's eyes flew open. Confusion set in as she gazed at a wall with a bizarre painting she didn't recognize. One couldn't tell if someone hung it upside down or even sideways. Yet, in the mere blink of an eye, the bewilderment disappeared. A feeling of peace replaced it. In that moment she knew her friend stood in the room with her.

Common sense took hold of her. It said she needn't fret over the unfamiliarity of her surroundings. The announcement over the intercom shouldn't bother her either. All she need do is look around and take stock of the situation.

Good enough advice. All right, I can do that.

She ignored the pain as she rolled onto her back and inched upward onto the stack of disheveled pillows. In a thorough search, she took in every inch of the hospital room she now occupied. She gazed at the IV tube that traveled from the needle taped securely to her hand, to the saline bag attached to the infusion pole. For a moment the incessant beeps of the monitor stole her attention. She watched the graphs as they bounced up and down. All the while she didn't see anything that would cause alarm on the screen. The comb, brush, and box of tissues on the bed tray deserved nothing more than a passing glance. She shifted her gaze to the night stand to her left, as well as the small counter top next to the sink. A variety of flowers in vases and pots cluttered both areas. Though quite beautiful, the most exquisite red rose she'd ever seen held her gaze far longer than anything else. She'd never, ever, seen anything like it before.

But why on earth did she wake up in this place? Did she get into an accident of some kind? She struggled for her most recent memory and—

Her dad's voice, just outside her room, cut into her thoughts. Who made him so mad?

"I don't think he'll come back now, Diane, so don't worry. First of all, I don't think he has the guts to face us. I know I wouldn't if I were in his shoes. Second, I'm pretty darn sure he knows I'll smash his face in if he does."

"I can't believe he would do such a thing to her. Not our Katie…" Her mom sniffed. "How could we have not seen it, Andy? I mean I knew something troubled her the day she came out to the ranch, but what about all the times before that? How long did she know about Chad and Heather without saying a word to anyone?"

Oh. That. Well, at least they knew without her having to tell them the sordid details herself.

A set of heavy footsteps drew close and then stopped short of the door.

"What's wrong, Diane?" Uncle Jake asked. "Why the tears? Is Katie all right?"

"She's fine. It's a…it's Chad," her mom said.

"Chad? Did something happen I'm not aware of?"

"Something happened all right. Seems the snake kept a mistress, and from all reports, for the better part of his marriage to Katie," her father spat.

Katie allowed herself a quiet breath of laughter. *Oh, he kept more than just one. Does Heather know that yet?*

"Now the happy couple is expecting a child. What do you think of that?"

Pregnant? That she didn't know. She danced around the idea and found it didn't bother her in the least.

"Aw, man! You've got to be kidding me," Jake said. "How do you know all of this?"

Her dad huffed out a derisive breath. "The twins told us. After they left the hospital, they stopped in for a bite to eat before heading back to the airport. As they walked into the restaurant, they saw them sitting together in a booth at the back. They were so cozy with each other they didn't notice them until Justin yanked him out of his seat and slammed him against the wall."

Jared and Justin were here? They had come to see her? How she wished she could've seen them before they left. Better yet, she wished she could've been with them when they spied Chad slobbering all over Heather. That would've been a lark because if nothing else, her cousins were blunt as well as fearless. All throughout her life they had protected her with a fierceness that could be downright scary at times.

"When they confronted the jerk, his lady friend jumped in to defend him—if you can believe that. To Chad's absolute horror, she spilled her guts about their relationship from tawdry start to the present. Chad told her to shut up numerous times but she didn't listen. She just kept going on and on. In a moment of defiance she told the boys they were in love. She said they planned to get married as soon as possible."

"Little hussy doesn't deserve to be called a lady," her mother hissed. "She isn't the least bit concerned over Katie's condition."

Their topic of conversation—though repulsive and unexpected—couldn't extinguish the amazing sense of elation she still carried inside her. In that moment she knew Chad didn't have the power to hurt her anymore. In fact, any feelings she may have once had for the man, both good and bad, had quite disappeared. Right now she only felt indifference.

"No wonder we haven't seen the sleaze ball during the past day or two. Does Katie know any of this yet?" Jake asked.

"She knows," her father replied. "Jared said the woman told them Katie walked in on them at Chad's office—and at the worst moment possible, if you get my meaning. She thought to excuse their actions by saying they had no idea Katie would stop by. Anyway, Diane and I believe that's the reason she came out to the ranch. I think she would've told us. She just didn't get the chance."

Katie remembered then. She did go out to the ranch yesterday. They were all outside listening to Toby's music and then—and then what? Why couldn't she remember?

"I think we need to pay Mr. McCrae a little visit, and let him know how we feel about the current state of his affairs," Jake ground out.

Her father chuckled. "There's no need. The twins administered a little Texas justice before they left. Last I heard they abandoned him in the middle of a hay field somewhere. In fact, they left him in nothing more than his underwear and without his cell phone or a way home."

"Good for them."

"Anyway, I just told Diane after all of that I don't

think he'll come back. At least he won't if he knows what's good for him. Remember, he hasn't faced her brothers yet—or me. I don't think he wants to either."

"Yeah, well, I still wouldn't mind running into him myself—if for nothing else than to drive the boys' message home," Jake replied. "I'd imagine he's probably too scared to show his face to me, though."

"You probably have that right."

"Maybe for Katie's sake, that's a good thing. She probably wouldn't approve of what I have in mind, anyway." Jake paused for a moment. "Tell me, has anyone checked in on her yet this morning?"

"I talked to her nurse a few minutes ago," Diane said. "No change. Anyway, we were just heading in there now. Come on in and keep us company for a while if you can."

The minute the threesome walked through the door, Katie greeted them with a smile and her arms outstretched. She laughed at the look on their faces. "What does a girl have to do around here to get a drink of water and a pitcher of ice? I'm dying of thirst."

"Katie!" Her mother flew across the room. As she gathered her into her arms she both laughed and cried. "Oh, Katie! You're back."

"I am? Did I go somewhere?" Her smile broadened as her dad leaned down and kissed her on the cheek. "Hello, Daddy."

"Welcome back, baby girl," Andrew whispered. "I've missed you."

"Yes, you were gone," Diane lamented. "For more weeks than I care to count—"

Her mouth dropped as she stared at each person in turn. "Weeks? What on earth are you talking about?"

They all spoke at once as they crowded around her. Somehow at the end of it all, she got the gist of the story. "Well, I guess I'm no worse for the wear. Other than a little bedsore, I must say, I feel pretty good. Tired, but good."

As the day wore on, she endured several interruptions by elated doctors and nurses who poked, prodded, and asked questions. Various conversations with an assortment of visitors—without any mention of Chad whatsoever—carried on until late afternoon. By then exhaustion had set in. Her mother noticed it, drew everyone's attention to it, and then shooed everyone out the door. Once they had all gone home, Katie stared down at her cell phone. Her mom had handed it to her with instructions to call if she needed anything. She could only think of one thing.

She picked it up and for several minutes she did nothing more than gaze at the screen. The joy she had carried since she woke up still hadn't diminished. If anything, it had inexplicably grown stronger. Would the phone call she had to make change even the slightest portion of that? Regardless of outcome, the task needed doing. *Might as well be sooner rather than later.*

Once she placed the call, she waited for him to answer. Just when she thought he wouldn't, the phone stopped ringing.

"H-hello?"

The very sound of his voice nauseated her. At the same time, his obvious fear amused her. She really should call Jared and Justin and get the whole story. "Hello, Chad."

"Katie?"

"Yep, it's me. Believe it or not, I'm finally awake

and doing quite well, they say."

"I'm so happy to hear that, we were all so wor—"

"Don't, Chad. Don't even pretend. I'm well beyond it. Now, I'll make this short and sweet. We need to talk. Now is the perfect time, and here is the perfect place. I promise I won't take much of your evening. I'm sure you have plans. If not, you should make some."

"Are...are you alone?"

"Yes, I am. You needn't be afraid of an ambush. There are no monsters, brothers, cousins, or angry father hiding underneath the bed with a loaded shotgun in hand."

He paused. "Give me twenty minutes."

Katie ended the call without saying goodbye and tossed the phone on top of the bed tray. She closed her eyes and waited.

Several minutes later, his distinctive footsteps echoed throughout the hallway. Chad rapped his knuckles against the open door and barged into the room without waiting for an invitation. A bizarre mix of emotions marred his face as he did so. She saw belligerence, insolence, cowardice, and curiosity as he gazed at her.

He stopped at the foot of her bed and gave her a curt nod. "Nice to see you awake. You had your family quite worried."

"That's what being part of a family that loves completely and deeply is all about, Chad. I'm grateful that during the days I spent in the coma, I had their support."

Chad dropped his gaze and shoved his hands inside his pockets. He jingled his keys and shrugged away the comment. "Well, you've got me down here, what would you like to discuss?"

"I didn't call you down here so I can help you name the baby."

Heat colored his cheeks and for a moment he had trouble meeting her eyes. He sucked in a breath and held on to it even as he spoke. "The thought never crossed my mind."

"I bet not." She cleared her throat in an exaggerated manner. "I suppose the word 'discuss' is a poor choice for what I have in mind. We can blame the weeks I spent in the coma for the inaccuracy of my request. In truth, I asked you for this visit so I could talk and you could listen."

He raised a brow. "So speak."

"Fine. You should know my lawyer has already prepared the papers for the dissolution of our marriage. If not for my accident, I would already have signed them and you would already have received them. He believes I've been more than fair. You can hire your own lawyer and contest the terms if you wish. Even if you choose that route, I don't think you'll do better than what I've offered. In addition, the quicker you sign the documents, the faster you'll be able to marry your— uh—present sweetheart and legally give your baby your name. Please remember, I'm not in the same hurry you might be in right now."

His eyes narrowed as he launched that annoying tic in his jaw. Finally, he shook his head. "You needn't worry, Katie. I have no intention of contesting the divorce. I'll sign your papers as soon as I have them and read them over, of course."

"I kept the words short and simple enough. You

should understand them without too much difficulty. I'm not worried either. Not in the least. I just thought I'd give you the heads up. The papers will arrive no later than week's end. See that you're around to sign for them. Oh, and uh, tell Heather I wish her the best of luck. She's going to need it."

As he spun around on his heels, Katie stopped him.

"One more thing before you go."

He turned around to face her. "What now?" he asked between clenched teeth.

"The doctors are kicking me out of here in the next day or two. Please have all of your things out of my house by the time I get home. Anything I find at that point will go in the trash."

"You can rest easy, Katie. I'm already gone."

"Good. I think the less we see of each other from here on out, the better off both of us will be. Wouldn't you agree?"

"I couldn't agree with you more."

"Goodbye, Chad."

The minute he strode out of the room, Katie looked down at the wedding ring on her left hand. With a smile on her face, she tugged it off, and tossed it into the garbage can next to her bed. The sound it made as it rattled against the bottom of it made her laugh. Who knew such a small, insignificant thing could make her feel this good?

Chapter Four

Month in and month out after her release from the hospital, William had steadfastly watched over Katie's progress. When she needed help over the rough spots, he held her in his arms as he kept her company. He supposed he carried a hope that somewhere along the way something would spark the memory of the letters he shared with her. So far though, nothing had. He found it obvious she didn't remember a thing. In his opinion, the further away from the dreams, the more likely they'd never be recalled. That caused him a great deal of anguish. So much anguish in fact, he finally sought the advice of his grandfather. In his mind, no one was wiser than Isaiah Griffin. Perhaps he could somehow help him through this? The hope took him to his grandfather's front door.

Isaiah welcomed him inside. "Well this is a pleasant surprise. To what do I owe the honor?"

"I need to talk to you," he said, coming straight to the point.

"All right. I'm listening."

Once he had shared his torment and uncertainty, Isaiah leaned back against the sofa and for a time, he did nothing more than gaze into his eyes. William waited out the silence.

"William, what you need is far more patience than what you have right now. You must keep in mind that

Katie is still mortal," he said. "She sees things through mortal eyes and with a mortal's perception. The thoughts and dreams you share with her, she believes are her own. In her mind, how could they be anything else? Of course she'll dismiss anything she doesn't understand. She'll wonder where the absurd thoughts come from and then pay them no heed."

"Well, isn't that just dandy," he groused.

Isaiah chuckled. "You did the same thing when I told you about the ultimate sacrifice you would make after you enlisted in the army. Do you remember?"

William nodded as those mortal memories flooded his mind. "Yes, I remember and point well taken."

"So, there you go."

"Then you're telling me that things will stay the way they are right now until she dies?"

As he leaned forward, he shook his head. "No, I didn't say that, boy. Listen to me again. I said you need patience. One day you'll find a way to get through to her. Especially if you're persistent and try any number of ways to make that happen."

"I don't know what else I could possibly do that I haven't already done."

Isaiah grinned. "I'm sure if you keep thinking on it, you'll come up with something new. Keep in mind, there's only one key that fits any given lock. Remember, no one knows Katie as well as you do. So take what you know and find the key that works."

Easier said than done.

William left his grandfather's home, deep in thought. Moments later, he stepped into Katie's realm. Once again he found her at her mother's house. The family had just finished a fine dinner of pot roast, corn on the cob, and mashed potatoes and gravy. They topped that off with her mama's homemade apple pie. The sweet aroma of apples, brown sugar, and cinnamon still lingered. She and her parents weren't in any hurry to leave the table. Then again, they never were on nights like this. This time though, a secret smile passed between Andrew and Diane. The exchange piqued his interest.

Diane dabbed at her mouth with her napkin and then set it on top of her plate. She turned toward Katie. Only a fool wouldn't see the twinkle in her eyes. "We've got some news," she sang out.

Katie giggled. "Good or bad?"

Diane bobbed her head from side to side. "Well, Daddy and I think it's pretty darn good."

Katie's gaze darted back and forth between them. "Are you going to share this news or are you going to make me guess?"

Again the smile passed between her parents. As Diane shifted her gaze back to Katie the smile broadened. "I suppose you could toss out a few guesses if you'd like. I'll let you know if you're getting warm."

"Mom—"

"Okay, okay. Here we go. Are you ready?" She glanced at Andrew and nodded.

"Austin is getting married!" Her parents shouted out at the same time.

Katie's eyes widened and her mouth dropped as she sucked in a breath. "You're kidding. My brother? The king of all matrimonial aversion and evasion?"

Andrew's nod coincided with a huge grin. "Yes indeed. I've never heard him more serious in my life. He says he can't live without her, so I guess that's that."

"Well who would ever have believed? Let me guess, is it Judy Weaver?"

"Nope," Andrew said.

"Then it has to be Sophie."

Diane shook her head. "No, it's not Sophie either."

Katie huffed out a breath. "Well then, who's the lucky girl? Anyone he's mentioned in any of his emails or phone calls?"

"No." Her mother's smile grew ever broader. "Since you'll never guess, I'll just go ahead and tell you. The lucky girl is a lovely woman named Lucina Neumann."

Katie's eyes sparkled with humor. "How do you know she's lovely?"

"Because I've talked to her, of course. She has such a fun and warm personality. I think she's everything Austin needs and then some. Not only is she a good fit for this family, she and Austin will be so great together. Wait and see."

"Then that's good enough for me." She pushed her plate off to the side. "So when and where will this miraculous event take place?"

"The sixteenth of next month, and in Germany," Diane said. "They said they can't wait a moment longer than that. We've been invited to attend of course, but I'm afraid Daddy won't be able to make it on such short notice."

Katie gazed at her father. "Seriously?"

"Seriously," Andrew replied. "There's no way around it. Austin and I have talked at length about it and he's okay with that, trust me."

Diane dismissed the comment with a wave of her

hand and once again turned her attention toward Katie.

"Anyway, in his place—" She paused as she moved the mysterious envelope in the middle of the table toward her. "I'm taking you with me. You'll find our itinerary and your ticket inside, so don't lose it. I also hope your passport is up to date and your calendar is clear for an entire month. If not, you better get them that way. If you have trouble with your job, let me know. I know the boss personally." She winked at Andrew. "He owes me a favor or two."

Andrew laughed. "More than that, I'd say."

Katie glanced at her dad and then settled her gaze on her mom. "A month? We're going for a whole month?"

"I figured we might as well. After all, I'll probably never get that way again. Therefore, I thought we should enjoy everything the country has to offer the tourists while we're there, don't you think?"

"Oh, you bet I do." Katie snatched the envelope. She clutched it to her breast and leapt to her feet. Her eyes filled with tears and as she hugged her mom, she cried. "Oh wow! I can't believe it—I really can't. I'll never be able to thank you guys enough for this—"

"Oh, sit down." Diane patted the table. "It's not that big of a deal."

"No, it really is. Don't you understand? Austin getting married is nothing short of a miracle, and I get to see it happen. On top of that, if I'm to maintain a shred of family honor and decency, I need to hand over the twenty bucks I'll owe him right after he says I do. If I hand it to him in person, he can't play stupid and say he didn't get it."

Her mother gave her a sideways glance. "You

didn't bet on that, did you?"

An impish smile matched the amusement that danced in Katie's eyes. "Yes, as a matter of fact, I did. I gave him until the ripe old age of thirty-five, mind you. However, it's one bet I'm so happy to lose."

Her mother let out a sigh. "I suppose I shouldn't be surprised."

"No, you shouldn't—and the sixteenth did you say? I've got to get home and see what all I should pack for a month's excursion." She looked over at her dad. "You're going to be okay with both of us gone for that long? I promise I'll make sure everything is caught up to date before we leave."

Andrew grinned. "I think we can manage without too much difficulty. If not, you're only a phone call and a computer away, right?"

"Right—"

The rest of their excited chatter escaped William. Given her excitement, he accompanied Katie all the way home. After all, for the joy of the moment, he didn't want her driving off into a ditch or something. Yet, all along the way he centered his thoughts on the upcoming trip and what it could mean to him. The vague idea at the back of his mind had taken root and sprouted in every direction possible. The more he thought on it, the more plausible the idea sounded. Try as he might, he found it difficult to subdue his excitement over something that might not happen. Nonetheless, Isaiah said but one key fit a lock.

One key only.

Did the possibility exist—even remotely—that he'd find his elusive key while Katie visited her brother in Germany? After all, Austin didn't live all that far from the French border. If he could get her that far, it shouldn't take more than a nudge to get her all the way to Normandy.

Chapter Five

Katie gazed toward the window as the jet taxied down the runway and took off. A few wispy clouds dotted the blue skies above. Below them, the wonderful colors only a New Mexico summer could offer. She had no doubt the scenery would change the closer they got to Frankfurt. The notion sent an exhilarating thrill down her spine. She still couldn't believe she'd soon be in Germany for an entire month. A year ago, it never entered her mind she'd ever travel anywhere outside the continental United States again. Circumstances changed all of that.

Diane gave her leg a little pat. "Are you excited, dear?"

"I am!" She gave her a smile. "Thank you so much, Mom. I still can't believe you invited me along."

"Well, you certainly didn't think I'd run off to Germany all by myself, did you?"

"Nah, you're too much of a coward for that," she teased. "Actually, I just figured Dad would change his mind at the last possible minute."

"Not with the calves coming. You and I both know all the hands are quite capable of carrying on in his absence. Despite that fact, he believes no one can run the ranch with the same care and competence he does. Besides, it devastated your brother when he couldn't come home after your accident. Therefore, he practically ordered me to pack your bags and bring you along whether your dad came or not." A slight smile touched the corners of her lips as she gazed at her. "You didn't know that part, did you? I suppose Austin wants to see with his own eyes that you're okay—really okay."

"That's sweet of him, all things considered. Still, you'd think Dad would want to witness the miracle of his oldest child getting hitched. More important, you'd think he'd want to meet the woman that accomplished the impossible."

"We'll have a video to show him when we get home. He'll make do with that. Keep in mind, it's just a quiet, simple ceremony and without any fanfare whatsoever. As you know, they've invited only a handful of friends and family to witness it. From all reports, the 'I do's' shouldn't take more than five minutes at best. Especially if Austin has his way."

"Speaking of the nuptials, just who does an army chaplain get to perform a wedding ceremony when said chaplain is the groom?"

Diane laughed. "Good question. I guess we'll find out shortly."

Katie dropped her gaze to her left hand. Even under the current circumstances, the missing ring didn't cause an ounce of pain or regret. Indeed, it only added to the sense of freedom and liberation that filled her when she finally took charge of her life. As time went on, and task by task, she put all the ugliness behind her. She did it without the difficulty she had imagined. The end result? She could now make decisions without fear of someone standing in her way. Decisions such as pursuing a college degree and attending her brother's wedding for instance. Chad would never have let her go back to school. He would've said they couldn't afford it. He would never have let her make this trip either.

****

The wedding itself passed in a lovely, short but sweet blur, as promised. Bouquets of beautiful orange lilies and edelweiss adorned the cozy living room. Lovely golden ribbons were tied to the stairway railings. Mini white lights adorned the tops and sides of the rustic fireplace. In addition, scented candles, decorated with silver and gold filigree, made the chosen venue quite festive. Austin, dressed in his army finest, had never looked so handsome. Lucina looked absolutely radiant in her lacy, form-fitting white gown.

A split-second after the minister legally and lawfully united them, the faces of the newlyweds lit up the room. Katie smiled at Austin's elation. A short while later he toasted his bride as exuberant spectators looked on. He said at almost thirty-two years of age he'd waited long enough to find his soul mate. Now that he had, he would never let her go. He also pledged to fill each of her days with love, laughter, lilies, and sunshine. Love sparkled from within Lucina's eyes as she promised the same in return—minus the flowers.

Tricia, Lucina's younger sister, turned toward Katie and giggled. "Aren't they cute? I think they really are true soul mates, don't you?"

"If such a thing truly exists between two people, then I think you're right," Katie replied. "However, I must say I'm not all that convinced there is such a thing as a soul mate."

Tricia's eyes took on a dreamy glow. "Oh, trust me, Katie—that kind of beautiful magic is out there. I know it and I can't wait to find mine. He and I will be so perfect together. Wait and see."

Soul mates. A pretty enough phrase, but did it have even a speck of truth behind it?

Many people accepted the notion without batting an eyelash. Did such a thing really exist, or should she file the conviction under fables and fairytales? Obviously if it truly existed, she'd never find hers. She'd never find him because she had no intention of looking for him. Never again would she trust herself to recognize her knight in shining armor. Not even if the man rode up on the white horse she imagined in all of her childhood dreams. Should such a moment arrive and said knight introduce himself as the man fate intended she have—she'd send him on his way. After she kicked Chad out of her life, she vowed she'd remain single and alone. She didn't think that such a bad thing though. The plans she had made for her future would surely fill the empty corners the promise of a family once occupied.

Toward the end of the small reception hosted by Lucina's mother, Austin made his way to Katie's side. He dropped an arm around her shoulders and kissed her on the cheek. "What has had you so deep in thought this evening, little sister?"

"Oh, I don't know. A bunch of things, I suppose. First and foremost, how happy I am that you found someone who would marry your ugly mug. That in itself is a miracle. Secondly, that despite the nightmare we experienced in going through customs, I made it to your wedding on time. I wouldn't have wanted to miss it for the world. Third, how pleased I am that I met Lucina here and now. To see for myself how perfect you are for each other, and finally—the twenty bucks I owe you is sitting on top of your chest of drawers."

"That's good. I wouldn't have wanted to send Guido out to collect the debt. Against all orders, he might've roughed you up a bit."

Katie laughed. "I'm glad I escaped good ol' Guido's attention then. Anyway, I also stood here wondering how on earth I would keep myself occupied once the two of you leave for your honeymoon. Not that I want to tag along, mind you."

He shook his head. "I don't understand. I thought you and mom had a whole list of things you wanted to do while you were here."

"We do and still will once you're back." She tilted her head toward her mother and raised a brow. "However, in case you haven't noticed, the mothers of the bride and groom have been giggling like a couple of school girls. They've indulged in this childish behavior from the moment you and Lucina said I do. If you had paid even the slightest bit of attention, you'd know Mom and Ingrid have made all kinds of plans for the entire week you'll be gone. Old lady plans I'd rather avoid, if you get my drift. Yes, I know I could either interfere with that or suck it up and tag along. I don't think I want to do either one of those though. They look far too pleased with themselves. So, how now, brown cow?"

Austin chuckled as he scrubbed a hand back and forth across his mouth. "Well, let's see. I have a couple of friends that have some free time. They could take you wherever you'd like to go and be happy to do it. I bet we could even rustle up a couple of horses you all could ride. We have a lot of interesting places out here you can only explore by hiking or horseback. I know this because I've checked them out myself."

"Friends, hmm." She gave him a sideways glance. "You're not speaking of single male soldiers in the hope of playing matchmaker are you, because if you are—" She finished the comment with 'the look.'

In turn, Austin appeared a little sheepish and more than a little grateful when Lucina arrived at his side.

"Who's playing matchmaker?" She glanced back and forth between them before settling her gaze on her husband. "What's going on?"

He threw his hands in the air. "Hey look, I'm innocent in all of this. Katie just pointed out that your mom and mine have made some plans this week. She didn't necessarily want to join them and I don't blame her. Therefore, I thought maybe we could get Hoffman and Fuller to act as her escorts. They could take her out to the—"

"Those two? Are you crazy?" Lucina huffed out a breath as she turned her gaze toward Katie. "Why don't you just take my car? I won't be using it. You can go wherever you want to go, whenever you want to go, and without the company of a couple of buffoons."

Katie sucked in a breath. "Oh, but I couldn't."

"Oh, yes you can, and you will." Lucina emphasized the edict with a firm nod of her head. "You're my sister now, and I won't take no for an answer."

Katie looked at Austin, seeking a bit of help out of her predicament. He shook his head. "If you don't use it, you'll hurt her feelings. You don't want to do that, now do you?"

"If you're both going to gang up on me, then all

right. I'll borrow it if you insist."

Lucina blessed her with a sweet smile. "I'll leave the keys on the table."

"You know what? I have just the place you can begin your adventure with too," Austin said.

"Good, good, and where would that be?"

"The Verdun Memorial. Lucina and I were there not too long ago. I know you'll love it for sure."

****

Once the celebration ended and she finally climbed into bed, Katie couldn't sleep no matter how hard she tried. For the life of her, she couldn't say why. Perhaps the thought of taking off unescorted in a strange country had something to do with it. That shouldn't bother her though, should it? She'd become quite independent during the past year and she took pride in that. So why the kaleidoscope of butterflies flitting around inside her belly? What made them dance all throughout the wee hours without reason? The puzzle kept her company off and on throughout the rest of the night.

****

As the morning arrived, the light that filtered in through the beige-colored bedroom curtains teased her awake. The bizarre restlessness hadn't gone away. Yet the lack of sleep didn't trouble her in the least. In fact, for the strange spark of excitement in the air, she felt marvelously refreshed and ready for adventure. She pulled on a pair of faded blue jeans and her navy blue top. After a quick bowl of cereal, she grabbed her backpack and Lucina's keys. She headed out the door to the battlefield of Verdun in Lorraine, where so many soldiers lost their lives during World War I. Austin thought she'd enjoy both the scenic drive and what the memorial offered. She could follow the simple directions well enough.

The beautiful green, hilly country stole away her breath until the breathlessness grew stronger. The air grew muggy, thick, and heavy. To make matters worse, without warning and from out of the blue, a series of spine-tingling chills made her tremble from head to foot.

In direct opposition of that chill, an exquisite feeling of wondrous heat wrapped around her body and shot through her. She had never experienced anything like it. Furthermore, it scared her half to death. The fear compelled her to get off of the road and stop the car. She turned off the ignition even as she put a shaky hand over her mouth and closed her eyes. Minutes passed. All the while she waited for the return of some kind of normalcy that didn't come. She couldn't venture the smallest guess as to the cause of the problem.

There's a special someone out there for everyone, Katie. Regardless of what you think right now, Heaven wouldn't be Heaven without everyone having someone to love and cherish.

Her eyes flew open. Though the words were only audible inside her mind, she could hear the voice as plain as day. A man's voice and one she somehow knew quite well, but couldn't place. She took in a breath and held onto it for dear life. Had she lost her mind? Perhaps the lightning strike had caused a health issue the doctors couldn't foresee—like an impending stroke, or heart attack even. Did she just experience one or the other of those issues? Should she dial the emergency number and ask for medical help?

Your soul mate? The notion you scoffed at last night? Well, like it or not, he does exist. He's also a man you've loved far longer than you can ever imagine. In fulfillment of his destiny, he gave up his mortal life while in the service of his country. This happened well before you were born. Even so, that doesn't make him any less real or any less yours—if you want him.

Katie again held her breath as she gave the passenger seat a quick peek. She almost expected to see someone sitting in the seat beside her. Instead of a person, a light that grew more brilliant by the second popped into view. The brilliance engulfed her. In the center of that light she saw a beautiful cemetery with manicured green grass, tall magnificent trees, and row after row of white crosses. She blinked several times but the stubborn scene remained.

Those crosses were quite common in American military cemeteries, right? She could now see herself running on and on for what seemed like forever through that graveyard. Through row after row, a force she couldn't describe guided her steps. At last she stopped and turned to her left. She didn't follow the path very far. How she knew the soldier's exact resting place, she couldn't say, but she did. She could see herself falling to her knees in front of his grave. Deep sorrow filled her heart as tears bathed her cheeks. Despite her attempts, the perspective the bizarre vision or hallucination offered, kept the name on the cross hidden from her view. Nonetheless, she knew without doubt, the body of her solider—her beloved soldier—rested there.

In response to the knowledge, the sorrow fled. In its place, her heart overflowed with love—a passionate, tender, magnificent love such as she had never experienced before or even thought possible—for this fallen soldier whose name she didn't know.

Wait just a doggone minute. Love? Passion? Her soldier? She'd somehow lost her mind.

She snatched her phone with every intention of dialing that emergency number.

His love for you is every bit as sweet and just as powerful, if not more so, than the love you feel for him right now. Aren't you the least bit curious? Wouldn't you like to know a little bit more about him?

All of a sudden, tears ran down her cheeks. Katie couldn't stop them. She couldn't stop the onslaught of emotion either, nor could she make sense of it. All she knew right now was that it both thrilled and frightened her beyond reason.

How long she sat in the car off the side of the road she couldn't say. A thousand fragmented thoughts assaulted her mind. She discovered a mountain of questions. Did the soldier she had just felt such passion for really exist? Was he buried in that graveyard? Or in some pathetic response to a failed marriage and her brother's wedding, did she make him up? Could the voice in her head in any way be real? *Don't be ridiculous. Of course I made him up. But if I did, why on earth would I? None of this makes any sense.*

Katie wiped away the last of her tears. She returned the phone to the side pocket of her backpack, started the car, and headed for the Verdun Memorial. Her quiet stroll through the cemetery didn't answer a single question. The white crosses marking the graves didn't match the ones in her wild hallucination-vision. If her soldier existed, he didn't lose his life during World War

I at the battle of Verdun.

No, he didn't, but you're on the right track. So don't give up now.

A shudder traveled down her spine. She shook it off and approached one of the curators at the museum.

He gave her a welcoming smile.

"Excuse me, sir, do you speak English by chance?"

"Yes, I do, Miss. Is there something I can help you with?"

"Well, I'm an American as you might've guessed. I'm on a quest to visit as many military cemeteries as I can while I'm in the area. Now that I've finished my visit to your wonderful memorial, I wondered what else might be in the vicinity. Can you help me?"

She left the facility with a list, a fistful of pamphlets, and a map in her hand. Katie nibbled a lip as she considered each of the names and locations. The quest would take several days if she visited each one and examined each cross. Did she really want to do that? She wavered for only a moment. She took her cell phone from out of her backpack and called her mom.

"Katie? Are you all right, dear?"

The panic in her voice brought a smile to her face. Good thing she couldn't see it. "I'm fine. I just wanted you to know I'll be gone for a few days and I don't want you to worry, all right?"

"I don't see how you can do that. You don't have your luggage with you, dear."

Ever practical. Katie laughed. "No, but I have my backpack and it has a few changes of clothing still in it."

"I can't imagine what's so important you have to go right now." She dropped a sigh. "I suppose you'll have your way though, you always do. You will promise to call me at least ten, maybe twenty times a day while you're gone? So I don't worry."

"Let's make that a couple of times a day. I found Verdun intriguing. So much so that I think I'll visit several more military memorials while I'm in France. We both know that's something you'd rather not do. You needn't pretend otherwise."

"Then I won't. But why don't you wait until Austin and Lucina return? I'm sure they wouldn't mind the trip."

"No, they've seen them all before, and we've already made other plans with them, so—"

"All right, if you're sure. In all seriousness, please call me a couple of times a day so I know you're all right. You are in a strange country, after all."

"I will, I promise."

"Oh, if you get down to Normandy, you might want to see if you can find your great-grand uncle Max's grave. He's buried there."

"I…uh…didn't know that. I'll be sure to look for him though."

Katie ended the call then wrapped her hands around her arms and rubbed them. Should she put the sudden intense chill down to mere coincidence or did the word 'Normandy' have anything to do with it? With the cemetery on her list, she'd know soon enough one way or the other.

****

On the third day of her journey, she pulled into the Normandy American Cemetery and Memorial parking lot. She felt more than a little foolish as she exited the car. The past few days hadn't yielded a thing. No crazy voices in her head. No ghosts. No visions or figments of her fertile, over-active imagination. Would this place be any different? Despite her doubts, she would finish this journey and put the matter to rest.

Katie glanced down at the brochure she held before turning her gaze toward the ocean below. A light breeze, carrying the aroma of sea brine, caressed her face. Under a blue, sunny sky the gentle swell of waves splashed onto a peaceful shore. On June 6, 1944, the day would've looked far different. The terrible scene described by all the history books made her shudder.

After several minutes, she turned away and headed for the cemetery. A thorough search of well over nine thousand graves seemed a daunting one. Nonetheless she would see this through, if for nothing else than to prove her vision-hallucination just that—a wonderful, wild, hallucination. Once she returned home and had her feet firmly planted on the ground, she'd laugh over this experience. She might even share it with her siblings and her Texas cousins. Jared and Justin could have such fun with it, even if at her expense. Indeed, they would never let her live it down. *Better that than being locked up in the loony bin somewhere, right?*

The moment she stepped onto the grass, her heart picked up its pace. The air around her now had a sudden heaviness to it. Moisture from the sea perhaps or just anxiety? Whatever the cause, she dismissed it. Instead, she concentrated on the rows of white crosses ahead of her, thousands upon thousands that matched the crosses in her bizarre vision. She knew without a name, she just couldn't do it. Yet at the same time, she couldn't leave either. How to reconcile the two?

Katie brushed her windblown hair away from her

face. She tugged at the hem of her emerald green, scooped neck T-shirt. All the while tears threatened to surface. She gazed all about the cemetery and didn't see anyone, anywhere in the near vicinity. Good. Because—

"I'm road-weary and bone-tired. I've had very little sleep since I arrived in Germany. I have found nothing that gives an ounce of credence to your existence during these past three days. More than likely, I'm stark raving mad. However, if this is not the case and you're somewhere out there, you better tell me which way to go. If you don't, I'm going to go back to the car. From there I'll head to the nearest medical facility for the mentally troubled. That, my friend, will be the end of my quest."

Did she just hear a masculine chuckle carried by the breeze? Her irritation intensified.

"Are you buried here or am I just wasting my time?" She tucked a hand inside the front pocket of her black jeans and waited for some kind of response. "Well? Are you going to help me or are you not?"

Head over to plot E, row 25. That's off to your right.

"Thank you." She had gone mad. Not only did she hear voices in her head, she believed what he said and followed his directions to the letter. As she approached the designated row, she slowed her steps. She turned left and stopped. Katie didn't ask for additional directions because she already knew which of the crosses belonged to her soldier. As she moved forward her gaze fell on a single rose in front of his grave.

The unique color—a shade of red and a beauty that defied all earthly description—matched the one she had pressed between the pages of a book at home. The one she had taken with her on the day they released her from the hospital, in fact. No one could tell her who sent the rose or any of the other roses that had appeared in her room each day. Not a soul had ever seen them arrive. They were always just there. Carol said she and the other nurses decided they were a gift from a kindhearted alien in another realm altogether. Perhaps they weren't far wrong.

She leaned down and picked it up. As she closed her eyes, she inhaled the rich, fragrant scent she knew so well. Somewhere in the back of her mind "Unchained Melody" played. This version of one of her most favorite songs came through loud and clear. So clear, in fact, she halfway expected the appearance of Inka Gold right there in the cemetery with pan flute and guitar in hand. She hadn't heard that song since—

Katie gasped as the sweet melody called up a precious memory she didn't even know she had until this very minute. A memory surely created in her unconscious state while in the hospital. One she now recalled with absolute clarity. Either that or her insanity had just intensified.

She needn't look at the name on the cross because all of a sudden, she knew it, though she couldn't say how. The grave belonged to Sergeant William Malloy Griffin. After taking in a much needed breath, she slowly opened her eyes and blinked. In fact, she blinked several times. Nothing in her line of sight changed when she did.

The ethereal companion she had known all her life, but never glimpsed, stood not ten feet away from her. How she knew that, she couldn't say. She just did. The interesting thing? He looked just as solid and real as anyone else wandering through the cemetery. Except none of the visitors she could see wore World War II combat fatigues. Not a single man out there could possibly be as fun to look at either. His dark, russet-colored hair framed the most compelling steel gray eyes she'd ever seen. Eyes she could get lost in if she wasn't careful. When he offered a flirty grin, the beat of her heart doubled its pace and shimmied up her throat. In addition, the kaleidoscope of butterflies took flight without knowing where in the world they were going. In fact, they kept bashing into each other.

Despite the ruckus, she returned his smile. "Good morning, William."

Could a ghost speak aloud?

He dipped his head forward and slightly to the left. "Morning, Katie."

They could.

"Thank you for the help. I'm not sure I could've found you without it." Is that the best she could do as she spoke to him for the first time? *Really? He must think me a complete idiot.*

"My pleasure." He didn't say anything else or even move for several seconds. She had the distinct impression he did that so as not to frighten her. His eyes danced with amusement as she looked him over from the top of his six-foot frame, past the broad shoulders, and all the way down to his combat boots. "Now that you've had a good look and you know I won't disappear, mind if I get a little bit closer?"

A breath of laughter accompanied the slight shake of her head. "Not at all. I'm not the least bit afraid if that's what you're worried about."

"Well, you never know." He closed the distance between them. "To at least some degree, most people are."

She knew what he meant. Ghosts, even the thought of ghosts, terrified the vast majority of mortals. Still, she couldn't resist a playful tease. "Well I can see why. You are kind of scary looking."

He grinned. "Think so, do you?"

In response, she merely lifted a shoulder and broadened her smile. All the while a question nagged, well, hundreds of questions actually. *How to phrase it without sounding like a dork?* "So now that we've been formally introduced, at least after a fashion, where do we go from here?"

His gaze swept over the park. "Good question. Care to take a walk with me so we can discuss that?"

Katie glanced at the cross that bore his name as the last strains of the music faded from her mind. Perhaps the marker carried with it some unpleasant memories from the battle he would have to have participated in on Omaha Beach? "I would love to take a walk with you."

He placed his hand on the small of her back as they strolled away from the cemetery. The slight pressure of it surprised her. How did he do that?

"Where we go from here is all up to you, Katie. If I make you uncomfortable, I can stay away from here on out. On the other hand, if you wish, I can become a bigger part of your life."

"Become? If you are who I think you are, then you've always been a big part of my life. I am right about that, am I not?"

The comment brought another smile to his face. "I've made an appearance from time to time."

"A little more than that, I'd say. I mean you've always been right by my side whenever I've needed a shoulder to cry on—if even a ghostly one."

He nodded. "If that's all you want, then that's the way it can stay. However, if you'd like to see me a little more often—get to know me better—I'll be more than happy to oblige. If not, with a heavy heart, I'll stay out of your life."

That's not at all what she wanted. She'd relied on him too much over the years. If he left, there would be a hole that nothing else could fill. She didn't want that. Not ever. "So how does this work? I mean now that you've introduced yourself in all your splendid glory, could you just drop by whenever I want you to? Or—would you still only visit me as you have in the past?"

He bobbed his head from side to side. "Probably for the most part I could come if you called out my name. At such times I might only be able to stay for a short while though."

"I need only call your name and you'll respond?"

"Yep, for the most part that should pretty much do it—you'd have to give me a reasonable amount of time to comply, of course."

"Even if I called your name every day?"

He halted their walk and turned to face her. A small crooked grin appeared as he gazed into her eyes.

Like a silly schoolgirl, her heart fluttered as a blush lit up her cheeks. *Why does he affect me like this now?*

"You'd want to see me every day?" he asked.

"Why would that surprise you? I mean, how else am I going get to all of my questions answered?"

Chapter Six

William laughed outright. He couldn't help himself. "You have some questions, do you?"

She stared at him as if he had quite lost his mind. "Don't be ridiculous. Of course I have questions and not just some. I have lots and lots of them. Wouldn't you if our situations were reversed?"

"I suppose you have a point. All right then, we may as well get started. Fire away."

"Okay." She traced the bottom of her lip with the tip of her tongue. "Are you one of those scary ghosts that stick around and haunt people or places? You know the ones I mean."

"Um, I'm afraid I don't."

"Ghosts that haunt for no other reason than it gives them a twisted sense of pleasure to see their terrified victims scream and run for cover. You aren't one of those, are you?"

It took everything he had not to laugh again. "No, I don't think so. I've never frightened you, have I?"

"No, I guess not." She narrowed her eyes as she turned her head to the side. "Do you have unfinished business? Business in which you need a mortal's help so you can bring it to some kind of conclusion then?"

"None that I can think of."

"You do know you're dead, right?"

"If you're speaking of the demise of my mortal

body, then yes. But come on, Katie, I think you already know all of this."

She shrugged. "Even so, it doesn't hurt to get the confirmation."

From all appearances, his answers satisfied her well enough. "Now we have all of that business out of the way, is there anything else you'd like to ask?"

She studied him for a minute. "If none of the above, why are you here?"

"That's obvious isn't it? This is where you are right now."

"That's not what I meant, but—" She took a half step back as she again looked him over from head to toe. "Wait a minute. Does that mean you followed me here?"

"Are you speaking of here in this particular cemetery, or here as in Europe?"

"Well, both, I guess."

"Then yes, I did, but not in the way you probably mean."

"Care to explain that?"

"Let's just say I knew your plans well before you boarded that plane in New Mexico. After you cooperated with the idea of checking out the military memorials, I'd thought I'd make my appearance here in Normandy."

"Why?"

"As you might suspect, there's an emotional connection to me in this location that far surpasses all others. Because of the intensity of it, I believed I'd have my best chance of finally getting all the way through to you here. I've tried many times before, you know. Obviously without the success I would like to have had."

"No, that's not right. I've seen you more times than I can count." She stopped short. "Well, not like I see you now, of course. Even so, I've always known when you were with me. I could feel your presence."

"Not good enough, Katie. Not only did I want you to see my spirit, I also wanted you to hear me speak. I want you to know who I am, what you are to me, and what I am to you."

"What I...I mean to...I don't—"

Her heartbeat accelerated even as a touch of color splashed across her cheeks. "Don't be afraid, Katie. You can say anything you want, or ask me any question you might have."

"I'm not afraid. It's just that—" She dropped her gaze as she nibbled at a nail.

He tilted her chin upward and gazed into her eyes. "Just ask it. I promise you it's all right."

"Okay. I think I remember something. A memory from the weeks I spent in the hospital. Well, either that or I've lost my mind, which is very possible. In fact, I may be delusional right this minute," she muttered.

He chuckled. "Is it a memory you'd like to share? Because if it is, I'm all ears."

"I believe you read me a letter—a letter from you to me, or did I make that up."

"If you're asking, rather than telling, then yes, I read you a letter and no, you didn't make it up."

"I have to know." She lifted a hand to her brow as she gazed into his eyes. "For the sake of my sanity, would you mind sharing it with me again?"

"I'll need a little bit more to go on than just that. I read countless letters to you while you slept."

"You did? I mean, you wrote more than one?"

"I have written hundreds of them, though some not as long or elaborate as others. As you already know and have so stated, I checked in on you from time to time. This is something I did from the early days of your childhood. So I kept a journal of my impressions, my thoughts, and feelings of those visits."

"Why?"

"Because it gave me a little of the comfort I needed at the time." The reply made her uncomfortable. William could see it in her eyes. He gave her a wink and hoped it put her at ease. "Now, about that specific letter you remember?"

"Yes. Okay, here goes. You spoke of a man named Isaiah and something about how he said you'd know when you found the woman destined to claim your heart?" Against another blush, her words tumbled out in a breathless sort of rush. "Do you know which one I'm talking about?"

He nodded. "Yes, I think so, but it probably needs a bit of an explanation."

"Okay."

"Isaiah is not only a great and noble man, he's also my great-grandfather. I'll also tell you he met me at the end of my mortal existence and acted as my guide as I stepped through the portal. He answered all of my questions. More important, he helped me adjust to a world far different than the one I left behind. As time went on, he became my confidant—someone to whom I could bare my soul, if you'll pardon the expression. Quite by chance, or so he said, he paid me a visit that coincided with a bout of self-pity. When he asked for the cause, I lamented over my solitary state. You see, everywhere I looked, I could see happy couples facing eternity hand-in-hand. That's something I desperately wanted, but didn't have. Indeed, I didn't think I'd ever have it since the opportunity passed me by during my mortal existence."

"He's the one that spurred your search even though he couldn't tell you how you'd recognize this mystery woman amidst the masses? Do I have that right?"

"Yep. That about sums it up, I guess."

"I see. Well, how did you know—or how do you know now—that you've found the right woman in me? You could be wrong, you know. The desperate desire to find someone could've clouded your judgment."

"No, I'm not wrong. This is very difficult for me to explain in a way you'll understand while still in your mortal state. Suffice it to say the unique light within your soul called out to me in a definitive way the first time we crossed paths. To this very day, it still does. Once attuned to that distinctive light of yours, I knew—and will always know—when you need me or when you call for me. Does that make any sense?"

"Some, I guess. If you don't mind my asking, where and when did this grand event happen? Finding me, I mean."

The simple question made him smile. "On a whim, a friend of mine and I visited the area of his childhood."

"Another ghost?"

"Yes, if that's the term you want to use. Personally, I prefer spirit. Nonetheless, keep in mind he lived out his mortality a century or so before I was born. Anyway, he wanted me to see some of the places he held a fondness for. Along the way, he showed me a place along the Rio Grande where he and his friends had spent countless hours. He said they fished, swam, dreamed of girls, and what their future might bring them. You know—that sort of thing. While we were there, you showed up with your extended family for a picnic. You were just a little girl at the time, perhaps three or four years of age. Your state of being didn't matter though. In that moment, the light of your soul interlocked perfectly with mine. I knew then as well as I know now, we are two halves of a perfect whole. To cowboy it up a bit for you, we are two peas in the very same pod."

A wistful smile touched her lips. "I wish I could remember the specific incident."

"One day, I'm sure you will."

"Really? What makes you so sure?"

"Because shortly after I found you, I remembered a few things I hadn't remembered before."

"Like what?"

"Sweet memories of things that happened between you and me. Moments that brought to light the powerful love we shared a long time ago. I'll just leave it at that for now if you don't mind."

"That's what you meant when you said I've loved you far longer than I could ever imagine?"

"Yes, it is." It perplexed him that she seemed more than a little uncomfortable with what he aid, "Are you all right with that? You aren't going to bolt on me, are you?"

"No, I, uh…"

The mix of pain and sorrow that filled her eyes pierced his soul.

"Please don't take this wrong. I just don't know if I believe it."

He nodded as he gazed toward the ocean. This wasn't what he expected or hoped for once he broke through the barrier that kept them apart. He at least wanted a chance. "Well, I can see where you might. I know I'm not any woman's vision of Sir Galahad or—"

She interrupted with a lift of her hand. A trace of dewy liquid filled her eyes. "No, William. You have that all wrong. What I find hard to believe…is that a man like you…could want anything to do with…with someone like me. I mean, look at you! You're perfect, while I'm so…so very flawed."

Relief filled him in the instant. That, he could work with. "I think one of the saddest truths mortals face is the ease at which they can be broken inside. One shouldn't let the actions of one reprehensible person, such as Chad McCrae, destroy all that is good and beautiful inside someone like you. Besides, you have that backward." He took hold of her waist and turned her toward him. He would've laughed over her look of wonder, if not for the serious tone of their conversation. "In my eyes you are the most beautiful, most perfect person ever created. My intention—indeed my very goal since I know you've forgotten your feelings for me—is to get you to fall in love with me all over again. Of that, you have no say in the matter. You can, however, choose to reject me once I've given it my best shot. Fair warning though, if you should do such a terrible thing, my heart will be irreparably broken. I'm afraid you'll have to accept the eternal consequences for that. I can testify the results won't be anywhere near pretty."

She widened her eyes and gulped. "Well, I don't think I—"

"Nah, I'm only kidding." He touched the tip of her nose. "I'm shamelessly playing on your fears and sympathies. Don't pay me any mind. I never do. However, I am dead serious about my goal."

"I see." Katie rubbed her lips together. "If you don't mind my asking, how will you set about accomplishing this lofty objective?"

He shrugged away the question. "The usual. Flowers, chocolate, and—let's see, what did that enchanted clock say in the cartoon you were so fond of? The part that always made you and your brothers roll on the floor with laughter when you were kids. Oh, yeah, something about not keeping promises. Except I do intend to keep all of mine, I so swear."

She gazed down on the flower she held in her hand. "Well, if the flowers you'll bring me in the future are anything close to this one, then I'd say you're off to a good start. Where do you get them?"

"From my garden."

She considered that for a moment. "I suppose that shouldn't surprise me. I've never seen anything on earth that could equal it."

"Then that's one up for me already." William dipped his head toward the left. "Come on, we've got company on the way. They could think you're a bit off balance if they hear you talking to the breeze."

Her gaze darted between him and the various visitors of the park. "They can't see you?"

"Not at the moment."

"I take it they can't hear you either?"

He shook his head. "Afraid not."

"Well that's probably a good thing. I hate to tell you this, but you do look a little out of place in your current state of dress."

"No doubt." He gazed toward the memorial and nodded. "Is there something else you'd like to see while you're here? I swear I'll be as silent as the grave while you enjoy what the park has to offer the visitors."

The offhanded remark made her laugh. "No, that's okay. I've done what I came here to do. Besides, I really should be heading back to Austin's house before my dear, sweet mother has a fit of the vapors." She peeked over at the small crowd moving their way. "The drive is a long one. So can you keep me company?"

"I'd love to keep you company. Perhaps you should at least visit the grave of your Uncle Max before we take off, though. After all, your mom might expect a picture of his memorial or something."

"You heard us talk about that?"

"I did."

She nodded. "You're probably right. Do you know where he's buried?"

He flashed a grin as he aimed his thumb to the right. "This way."

****

Even with the delay, the journey back to Austin's didn't last very long. At least not in William's eyes. But now the promise of other such adventures lay ahead of them both. All throughout the drive, Katie asked him countless questions. She now knew he favored the shade of blue that matched her eyes and that he loved sunrises and sunsets. He told her he loved wide-open fields, the smell of freshly mown hay, and damp earth after the rain. Katie could now name the small town he had once called home and even knew where to find it. She found delight in the fact that he too—let's see, how

71

did she put that?—grew up on a horse, behind a cow.

"Sarge!"

The greeting, if something said with such obvious exasperation could be called a greeting, sliced into his thoughts. He turned half-way around. Richard Barnett waved a hand as he lengthened his stride. Once he caught up, he fell into step beside him.

"Hello, Rich, nice to see you."

He rolled his eyes skyward even as he shook his head. "You realize, don't you, that I've only called your name three different times now? What's the matter, got cotton in your ears or something?"

He warded off the silly grin that screamed for release. "The 'or something' might be a better fit. How are you doing? I haven't seen you in a while."

Richard's own grin slowly broadened as he pinned his gaze to his. "You know, I think I'd rather know how you're doing."

He returned a nonchalant shrug. "Couldn't be better."

"Um-hmm and if I had to guess, I'd say that has something to do with your lady. Am I right?"

He couldn't contain the joy within him any longer. "You are."

Richard whooped in excitement. "You finally got through to Katie! You did, didn't you?"

William nodded. "Yes, I did."

"She can see you? She hears everything you say?"

"She can, and every word."

"Does she know who you are?"

"I told her."

He gave him a sideways glance. "How did she take it?"

"Well, she didn't run for the nearest exit if that's what you're asking."

"Now that, my friend, is incredible and for so many reasons. The guys will want to know how all of that came to pass. Mind if I gather them up and we can drop by your place a little later?"

He hesitated. The need to shelter and protect his boys had never waned. If anything, it had grown stronger and not just for the special ones he led through the portal on D-Day. He gave every soldier that followed the same consideration, compassion, and care. How would Donald Martin react to his success?

Richard knew his thoughts and shook his head. "I think it will give all of us in the same boat a little bit of hope—including Don. Don't you?"

****

Despite her fatigue, Katie couldn't sleep. Her chaotic thoughts wouldn't let her. Did she really just spend the most incredible day of her life with a ghost who professed to love her with a passion second to none, past, present, or future? Or more likely had she lost her mind? Such a thing wasn't unheard of. Psychiatric hospitals were full of people who lived with their delusions twenty-four hours a day, seven days a week. For the most part, the world pitied them. Did she need their pity as well?

On the other hand, did she have the kind of fertile imagination necessary to conjure someone as unimaginably perfect as William Malloy Griffin? A short while ago she didn't think such a man existed. Doubt gnawed at both heart and mind. After all, anyone could roam through a cemetery, stop at some random grave, and say, "Aha! I know who you are! You are my long-lost love. There is no escape now. I hereby decree we shall be together forever."

The thought led her forward. Did some kind of proof exist that she in fact saw the spiritual form of the man buried inside that grave? No doubt she could find information regarding the Sergeant Griffin buried in Normandy on the internet. That should be easy enough. But could she find a picture of his face? If she did, would that face match the one she had spent the entire day with?

She tossed the covers off to the side and got out of bed. After she donned her blue silk robe, she tip-toed to the living room. Stubborn determination accompanied her toward Austin's computer in the corner. Katie sat down, turned it on, and typed in her query. The search engine returned thousands of sites she could explore in regards to the casualties of D-Day. No surprise there.

She rubbed her hands together. "Okay, Katie, let's get this show on the road."

After several unlucky site searches, she found a D-Day site that focused solely on the Americans who died in that battle, a site that boasted a ton of photographs. Without doubt, his profile would be in their database, but would it have the picture she needed? She held her breath as she clicked on the search box and typed in his name. One more click and she arrived at his personal file. She gave the breath she'd held a slow, uneven release. At the same time, she clasped her fingers together and raised her trembling hands to her mouth. All the while tears filled her eyes as she gazed at the black and white photograph. Sergeant William M. Griffin, so very handsome in his dress uniform, gazed back. Her butterflies once again began a wild ruckus.

The profile told her he voluntarily joined the army at the age of twenty-eight. He signed on from his hometown in Arizona, just as he said earlier. Not quite two years later, death claimed him on the shore of Easy Red Sector, at Omaha Beach. The pictures the site had of that bloody battle turned her stomach. Especially when she thought of him lying there, broken and bleeding. On a whim, she ordered his Individual Deceased Personnel File from the United States Army, via the Freedom of Information Act. Along with the IDPF, she also ordered his Military Service Record. The files would give her far more information than any D-Day website provided.

Once she copied his photograph to her phone, she shut down the computer. Right now, she wouldn't share William with anyone. Not even her mom. A time for that might come, but not now.

"Katie?" Her mother sounded surprised and perhaps a little frightened.

She swiveled around in the office chair and faced her.

Diane put a hand over her heart as she gulped. "What are you doing up so late? I thought someone had broken into the house."

Katie dismissed her concern with a wave of her hand. "Don't be silly. I don't think anyone would dare break into Austin's house. They'd fear the consequences of such a foolish act, I'm sure. After all, he's an expert marksman and heavily armed. Now, as to what I'm doing? Well, I couldn't sleep and thought I'd do a little military research."

"I'm sure that could've waited until the morning."

"Yes, it could've, but I needed something to do that

would knock me out. Reading usually does it."

"Maybe some warm milk might help. Would you like me to get you a cup?"

Katie laughed. "Now that's something you haven't offered me since grade school. And just to let you in on a little secret? I didn't like it even then."

"Well, how about some herbal tea instead? Austin has some chamomile and valerian in the cupboard."

"That I would take, but only if you'll join me."

Once they settled onto the sofa with cups in hand, Katie took a sip and nodded. "This is good."

Diane wrinkled her nose as she gazed down at the contents. "I've never cared much for it."

The comment made Katie smile. "Then why are you drinking it?"

"Well, because you asked me to."

The smile turned into a quiet giggle. "I'm sure you could've found yourself something a little more agreeable."

"Perhaps." Despite her obvious distaste for the beverage, her mom took a couple more sips. "Anyway, would you like to tell me why you can't sleep?"

"What makes you think there's a specific reason?"

"Because you can sleep like a log and at the drop of a hat when you've a mind to. So what's the reason? Is something wrong?"

"I think it's just the emotion of the last couple of days." She paused as she gathered her thoughts. "You know, as I walked through all of the cemeteries, I read countless names of soldiers whose lives were cut way too short. Many of them were still in their teens. Others surely left young widows and families behind. I couldn't help but think of all they didn't experience during their lifetimes and it made me sad."

Diane nodded. "Now you know why I avoid those places."

"Yes, but haven't you ever wondered what happens to them?"

She knit her brow. "What happens to them? I don't know what you mean?"

Katie set her cup down on the tea table and drew her legs up onto the sofa. "Oh, come on, Mom. You've read numerous books on near-death-experiences. Your library is full of them. In addition you've watched just as many television shows where life after death is the sole topic. You've always had a passion for that sort of thing and shared it with anyone who would listen. After all of that, haven't you wondered what happens to those who didn't have a chance to live a full life? You think they just flit around Heaven with golden harps in hand and never fall in love with anyone? Do you think they even care about such things?"

"You're serious about this, aren't you?"

"Dead serious."

Diane placed her cup on the coaster beside Katie's and leaned back against the cushion. She searched her eyes with an intensity that made her a bit uncomfortable. Did she look for something in particular? If so, Katie didn't have a clue as to what.

"You know, ever since your accident, I've wondered if perhaps you had an experience of your own. You never said, and I thought if you did, you would tell me about it when you were ready. But the questions you're asking tell me you don't remember anything at all that happened during the time you were gone from us."

She shook her head. "Sorry, I don't. Those minutes are a complete blank."

"That's too bad. I would've liked to get your perspective, and well—" She shrugged. "Okay, you want to know what I think. I don't think Heaven would be Heaven without someone special to share it with."

Intense chills raced up and down Katie's spine as her mother all but repeated the same statement William had made.

"The opinion is my own, of course. But I can't help but believe in my heart of heart's there's at least a bit of truth to the notion, if not a whole lot of truth. I just can't imagine a life in a Heaven that didn't include your dad by my side."

Long after the conversation ended, Katie wandered out onto the patio. The brilliance of the night sky stole her gaze as she sat down on the white wicker rocking chair. While the melody of nocturnal creatures kept her company, she thought about what her mother had said. Her thoughts, beliefs, and insights surprised her. Perhaps one day she could tell her mother about William. Maybe she might even believe her. If she did, what would she think of William's intention to win her heart? What would she think of him? Would he ever allow her to see him? Better yet, could he? Did her own "near-death" experience have anything to do with her ability to see her William now?

Her William. But was he really hers?

What would become of them in the end? An unconventional relationship between a ghost and mortal just didn't sound reasonable. Yet he acted as if such a thing was a normal, everyday thing to do. Was it? Were there mortals out there right now in love with ghosts? If so, would she be one of them? Did she love him already and willfully denied that truth regardless of the brief wave of intense emotion she felt during her vision? Did she fear it? Without a doubt she felt a powerful connection to him, but then again, she always had.

She retrieved her phone and brought up his picture. For a time she studied every detail the old photograph offered. The thoughtful but serious expression he carried made her wonder if he somehow knew he wouldn't make it home.

"That's not the best picture I've ever taken you know. I think I could rustle you up a better one if you'd like. One more in my element."

A rush of liquid excitement filled her as she turned toward him. "William! I didn't expect a visit from you quite this soon or at this hour."

He grinned as he offered her the flower he had in his hand. Though not quite at half-bloom, its exquisite outer petals were an iridescent shade of lavender blue with shimmering pink undertones. Even so, the feeble description didn't do the flower, or its colors, justice.

"For you."

"Wow, you weren't kidding about the flowers."

"No, ma'am."

"I've never seen one quite like this." The moment she had it in hand she took in a deep breath of the potent fragrance someone ought to use for a prestigious line of perfume. "Umm. Smells so good. From your garden?"

"Yep, I thought you might like it. Unlike the one pressed inside your book, or the now battered and wilted one you carried here today, this one is fresh. Might last longer than you think it should if you put it in some water."

"I love it, thank you—and of course I will." With a sweep of her hand, she offered him one of the empty chairs. He chose the one beside her. "As I said, I really didn't expect to see you quite this soon."

"I know. But since you were awake, I thought I'd stop by since I probably won't get another chance for a little while."

Her heart dropped even as her throat tightened. Did he think better of his avowal to court her and decided in this way he could let her down easy? Such a thing wouldn't surprise her. In fact she had half-way expected him to cast her off—just like Chad did. "Oh, I see."

Somehow he took hold of her hand without passing through it, gave it a gentle press, and then released her from his grasp. How did he do things like that?

"No need for thinking what you're thinking. In fact you're way off base."

"How would you know what I'm thinking?"

"Regardless of the emotions you keep hidden from the world, you have the most expressive eyes I've ever seen. They're quite informative if one cares to look. And trust me, I've never tired of looking."

A blush stained her cheeks. She could feel the heat. "If you don't mind my asking, why can't you—"

"I've already told you I don't mind your questions," he cut in. "Don't ever be afraid to ask them, okay?"

She gave him a half-hearted smile. "Okay."

"I'll be gone for awhile because I have assignments I must take care of, that's all. Though possibly hard for you to believe, I do have far more important things to do than float along on some billowy cloud while I strum a harp."

The image her mind had conjured earlier of him in that very pose made her laugh. "That's probably good. You don't look like the harp-strumming type."

"No?"

"No. So as an alternative to that, what do you do in this heavenly realm of yours?"

"Well, let's see. How shall I put this?"

He paused far longer than she had anticipated. Had she stepped into forbidden territory?

"In one way or another, soldiers, past and present, die every single day, Katie. I'm sure this is something you're well aware of. Because of my own background and experience, one of my duties—as well as my greatest honor and privilege—is to help some of them when they cross over. Most especially those soldiers who have suffered horrendous trauma in the moment they die. A handful of those individuals need a little more help and understanding than most. Under the directive of General George Henry Thomas, I belong to a company of men and women that give it."

"You do?"

William nodded. "I do."

As she mulled that over, she discovered the notion didn't surprise her. After all, she had experienced his understanding and comfort many times over. She smiled. "I can see why you'd be given an assignment like that. You're very good at it."

Chapter Seven

William craved a visit with Katie like he never had before. He hadn't seen her for several weeks and he missed her. Now that he had some free time, he'd step into her realm and take her into his arms. But he couldn't. At least not yet. Not before he checked on Don.

As expected, William found him in the park near his home. He sat underneath the majestic oak tree, resting his back against the trunk.

"I thought you'd be here. You seem to favor this spot." William placed a hand on his shoulder and gave it a squeeze. "How are you doing, my friend?"

Don didn't turn around. His gaze remained fixed on the ice-blue lake that glistened like diamonds underneath the golden sky. With an indifferent shrug, he acknowledged his presence. William sat down beside him. For awhile, they watched the elegant white swans glide across the water in a slow, graceful dance. After a time he nodded at the birds that had settled near the grassy shore with their necks entwined.

"Funny, isn't it? Even the birds have a special someone. They're so engrossed in each other they haven't even noticed we're here."

William understood his feelings of resentment. He had them himself a short while ago. Not that reminding him of that detail would bring his friend the comfort he needed. If he said such a thing, Donnie would bring up his recent success with Katie. In turn, his bitterness would increase by leaps and bounds if it hadn't already. William understood this. How many times had he witnessed the success of others without having any of his own? Perhaps if he tried a different tactic?

"You know Don, you shouldn't give up hope so soon. All things considered, you haven't been here nearly as long as some who are still searching. Your companion is out there. You know this just as well as all of us do. You've seen it time and again. Sometimes discovering who that person is takes more time and effort than we might otherwise desire. Look at Bartholomew. He died during the Revolutionary War and he's still search—"

"I'm way past the discovery stage, Sarge," Don cut in. "I've never said this to anyone else, so I would appreciate if you didn't either. I know who she is. You see, some of us don't get the chance at a happily ever after like you do with your Katie, even if so decreed by Heaven. Maybe if you take a good look around, you'd notice it."

The confession surprised William. "You know who she is?"

Don firmed his jaw. "Yep, and without any doubt whatsoever. I've known that cold, hard fact since my junior year in high school. What do you think of that little tidbit?"

"I don't understand."

"You wouldn't." Don vaulted to his feet and strode toward the strand without giving him a backward glance.

Despite the obvious dismissal, William followed

him anyway. "I know it's none of my business, but I'd like to understand whatever it is you're going through. Perhaps I could find a way to help you."

Don scoffed. "There's nothing you can do. There's nothing anyone can do. Don't you get it? We're all free to choose, isn't that right? Even if some of us make the wrong choices?"

"Yes, I can agree with that."

Don nodded. "Now don't get me wrong. You don't know how happy I am you and Katie are finally together. I'm happy she can both see and hear you now. Since you've overcome that final obstacle, I wish you every joy and happiness. Believe me when I say your triumph is the one bright spot in my existence right now. That being said, what will you do if somewhere along the way she rejects you? She's still young, isn't she? What if she decides your ghostly form isn't enough for her? Given enough time, Katie might love you more than she could ever love anyone else. But what if she settles for someone with a warm, tangible body she can feel, embrace, and cuddle up with at night instead? She might want someone she can have children with, you know. Most women want a family, don't they? Sometimes people just settle for—and are content with—second-best."

Not that those thoughts hadn't crossed William's mind more often than he could count, but— "Is that what happened to you?"

"After a fashion."

"What do you mean?"

A faraway look entered his eye. "We were happy once, Rachel and I. In those days we were the envy of every kid and couple our age in the whole entire town.

'Look,' people would say. 'There goes Donnie Martin and Rachel Jameson. Did you ever see anyone more perfect for each other than what they are? They look so happy, so in love with each other.' Then the blasted Vietnam War began and wouldn't you know? During the first wave I got my draft notice. In the weeks that followed, Rachel spent more than one evening crying in my arms. Before I left for boot camp, I asked her to marry me. I'll never forget that night. We stood underneath this big, old, moss-covered oak tree in her front yard. A full Texas moon bathed her face with radiant light. I'd never seen her look so beautiful. With tears shining in her lovely doe brown eyes and a smile on her face, she said yes. I put a ring on her finger—a brilliant diamond that I'd worked and saved for well over a year to buy her. Why did I do that? Because she deserved such a ring. When we parted at the bus station, she said she'd write every day. For a while she did. Once I got overseas, but for one lousy letter, they all stopped."

Don shook his head. "Like an idiot, I kept writing though, you know? I thought maybe her letters to me had gotten lost as I moved around from place to place. After a while—a long while—the excuse didn't hold water anymore. After all, the other men received their forwarded mail just fine. I finally faced the fact she'd ended our relationship in the way that suited her best. The pain of that knowledge never went away, but I learned to accept it. I figured after the war ended I would come home and knock on her door. I'd ask her why she didn't write because she owed me that much. She should've told me if she had found someone else or if she simply changed her mind for one reason or another. I wanted to tell her a letter would've been far kinder than silence. But—I never got the chance."

"I'm so sorry, Don." His chaotic thoughts raced far ahead of what he said aloud. "I guess you must not know where she is right now either, do you?"

"Nah, I haven't looked. Why should I? Given her age, she's probably still alive. If some horrid disease or accident took her early, I haven't run into her. I think that's for the best. As my daddy always used to say, let sleeping dogs lie or you might get bit. Besides, I don't think I could take the pain of seeing her with a husband she loves, their children—maybe even their grandchildren—at her side."

Long after they parted company, the conversation he had with Don weighed heavy on his mind. He worried something like this might happen after the gathering at his home. Richard had been partially right. His success had given renewed hope to the soldiers who had found their soul mates within the earthly realm and hadn't yet gotten through to them. They were now more determined than ever to break through the barrier. But Don had fallen deeper into despair. He couldn't have excluded him though because sooner or later he would've found out about him and Katie anyway. Better he found out surrounded by his friends. Right?

Still, something about his story didn't add up. Most women didn't have any qualms at all about writing a Dear John to a soldier. He'd seen plenty of examples of that once he enlisted in the army. The letter ended the relationship without the need for a face-to-face confrontation. With pen and paper, the girl could avoid all evidence as to the pain she inflicted upon the man who received it. In turn, that would lessen her guilt.

Yet if Rachel had accepted his ring, would she really have ended their relationship without returning it or at least offering to return it given its value? Would Don have fallen in love with someone that cold-hearted? If loneliness drove her into the arms of some fool, did she later regret it? He thought of Katie and Chad. She had been so young when she married the man. In fact, too young to make the decision she did. It didn't take her very long to wish she hadn't. Could something like that have happened to Rachel Jameson? Did she still love Don and mourn his loss every bit as much as he mourned her? Could she have met an untimely death as well? Did the possibility exist that she sat somewhere in the farthest corner of heaven crying her eyes out? What if he could somehow find out?

The voice at the back of his mind said it wasn't any of his business—that no one assigned him the job of matchmaker. He knew that, but at the same time he couldn't leave Don in such pain either. Not if he could find a way to help. If he failed in his quest, if he found she preferred another, Don need never know he tried, right? At once he dismissed the idea as ridiculous. He didn't have a clue as to what the woman looked like. How would he ever find her?

No, wait a minute.

Katie had found his photograph, she said, simply by looking for it on the internet. In the same way, could she find a picture of Rachel Jameson? Would there be a record of her whereabouts if she still lived? A record would also exist if she had died, wouldn't it? Perhaps he could even find out more than that. For Donnie's sake, he would at least explore the possibility. Without any doubt whatsoever, he knew Katie would help him in his cause. His sweet, precious Katie.

She had never strayed far from his mind even while fully occupied with the newest arrivals under his care. He missed her more than he thought possible. He'd fix that problem right now.

William found her in the middle of the floor of her small living room. She had spruced it all up in the country colors and style she loved and Chad abhorred. All evidence of her time with the man had disappeared. That suited him fine. What's more, it suited her as well. She looked happier and more radiant than he had seen her in a long while.

Right now "Unchained Melody" held her captive. With her eyes closed, she danced to the slow, easy rhythm of the music. He smiled at the scene she presented. As he positioned himself behind her, he gathered her into his arms and followed her steps— what there were of them anyway.

She gasped and all but stumbled as she whirled around to face him. The smile in her eyes matched the one on her face. "William!"

"No need to stop on my account." With a bit of gentle pressure on her waist, he swept her back into the dance. She didn't quite know what to do with her hands it seemed, but other than that she kept up well enough. "I can't tell you how many times I wanted to dance with you over the years."

Her eyes widened as she gaped at him. "You did?"

"Yep. Since I couldn't, I took my pleasure in watching you move. You dance better than anyone I have ever seen."

"Oh. Well, thank you." The compliment brought a

blush to her cheeks. "You like to dance?"

"Love it—at least I did. I haven't taken the opportunity where I find myself now." He twirled her around as the song ended. "One of these days you'll have to play some Sinatra, Crosby, or even Benny Goodman for me. If you do that, I'll teach you the Jitterbug."

"You'll teach me the what?"

William chuckled. "The Jitterbug—it's a fabulous dance from back in my day. I think you'd enjoy it though. Especially with me as your dance partner."

Her eyes sparkled with mischief. "Is that right? Well who on earth could resist that offer? I'll try and have some good ol' Sinatra ready for you next time you visit. I think my mom has an old CD or two buried in a deep, dark, and dank corner somewhere. If not mistaken, they used to belong to my grandmother, or was it my great-grandmother?"

"Come on now, CDs aren't that old and neither am I."

"Oh, yes you are. In case you've lost track, you were born over a century ago." She plopped down on the sofa and patted the cushion next to her. "Now, come sit down beside me and tell me what you've been up to."

She looked a bit mystified as he crossed the space between them and sat down.

"What?"

"I just can't figure out how you do that."

"Do what?"

"Look, well—alive. I mean, you're not anything I ever expected to see in a dead person."

Once again it took everything he had not to laugh.

Somehow he kept the grin at bay as well. "Really? Exactly what did you expect to see in a dead person, if you don't mind my asking?"

"You're laughing at me." She leaned away from him.

"No, I'm not. I swear."

"Oh, yes you are. I can see it written all over your face." A bit of suspicion and a whole lot of recrimination filled her beautiful eyes. "I thought angelic beings always told the truth and here you are telling a bald-faced lie."

"Angelic beings do tell the truth. However, I, my precious darling, am not an angel. Far from it, actually. Even so—as I said—I'm not laughing. I'm merely amused. There's a difference you know."

She shook her head as she placed a hand against her temple. "I don't think I'll ever figure this whole ghost thing out."

The grin emerged despite all will against it. "That's the beauty of it. You don't have to. At least not yet."

She rolled her eyes skyward. "Whatever—and you didn't answer my question."

"What question?"

"How you move, look, and speak like any mortal being on this earth. I mean, I always thought if ghosts did exist—and if I actually saw one—I'd see right through him or her. I certainly didn't expect the entity to walk, much less dance. I thought they'd glide along the floor or hover with scary faces, rattle rusty chains, or do something else icky. You know, like they portray them in the movies and television shows?"

"I suppose you could encounter a few disembodied beings who might present themselves in such a foul manner and for whatever twisted their reasons. Best you can do with that kind is to ignore them."

"I'll keep that in mind."

"As far as projecting myself so you can see me as I was and in all reality, still am? It comes from the desire to master the skill, combined with a whole lot of practice. The fact you didn't close your mind off to the possibility is also a factor."

"Oh. I see—I think."

"Good. Anything else?"

"Yes. How is it I can feel it when you touch me, but I can't touch you without going straight through your body?"

He lifted a shoulder. "What can I say? Because I have a gifted spiritual body that can do these miraculous things, while you have an ordinary mortal body that can't?"

"Oh, that's brilliant."

"I do have my moments of genius." He squeezed her hand and then let it go. "Come on now, there's no need to get all huffy on me. I'm just teasing. In all honesty, I think the problem lies in the human condition."

"Explain that, please."

"Well, the mortal body is one that is tangible—made of solid mass like flesh and bone, right? So when mortals touch each other, they encounter the physical elements of that body. In a natural way, they simply stop moving forward without giving the process any thought whatsoever. Once one leaves their physical body behind, they find their spiritual form is also tangible. It's just made of a different composition than the mortal frame they were accustomed to. You see, spirits don't have any problem interacting with each other in the same ways mortals do. We feel the surface of our spiritual body in the same way we did our mortal one. On the other hand, when a mortal and spirit encounter each other, the mortal—knowing only the more tangible frame—has difficulty perceiving the barriers of the spiritual form. Does that, in any way, make sense?"

"Yes, I suppose it does." Katie first studied his face and then gazed at his hands. "Do you think that's something I could overcome?"

He swung his head to the side. "I don't know, but I'd sure love to see you try."

Katie's quiet laughter settled into an enchanting smile. "Okay then, I'll see what I can do."

"I'll look forward to it. Now, do you have any other vexing questions you'd like to ask while on the subject?"

"Actually, I do have one that's related. I—uh—just wanted—can you tell me about those newest soldiers of yours, or is it not the business of a mere mortal that hasn't a clue about how things work in your realm?"

****

Katie waited for what seemed like forever for his answer. He didn't seem unwilling, just hesitant. Maybe even a little sad, and that sadness touched the deepest part of her heart. She shouldn't have asked.

"A few of my boys are having a harder time than most. I have one that died in Afghanistan just as you and I parted company—a roadside bomb—he didn't know what hit him. He didn't realize death had claimed him either. His confusion took a while to sort through. He told me many times over he had a lot to live for and he didn't want to die. More than once he asked if he could return. Unfortunately, he didn't have that option."

"Are you saying some of them do?"

He nodded. "Every now and then that choice is open. Some take it, some don't. In this case, he didn't have that option."

"Then what you're telling me is that near-death experiences aren't hallucinations after all," she murmured. "Did you have the option?"

"No, no, I didn't." William cocked his head to the side and grinned. "Now what?"

"Nothing, it's just—can you tell me about your experience, or is it too painful a subject?"

"What would you like to know?"

"Oh, I don't know. Everything, I guess." She paused. "Did you die instantly—like they say I did after the lightning strike?"

"No. I made it as far as the hospital ship."

Katie gulped. "Were you in a lot of pain?"

"No, not really."

"That's good. I would've hated it if you suffered." She dropped her gaze for a moment. "I don't know quite how to phrase this, but since I stepped into that realm myself, if only for a few minutes, I've often wondered what happens when you die. I mean, what is it like?"

William picked up her hand again and this time he held on to it. "I'd say very much like the stories your mom has shared with your family over the years. While the medics worked over my body, I stepped into the infamous all encompassing tunnel of unearthly darkness. For whatever the reason, I didn't fear the gloom of misty shadows, though. Once deep inside it, I no longer heard the voices of the medics or the sounds of the battle. Everything outside my physical body disappeared, and that's when the review began."

"The review?"

"Yep, the story of my entire life laid out before me in panoramic, high definition color. I saw my moments of sorrow, joy, and rip-roaring fun." A far-away look entered his eyes. "You know, I had completely forgotten most of those memories, so I found the whole thing kind of entertaining. At least I did until I relived the crossing of the English Channel. After all, the memory wasn't all that old and I think I could have done without it."

"I'm so sorry, William."

"You needn't be. The event happened a long time ago and is well behind me now. Anyway, after the review, this brilliant, iridescent light cut through the darkness. I marveled over the beauty and power of it. I couldn't resist that power of light any more than what an enchanted sailor could who hears the deadly song of the siren. So I moved toward it and the man who waited for me at the end of it. Yet midway in my journey, the cries of pain and fear from the wounded soldiers on the ship captured my attention. Somehow I could take them all in with a single glance. Their suffering hit me hard and I wondered then about my boys back on the beach. Did they make it past the relentless hail of gunfire? Were they just as frightened as the casualties here on the ship? I had to know. Then, in the blink of an eye, there I was."

"On the beach?"

He nodded. "Right in the middle of it. Amidst the devastation, and for miles on end I watched ocean waves as they lapped at the abandoned weapons of the dead. I saw empty, battered helmets and various canvas bags that had washed ashore. I spied pieces of clothing adrift on the surf—a sock here, the fragments of a shirt over there. I even watched a pair of broken glasses bob along the turbulent swell. Then there was this solitary boot that tumbled out of the water. The waves reclaimed it and then spat it back out again as if the sea found it distasteful. I wondered about the soldier it belonged to."

For the picture he painted, Katie could see the awful scene herself, if even her version of it.

"Someone called out to me then—not by name, but by rank. I turned around and found a small group of disembodied soldiers walking toward me. They all looked lost, confused, and so very terrified. The young man at the forefront of the group told me the other soldiers didn't wait for them—that they'd all gone ahead. He said they had lost their way and didn't know where to go. All of them looked so young. Too young. Anyway, I told them to follow me and that I would lead them home."

"Did they follow you then?"

He nodded. "Even though most of them weren't ready to die, they followed me without any hesitation whatsoever."

"Yes, but is any soldier on a field of battle ever ready to die?"

"Probably not. Even so, most individuals who enter the service accept the fact they might not come home. I still carry a vivid memory of the soldiers in my boat as we journeyed toward our assigned destination. Every one of them scribbled out their wills as we crossed the channel in a boat so crowded not another soldier could fit inside. Each of us prepared ourselves for such a need. I can tell you that does something to a man. Nonetheless, those that live through the horrors of war and go home are never quite the same either. Most, if not all of them, return to us bearing the same weight. They return carrying the same post-traumatic stress they lived with on a daily basis throughout their mortal life. This I've already mentioned."

"Yes, I remember—it broke my heart."

A small smile touched his face as he nodded. "That's because you have such a loving and compassionate one."

"I'm happy you think so." She cleared her throat. "I must confess that after you left, I thought a lot about what you said. I discovered this burning need to help them if I could. So I decided I would change my major. I thought perhaps instead of pursuing a bachelor degree in history, I could become a counselor instead. That degree will take quite a bit longer to achieve though. Do you think I've waited too long to begin that kind of journey? After all, with the limited time I have for school, I'll probably be in my mid-thirties before I can get my doctorate degree."

"I not only think you're a marvel, I think you'd be a natural at it."

"That's good, because I've already made a few class changes for the fall semester."

He cocked his head to the side as a look of deep contemplation entered his eyes. All the while he didn't say a word.

"What? Did I say something wrong?"

"No, quite the contrary. With this newfound desire

of yours, how would you like to help one of my boys right now?"

Her mouth dropped as excitement filled her. "Yes, and I would love to! But how?"

"By doing a little bit of detective work."

Not quite what she expected, but— "Okay. What do you need me to do?"

"I need a picture, if one exists, of a woman named Rachel Jameson. If possible, I would also like to find out if she's still alive or if she has passed. If she's alive, it would be helpful to know where she is now and maybe a little something about her life."

"Does this woman have something to do with the soldier in question?"

"Yes, she does."

"Something like you and me or altogether different?"

He chuckled. "In some ways very similar to you and me. In some ways not so much."

"Now you're confusing me."

"Unlike you and me, they knew each other while in mortality."

"I see. Well, I think I can help you with that. At least I hope so. I'll need a little more to go on though. I'm sure there's more than one woman in this world named Rachel Jameson."

"What kind of information?"

"Her birthday if you have it. If not, something as close to it as you can get. To have any real hope of finding this lady, I'll need a place of birth—or at the very least—know where she lived."

"I don't have an exact birth date, but more than likely she's somewhere between sixty-one and maybe sixty-five years of age, give or take a few years either way."

"Oh." She paused for a moment. "This must mean your soldier served during the Vietnam War."

William nodded. "In this case, yes, he did. But to keep things in perspective for the future, I dwell among soldiers from every age that died in service to our country. Many of them still search for their soul mates."

"Of course. I guess I just didn't think about that. Did he die in Vietnam?"

"Yes, in 1965."

"I'm so sorry." She took in a deep breath and let it go. "I think you were going to tell me where Rachel lived?"

"The best I can do is tell you at one time they both lived somewhere in the county of Brazoria, Texas."

"Did the soldier know Rachel well or were they just mere acquaintances?"

"I'd say he knew her pretty well."

"Were they around the same age?"

"Fairly close, I'd say."

"You know—you're making me feel like I'm on a game show and we're doing twenty questions." She shook her head. "I mean, none of this is making any sense. Why does he need you to find her? Why can't he find her himself like you found me? That goes double if he knew her. If for some strange, unearthly reason he needs help, why don't you just ask him for the details I need—and what in the world is his name anyway? I'm already tired of referring to him as your soldier."

The most charming grin she'd seen to date stole across his face.

"Let's just say what I have planned is a surprise. So

no, I don't really want to ask Donald Raymond Martin for the details unless it becomes absolutely necessary."

"Donald Raymond Martin—and a surprise is something I can understand. I'll see what I can do. Keep in mind this might take me a while."

"That's not a problem. Time is something I have plenty of—at least where I'm at present anyway. Now enough of all that. How would you like to go for a horseback ride? If *you* have the time, that is."

She gave him a sideways glance. "You can ride horses? I mean, in your current state?"

"Without any problem whatsoever."

"Well—how do we do this? Do I need to get one of mine ready for you or—"

He laughed, rose from his seat, and tugged her to her feet. "Nah, I'll go get my own while you get your mare ready. A ghost should ride a ghost horse, don't you think? I'll be back before you know it."

The ride with William both thrilled and exhilarated her. He appeared in the pasture on top of the most gorgeous silver Morgan she'd ever seen. Never in her wildest imagination did she think a ghost would show up on her little acre, riding a ghost horse. In addition, he had somehow changed out of his combat fatigues. At least for now her cowboy knight wore a pair of faded blue jeans, navy blue western shirt, black boots, and a black cowboy hat.

Oh my.

Once again her blundering butterflies took flight without knowing where they should go or why they were even going. *Stupid, pathetic bugs. Why couldn't they stay put?* The knowing grin on William's face increased the commotion as well as the chaos.

Beyond flustered, Katie blurted out the question that weighed heavy on her mind. "William, how many ghosts would you say are in some stage of a relationship with mortals right now and vice-versa?"

"Sorry?"

"The question shouldn't be that hard to understand, should it? From our various conversations, you've implied that you and I—and Rachel and Donald for that matter—are not the only such couples roaming the earth. So I wondered how common such a thing really is."

"Far more common than you might think."

"Would you say it's in the hundreds, maybe even thousands?"

"I can't put a number to that, Katie." He shrugged. "I can only tell you that many men—and even women—within my realm, have soul mates that are alive right now."

"Well, wouldn't it make more sense for those who have passed on to form relationships with others who have passed? I mean, you said it yourself—countless young men and women have died in wars, plagues, and whatnot throughout the ages. Wouldn't it make more sense if they found someone to love in their own realm?"

He shook his head. "That's not how it works. Like I've told you before, we each have a special someone. Now it's true that sometimes spirits find their special someone in my realm. Even so, I'd say the great majority find their special someone during their mortality. Your parents, as well as my own, are prime examples of that. However sometimes, like in the case of you and me, our individual destinies separated us.

Now I suppose I could've waited until your earthly demise to stake my claim on your heart. However, my lack of patience, my need—as well as my desire to work on our future now—overrode all else. Given the vast number of other couples such as you and me, I guess I'm not alone in that desire."

The notion brought a smile to her face. "I not only think that's amazing, I think it's beautiful. Kind of like a storybook fairytale."

He reached out, grasped her hand, and gave it a gentle press. "That's good, because whether you like it or not, you're stuck with me now."

"I am?"

He returned a firm nod. "Yes, ma'am, you are. Forever and ever onward."

"Could I ask you another question along these same lines?"

"You know you can. What would you like to know?"

"Why did you enlist in the army? I mean, according to history, at the age of twenty-eight, you didn't have to."

"I don't know. Just seemed the right thing to do at the time."

"The photograph I have of you—the look in your eyes made me wonder."

"Wonder what?"

"Did you know you wouldn't come home from the war?"

"Yes, I did."

"And still you went anyway."

He shrugged. "Like I said, it seemed the right thing to do."

****

After the ride he talked her into another dance. For the lack of anything resembling Sinatra, she chose Kris Kristofferson's "A Moment of Forever." Right now, the song seemed a fitting one.

As he took hold of her waist and gathered her into his arms, she gazed into his eyes. "I don't know if this is such a good idea."

"Why not?"

"Well, what if I step on your toes or something?"

He flashed a grin. "I promise I won't feel a thing."

"On top of that, I don't know where to put my hands just yet," she blurted out.

William chuckled. "Just close your eyes, Katie. Give your hands free rein. Relax, listen to the music, and follow my lead."

"All right, if you insist. I'll give it a try."

At first they merely swayed to the slow tempo of the music. With her eyes still closed he guided her forward, back, and side-to-side before their steps grew a little more complex. She mastered them with unexpected ease. Magic. Nothing else could explain this enchanted moment, nestled in William's arms. For the way they danced, they may as well have been partners forever.

All too soon the song ended. He released her from his arms and as he stepped back, he grinned. "Now, that wasn't so bad, was it?"

"I've endured far worse. So if you're ever game to try it again—" She gave him an "I dare you smile" and let the sentence hang.

He took hold of her hand and tugged her a bit closer. "Oh, I'm game all right and to prove it—how about one more before I go?"

After several dances, William finally bid her goodnight with the promise of seeing her sometime tomorrow evening. For the way he looked at her after he said it, she could do nothing more than suck in a breath and nod. In that moment he made her feel far more cherished than any other man ever had.

Once he disappeared from her living room—and the pace of her heart returned to normal—her thoughts turned toward the mysterious Rachel Jameson. Katie headed for her computer and turned it on. After she sat down she grabbed a notebook and pencil.

"All right," she said aloud. "Let's see if I can find our mystery lady for William."

What she thought would take several days took no more than a couple of hours—if she had the right Rachel Jameson. This one came from a very wealthy, well-known family. They had settled near West Columbia during the early part of the nineteenth century. A great deal of historical information could be found on her ancestors. The bulk of the information centered on the sugar cane plantation they owned and operated for well over one hundred and fifty years. Rachel's parents were Gustavus and Thalia Clark Jameson. She had one brother named Quinn, who died in a freak accident at the age of seventeen. His death made Rachel the sole heir of the Jameson fortune. The family estate, a beautiful, historic home, still existed. According to the information she found online, Rachel still owned the property, which she kept private. No tours or tourists were allowed on site. She didn't find anything that indicated she had died or that gave her current whereabouts. Did that mean she lived at the mansion? What about a husband? Did she ever get married? After all, a lot of women kept their maiden names, especially those from high society. Perhaps she could find out more if she went through the various newspaper archives of Brazoria County.

As far as a photograph, so far she had only found one. About fifteen years ago, someone had taken a group picture at a social gala hosted by the Texas State Historical Association. Rachel, a lovely, middle-aged, brown-eyed brunette, stood in the center. Everyone smiled for the camera, but the smile didn't quite reach Rachel's eyes. Katie gazed at those eyes for several minutes and couldn't see any emotion of any kind. They just looked—empty. Then again, maybe her tired, befuddled mind saw things that didn't exist.

Katie hid a yawn behind her hand as she glanced up at the clock. The midnight hour had come and gone long ago. She needed some sleep if she had any hope of feeling half-way human come tomorrow. At least now she had something to show William. Would it be enough?

Chapter Eight

Katie swung around in her chair. As her hand flew to her shoulder, she met William's playful gaze. "Oh, it's you! I thought for a split-second there some hideous spider had crawled up my arm and for one reason or another gave me a hug."

"Really? That would be some huge spider with pretty impressive skills if you ask me."

She waved the comment aside. "No matter, you're just the man I've wanted to see all day."

William straddled the wooden table chair beside her. Once he sat down, he rested his arms on top the back of it and grinned. "I hope I'm the only man you've wanted to see all day."

Her lips twitched as she dropped her napkin onto her empty dinner plate. "Well, for the moment you are."

"Now that cuts to the quick, Katie. But—if that's the best you can do, I guess I'll have to take it. After I lick my wounds, of course."

Her nonchalant shrug accompanied the snooty lift of her nose. "I don't see where you have much choice in the matter."

For the next couple of seconds he did nothing more than gaze into her eyes. All the while his eyes sparkled with amusement. "Nice to see the lightning strike didn't take away any of your sauciness. Since I haven't seen more than a smidgen of it here of late, I mourned the loss."

"Did you now?"

"Yes, I did."

"Well, you shouldn't have. Didn't you know? The trait is a genetic defect inherited by all those who carry even a drop of Adelton blood. Therefore, it's impossible to root it out. Many have tried and I assure you, many have failed."

"I can't tell you how much that eases my mind. So tell me, did I make such an extraordinary impression on you with my abundant charm and good looks that you just couldn't wait to see me again or what?"

She laughed. "Oh, I don't know—that might've had something to do with it. Not to mention, I've a pitiful weakness for men in uniform. All that aside though, I wanted to show you what I unearthed about the Jameson family."

"You found something already?"

Katie rose from her chair and headed toward her computer. With a wave of her fingers, she beckoned him along. "Well, I found a Rachel Jameson in the area you mentioned. To be certain she's the one you're looking for, I'll need a little more proof than what I have right now. That means you can't get too excited just yet."

He crossed his heart. "All right, I promise not to get too excited. So show me what you've got."

As she turned on the screen, the photograph of Rachel popped into view.

"This picture of Rachel Jameson is the most recent one of her I've found. Just so you know, the photograph is well over a decade old." She tapped on the screen. "As you can see from the caption, she's the woman in the center. She is also, I might add, the heiress of the vast Jameson fortune. What do you think about that little morsel?"

William studied the picture. "The Jameson fortune?"

"Yep. That's the reason I found as much as I did as quickly as I did. According to all the historical records I plowed through last night—and all day today, I might add—the Jameson family settled in Brazoria County in the early eighteen-hundreds. They accumulated a great deal of wealth and social standing by operating a very successful sugar cane plantation. Each generation that followed the first, kept the plantation going as well as growing. They did this by branching off into other businesses. Some related, some not. However, no one did that with the same gusto as Rachel's father, Gustavus Jameson. I swear that man had his fingers in everything but the local gas station."

"Yeah, I've seen that type before."

"I suppose every county in the union has at least one. The thing I found interesting though, is that Gustavus didn't marry until he reached the ripe old age of forty-eight. I thought perhaps he put off marriage so he could build his empire unhampered by the needs of a high-maintenance wife that nagged. On the other hand, Rachel's mother, Thalia Matilda Clark, was just nineteen when the couple said 'I do.' The newspaper dubbed their wedding the social event of the year. Every person of importance for miles around attended—or so the article claimed."

"No surprise there."

"Right, but you know what? I couldn't help but wonder if he married such a young woman so he could produce an heir, or if he married her because given his wealth, he knew he could."

"I expect either one is a possibility. But here's another one for you, and hang on to your hat because it might be a shocker."

She laughed. "All right, I'm hanging on tight with both hands."

"Despite the age difference, perhaps they actually loved each other." He winked.

"That's a possibility, I suppose. Whatever their reasons, I hope all throughout their marriage Thalia lived a happy life."

"Why wouldn't she?"

"Because in every single picture I've seen of Gustavus he looks cold and stern—even in family portraits. Here—let me bring one up for you." She brought up a family photo and put it side-by-side with the first. "His son is just a baby in this picture. You'd think that having a boy would've made him ecstatic, but look at those eyes."

"I see what you mean."

"And the older he got the more cold and stern he appeared. All that aside though, the death of his son left Rachel the only surviving member of the family." Katie put the second photograph away.

"What happened to him?"

"The article in the newspaper said he somehow fell from the barn loft and landed on the sugarcane harvester parked just below it. Some blame the wind, some put it down to pure clumsiness. Either way, they said the force of the fall broke his neck. He had just turned seventeen when the accident occurred."

"That's too bad."

"Yes, it is. As a result—and as recorded by the most recent records I could find—Rachel owns all the properties connected to the family. That includes the beautiful historic mansion her ancestors built in West Columbia."

"Hmm."

"That's it? All you have to say after I've slaved over my computer for hours on end is 'hmm'?"

"Well, no, it's just that the information surprises me a bit."

"Why?"

"Because in most cases, wealthy heiresses don't associate with the—um—poorer working class, if you get my drift. Don fits in that group. Well, at least he did. Back in my day, the rich hung out with the rich, and the poor hung out with everyone else. I suppose that could've changed with time though."

"Like I said, I want far more proof myself. Particularly now that you've suggested Donnie might not have been part of her social circle. So far though, I haven't found any other Rachel Jameson in the area and in the time frame you've given me. That's not to say I won't. There could be one out there that isn't as well known as this one. She'll just be harder to find." She paused as she gazed at the woman's image. "Still, this Rachel is lovely, don't you think?"

William gave the photo a cursory glance. "Yeah, I suppose she is. Do you know if this woman ever married?"

"No, I don't. The fact she's identified by her maiden name in the picture doesn't mean she didn't. Some women don't take on their husband's name for one reason or another. If she did, and then divorced him, she could've petitioned the courts to reinstate her maiden name as well. As you can see, her right hand is covering her left, so I don't know if she's wearing a ring or not."

"How do we find the missing information?"

"By a lot more snooping into other people's business, of course. I've already gone through all of the local cemetery records available online. In them I've found this particular Rachel's parents alongside her brother and a great many of her ancestors. They're all buried in or near an ornate and very expensive looking mausoleum in the center of their church cemetery. No surprise there. However, she's not buried among them. This gives credibility—alongside the property records—to the belief she's alive and well. I've also looked through the available marriage records for Texas. There's an index online spanning 1837 to 1977, but according to the site, it isn't complete. I didn't find her there. Perhaps her record is one that's missing. On the other hand, she could've married someone in a different state or in a different time frame. Given her wealth, she could easily have married in another country altogether. If she did that, it would be like looking for that teeny tiny needle in the great big haystack."

"I see. Do you know if this woman still lives in the same community now?"

"Sorry, I don't have a clue. I haven't found her name mentioned in any of the online newspapers for the past five years or so." At the disheartened look in his eyes her hand drifted toward his face and taking the greatest of care, she traced her fingers down the side of it.

Her attempt made him smile.

"Don't worry, I promise, one way or another, I will find out. I still have a lot of records to sort through."

William shook his head even before she finished her sentence. "Not right now, you don't." He extended a hand as he cocked his head toward the front door. "There's a full moon out tonight, and the stars are especially brilliant. Care to take a walk with me and see them for yourself?"

She glanced at the dirty pans on her stove. "I should do the dishes first. There aren't many and it'll only take me a minute."

"They can wait, the full moon won't."

"Not even for ten minutes?"

"Nope. If we don't leave right now, you'll miss its most impressive display of the night. That will make the moon sad."

His flirty grin was her undoing. She placed her hand in his. "William, I think you're a very bad influence on me."

"Yes, but only in the most positive way possible."

Just as he said, the moon and stars were exceptionally beautiful. For a while, neither of them said anything as they strolled down the row of lush majestic trees leading away from the house. The sweet scent of honeysuckle filled the air. All the while, the lilting call of elf owls made for a lovely serenade. The silence between them in no way felt awkward. Rather it felt just as natural as it did comfortable.

She broke the silence first. "I'm so glad you asked me to do this. You know it's been a while."

"I do know."

She turned to face him. "You do?"

"Um-hmm." The lop-sided grin she'd come to love made an appearance. "I know a lot more about the things you do than you think I do."

"Is that right? Like what, for instance?"

"Oh, that you stop and smell the flowers when others wouldn't take the time. I know you can't walk past any four-legged critter without giving it some attention. You kick your shoes off at the first sign of water just to dip your toes, and the last time you walked underneath the stars you were happy."

"Well what do you know? Okay—I'll have to admit you're right on all accounts, even if I must do it grudgingly." Katie remembered well the walk of which he spoke—that day the judge restored her maiden name and freed her. He freed her of the miserable life she had led for over four years and freed her of Chad McCrae. "What else?"

"I've been around when you've laughed and I've counted the tears when you cried. The one I took pleasure in, the other—not so much."

She dropped her gaze for a moment and nodded. "I think those were the times I sensed your presence most."

"I'm glad." He paused. "What or who did you think I was—if you don't mind my asking."

"In truth, I didn't put a whole lot of thought into that. I don't know why. In my mind you were just my friend, and whatever else you were, didn't really matter."

He halted their walk and turned her around to face him. The look in his eyes right now reduced her to a tumultuous puddle of heated slush that her butterflies were drowning in.

"I hope it matters now."

Her heart began a slow dance as the heated slush slithered through and filled every part of her body. Words fled her mind as he gathered her a bit closer.

"Do you have any idea how long I've waited to be here with you like this?"

Oh boy. She gulped in a breath as he leaned down, tipped her chin upward, and kissed her. At once Katie fell headlong into the depths of exquisite emotion and stayed there. One kiss turned into so many more. Electrifying. Magnificent. Soul-shattering. Kisses. Not until he finally released her from his arms and stepped back did a small drop of conscious thought return. She gazed up at him in wide-eyed wonder. All the while she sought to catch her breath.

"Wha...I mean, how?"

He chuckled. "You've done this many times before, Katie, and much to my dismay I might add. Therefore, I know you know the how of it."

"But...but you're...you're a ghost...a...a spirit, I mean," she sputtered. "How can you make me—"

"Works the same way, I assure you," he cut in.

If it would've had any impact, she would've smacked him in the chest. "You know that's not what I'm talking about. I'm talking about the intensity of it. I've never experienced anything like it before. Not ever. I didn't know a feeling like that even existed."

"Don't over think it, Katie, just enjoy the gift." Once again, he gave her *that* grin. Did he know how it affected her? His lips hovered just above hers. "I know I am."

Throughout the remainder of the evening, and as she finally crawled into bed, his words played over and over again in her mind. William had stayed with her far longer than he intended, or so he said. He apologized when the clock chimed the three a.m. hour, despite all of her protests. A few minutes later he took his leave, but not before he gave her one final, incredible kiss.

Despite her fatigue, she couldn't fall asleep. Her willful heart and mind insisted on reliving the way he looked at her tonight. The laughter they shared. Each kiss that stole away any attempt at rational thought. She recalled every word he said. Words that engraved themselves deep within her heart's secret treasure chest where they would remain, forever safe.

William, as a friend and comforter, had always meant a great deal to her. No question about that. Now though, her feelings for the man had shifted in a much different direction. She knew that as well as she knew anything else. At the same time, she didn't give those feelings a name. She couldn't. Not right now anyway. The thought of naming them scared her half to death. For the time being, she wouldn't scrutinize them too closely. Instead, she'd do as William advised—she would simply enjoy the gift.

Chapter Nine

Katie tugged back on the reins and swept her wind-blown hair away from her face. The morning sun had painted the clouds in spectacular colors of red, pink, and orange. The breathtaking sky against the green, rolling grasslands made for a wonderful view.

She grinned as she leaned forward and patted her mare on the neck. "So tell me. Are you tired of listening to me ramble on and on about William?"

Right on cue, Shahar nickered and that made her laugh.

"All right then, since you were so very patient with me, how about I let you run just as fast as you can, all the way home, hmm? Let's see if you can beat that old record of yours. Are you ready?"

With just the slightest pressure from her heels, Shahar took off. The mare's high spirits matched hers as they raced along the twists and turns of the trail heading home. At the end of the exhilarating ride, they were both out of breath, but quite content. Katie dismounted and removed the tack. She led Shahar into the pasture, brushed her until her coat glistened, and finished up with a handful of oats.

All throughout the routine tasks, her thoughts wandered away from William and over to Rachel Jameson. What records might she have missed that would give her more information than what she had?

Where else could she search that she hadn't already searched? Did any proof exist that the wealthy heiress, once upon a time, loved Donnie Martin?

As she stepped onto her porch and retrieved her mail from the mailbox, Rachel disappeared from her thoughts altogether. Instead, the IDPF file she ordered from the US Army resources concerning William's death captured her full attention. Guilt swept over her as she gazed at the label. She never told him she ordered his personnel records. Right now, she didn't have any desire to bring it to his attention, either. After all, they had already discussed his death. Why remind him of it again?

She carried the large packet to her computer and sat down. Yet now she had the envelope in hand, did she really want to know the details of William's death that he had left out? When she ordered the file, she hadn't fully convinced herself that her soldier truly existed outside her own delusions. But now—now she saw him as a man in every sense of the word. Her man.

Katie abandoned the packet and headed for the kitchen. While she ate lunch, her gaze wandered toward the envelope many times over. The contents promised a plethora of information concerning William's two years in the military. The information might answer the questions she couldn't bring herself to ask. On the other hand, it could also give information she didn't want to know.

Don't be such a baby. I can do this. They're just words on a piece of a paper, after all.

Despite the pep talk, she did the dishes first. She put in a load of laundry and even vacuumed the floor before she made it back to the computer. Her heart raced as she ripped open the envelope and withdrew the hefty contents. She tossed her order receipt to the side and gazed at the first page of the file.

The official title read "War Department, the Adjutant General's Office, Washington, Report of Death. The brief form didn't say anything she didn't already know. Next, she read the Inventory of Effects, all the letters that accompanied it, and notice of shipment. The short list included his wallet, some snapshots, a fountain pen, and a pocket comb. Did those few items really warrant the vast amount of paperwork involved in returning them to his parents? One form and one letter could've sufficed. That might've spared his family the heartache of losing William with constant reminders in the mail. Still, his parents probably treasured each item William carried into battle.

An autopsy report of sorts followed, complete with red markings on the paper drawing of a body. A shudder raced up and down her spine. She didn't read what it said. Instead, she averted her eyes and put it through the paper shredder where it belonged. A page with his fingerprints followed that report. They even sent a copy of his dental records. If nothing else, the army was thorough.

The Request for Disposition of Remains came next. Although his parents had the option of returning his body to the United States, they chose to have him buried in a permanent American Military Cemetery overseas. The Report of Burial, and accompanying certificate, provided William's burial location. A location she had visited. Did his parents ever get that chance? Katie skimmed over the various certificates that documented his awards and rank promotions. They also included documentation of William's Purple Heart. She read the official Transmittal Sheets, personal letters to the family from his superior officers, and the heartbreaking telegram sent to his parents.

She closed her eyes as an uneven breath passed through her lips. How difficult this ordeal must've been for his family and his friends in knowing he would never come home. Not ever. Had she been there, she might never have recovered from the loss. Katie tucked the telegram underneath the stack of pages. As she did so, her gaze fell on a handwritten letter to the army, dated August 28, 1944.

Dear Sirs,

I am writing for and in behalf of Sergeant William Malloy Griffin's parents, Mr. and Mrs. Peter Griffin. I am a very close friend of this family and they have asked me to write this letter. We appreciate your efforts in collecting William's personal things and returning them to us so quickly. I am sure such an effort isn't easy as battles are still being fought on distant shores and our men are dying on a daily basis.

Regardless of the current conditions, please know that here at home, our hearts are broken. It wasn't easy for any of us to receive the news of his death. William was beloved by all who knew him and he will be deeply missed. Besides our fond memories, and a few precious photos, all we have to remember him by is what you have sent us in that small box.

I tell you this because some of William's things weren't included in the shipment. We know he carried a small Bible with him at all times. This Bible meant a great deal to him and therefore, means a great deal to us. He also had a silver wrist watch, which had his initials engraved on the back. You should also have found a small pocket knife, which once belonged to his grandfather. In a letter, he also mentioned a foot locker. Could the missing items be inside it?

If at all possible, we would like to have these items located and returned to the family. They are of great personal worth. Of course, if you come across anything else that belonged to William, we would appreciate the prompt return of these items as well. Your efforts would mean so much to this grieving family.

Sincerely,

Laura Lea Erickson

A single teardrop fell from Katie's cheek and splashed onto the bottom of the letter. She sniffed and wiped the others away. Funny that a moment in time that happened so long ago could hurt this much—especially since she didn't live through it like his loved ones did. Without doubt, had she lived and known William then as she did now, she too would have wanted something of his she could hold close to her heart.

With a bit of trepidation, she went through the remaining documents. Among them she found the notice of a second shipment that arrived much later. This shipment contained the missing items Laura mentioned, as well as a few books William must've picked up while in the service. Did those in charge try a little harder to find his possessions after her letter? If so, then thank Heaven for Laura Erickson.

Laura Lea.

Just who was she anyway? A friend of William's parents? A friend of William's or the entire family in general? No matter. It wasn't like she could call her and thank her now. The woman wrote the letter seventy plus years ago. Katie sighed as she grasped the stack of papers, straightened them out, and put them back in the envelope. Once she tucked it away in her file drawer, she turned her attention away from William and placed it solely on Rachel.

She clicked the file on her desktop and for the umpteenth time, studied the contents. It occurred to her then that she hadn't Googled the woman's name alongside the year of her birth, coupled with county and state. At once she placed the information in the search engine and hit enter. The top of the page indicated about 350 results, most of which she'd already gone through. Then on a whim, she added the name "Donald Martin" and entered again.

Excitement consumed her as she gazed at the single link at the top of the page. She clicked it. Katie couldn't help but laugh out loud as she gazed at the page. She drew her clasped hands to her chin and nodded.

Bingo.

Chapter Ten

William gazed at the latest entry in his journal and grinned. The words in his letter to Katie could've been penned by some love-sick teenager with his first crush. That's the way she made him feel, though. How could it be otherwise when she had entered this newest chapter in their relationship with the same joyful enthusiasm he did?

As he reread the words that detailed the last evening they had shared, he stopped at the passages that spoke of Rachel Jameson. This time, the comment Don Martin made about working a full year for her ring came barreling to the forefront of his mind. Could he have meant—at least in part—she deserved a ring suitable for a wealthy heiress? The more he thought on it, the more plausible it seemed. Could he somehow find out without being obvious?

At once he closed his journal, returned it to the desk drawer, and headed for Don's house. He stopped just outside the gate. Second thoughts kept his feet planted there. In the instant he turned for home, Don opened the door.

"Are you just going to stand there and gawk at the bushes, or are you coming in?"

William chuckled. "You know, I stopped right here so I could debate that very thing."

"Were you winning or losing the fight?"

"I suppose that depends upon your perspective."

Don shook his head and rolled his eyes skyward as he invited him in with a wave of his hand. Once they were seated, he clasped his hands together and leaned forward. "Is there someone you need my help with and found you were reluctant to ask?"

"No, well—at least not right now anyway."

"Do we have another rash of incoming and it's all hands on deck then?"

"No, it's not that either. At least not yet. I just hadn't seen you for awhile and wondered how you were doing. That's all."

"Ah." Don pinned his gaze to his and nodded. "After we last spoke I figured that sooner or later you'd show up with that very question on your mind."

"Did you now."

"Yep. You can't help yourself—it's in your nature." He shrugged. "Of course, that's not such a bad thing, mind you."

"Okay, so now that we have your evaluation as to my character out of the way, how are you doing?"

"Oh, I'm all right. You know, the last time we spoke you caught me at one of my lowest moments in this fine existence of mine. I'm sorry about that." He paused for a moment. "Then again, if someone had to witness my bout of self-pity, I'm glad you were that someone."

William leaned back in his chair as he gazed at his companion. "I know what you mean. I chose Isaiah as my hapless victim when I ranted and raved over the unfairness of my life. I felt much better after we talked though. I realized then that sometimes the things that fester deep inside our souls have to come out sooner or later. When they do, it might as well be with a friend."

"Yes, well—I thought about my emotional state for quite some time after we parted company. Far longer than you might guess. Thoughts and feelings, both good and bad, tangled themselves up inside my mind and wouldn't let go. It took a while to put them in order and lay some of them to rest."

"What did you conclude, if you don't mind my asking?"

"As strange as it might sound, I don't hold any real animosity toward Rachel. Quite the opposite actually. I'd appreciate it as well if you didn't think ill of her either. Despite the way our relationship ended, I still find her the most wonderful, most amazing woman I've ever known. That's the part I'll keep in my heart. That's the only part I'll choose to remember in the future."

"Given the circumstances, I'd say that's very charitable of you, Don."

"Nah, it's just something my grandmother once said. Something long forgotten that surfaced during my inner reflection after you left."

"Really? What profound thing did she say?"

"In order for it to make sense, I should tell you my granddad died when my mom was just a little girl. So little in fact that her memories of the man are few in number. One day as my grandma dusted off her wedding portrait, I asked her why she never remarried. I never saw a sweeter smile cross a woman's face as I did in that moment. She gazed at the image of my grandfather. As her fingers glided over his face, I could almost see the flood of recollections she must've relived in that moment. Tears filled her eyes as she turned to face me. Once again she smiled and I swear that smile erased decades of wear from her face. She said she had lived—and could happily live forever if needs be—on just her memories. I suppose I can do the same."

"Can you really?" he asked.

"I hope so." A soft chuckle accompanied the shake of his head. "You know, given her privileged status, Rachel shouldn't ever have given someone like me a second look anyway. Yet she did. Never once, in all of our time together, did she treat me as anything less than her equal. During the brief years we shared, she made me happy. That's what I'll hold on to when the bitterness rears its ugly head—as I know it surely will."

"Privileged status? Are you saying your Rachel came from a well-to-do family?"

Don's smile broadened. "That's putting it mildly. You should see the Jameson estate—it takes up an entire city block. That doesn't count the farm property they own either. If either of them still exists, that is. I haven't visited the area since my death, nor do I have any plans to do so in the future. Better to leave it at just the good memories, right?"

William hoped he responded in an appropriate manner to the comments as well as the remainder of their conversation that shifted away from the Jameson family. He couldn't keep his mind on any of it. Not when Katie needed to know what he found out. The moment he left Don's home, he headed straight for her inner light. He found her outside, tending her garden.

"Katie?"

She whirled around to face him. A radiant smile lit up her face as she met his gaze.

"Guess what I found out," they said in almost

perfect unison.

Katie laughed. "You first. What did you discover?"

"That you found the right Rachel Jameson after all." He dropped a kiss on her lips. Though he craved more, he stepped back. "Your turn."

The sparkle in her eyes matched her sunny smile. She pulled off her gloves and laid them on the outdoor table. "Come with me and I'll show you."

Once inside the house she sat down at her computer. Her hands raced across the keyboard. With the one final tap, she turned the screen toward him. "In confirmation of what you already know, here's a photo of the happy couple in their online high school yearbook. As you can see, she's standing hand in hand with your Donnie Martin. She looks properly blissful as the newly crowned prom queen with her tall, dark, and handsome king. Don't you think?"

"Yes, indeed she does." William paused as he gazed at the couple smiling back at him from the pages. "Have you found out anything more about her?"

"No, I'm afraid not." She turned away from the computer and settled her gaze on him. "Are you ever going to tell me their story, or are you just going to make me wonder why Don isn't with this woman right now? Is it that for some reason she can't see him or even feel his presence?"

"Those types of barriers do exist between couples and far more often than you might guess as you already know. However, in this case, I'm afraid their story isn't nearly as joyful as mine has been here of late." For the next little while William told Katie just enough to satisfy her curiosity, but still keep most of Don's confidences. At the end of his tale a thoughtful look entered her lovely eyes as she nodded more at some inner reflection than at him.

At last she spoke. "We need to find out what happened to her, don't we."

"If at all possible, I sure would like to."

"You know, despite all of the decisions she's made throughout the years, Donnie could still be the love of her life. Right? I mean, they look so in love in that photograph. Time can't have erased that entirely."

"If not for that possibility, I wouldn't have asked you to look for her."

Determination firmed her jaw. "You don't have to worry. One way or another, I'll find her. You can count on that."

"That's my girl." He leaned down and gave her another kiss. But then when he would've given her more, she held up a hand.

"Wait a minute, I have a question to ask before I forget. Do you know where Don is buried?"

He shook his head. "No, I'm afraid I don't. Why?"

"Well, because I had a thought. If she still loves him, she just might visit his grave. Often. If she does that, then someone may've seen her. Like a caretaker for instance. If so, perhaps the caretaker may've struck up a conversation and know something useful."

"That's a very good possibility. Do you think you can find out where they buried his body?"

"I think I can, even if I have to write to the National Archives in order to do it."

"Good." He drew her to her feet and turned her to face him. "Now, do you have any more comments or questions regarding this quest of ours?"

"No, I don't think so. Why?"

"Because I want a little bit of uninterrupted time for this—" He leaned down and touched his lips to hers. The sweet, gentle kiss turned into several more that went far deeper and became far more meaningful. Kisses that spoke of the deep love and devotion he had for her. Could she feel them as he intended her to feel them? Better yet, did she know she gave as well as she got?

"Sergeant Griffin? You're needed right away, sir. A young soldier has made an unexpected arrival with a soul deeply wounded. He is in desperate need of your help."

With more reluctance than he thought possible, he released her from his arms. "I'm afraid I have to go now. I can't be certain when I'll be back."

She locked her gaze with his and for a time, she searched his eyes. Her expression changed to one of tender concern. She lifted a hand and touched the side of his face. With the greatest of care, her fingers glided down the length of his jaw and then she smiled. "I'll be here waiting when you do."

Chapter Eleven

Sleep wouldn't come. She wouldn't pretend otherwise. Katie tossed her covers off to the side and abandoned the comfort of her bed. In the hours that followed, she all but carved a path on the plush, teal-colored carpet beneath her bare feet. As she paced, the image of PFC Donald R. Martin's small cemetery stone haunted her. In the moment the photographer had taken the photo, a bunch of wilting violets had adorned his grave. Did Rachel put them there? After all, it couldn't have been his parents. Both were deceased and buried beside him. Don's obituary didn't mention any siblings. Could the flowers have come from an aunt or an uncle perhaps? A cousin? A kind stranger with a deep respect for those who died in service to their country?

The question kept her company until the faint colors of dawn seeped through the white wooden slats of her bedroom window blinds. Without doubt, she wouldn't rest until she found an answer to the many riddles that plagued her. She knew of only one way to solve them.

Before she lost her nerve, she booked the first available flight to Houston. William hadn't in any way asked her to take her investigation this far. He probably wouldn't approve. Nonetheless, if she didn't take this next step, her search wouldn't go any further than it already had. Her heart hammered inside her chest as she picked up her phone and placed the call. Jared answered on the second ring.

"Well, I'll be a son of a beachcomber if it isn't our lovely Katie! To what do I owe the pleasure on this fine morning?"

Justin hollered out a hello over and over again in the background, all in tones from a screechy high to the boom of the lowest low he could muster. His antics made her laugh.

"Well, I'm looking for some cahoots partners. If either one or both of you can spare a bit of time during the next two or three days, I'd love it to be you. And for Heaven's sake, tell Justin I said hello before he hurts himself."

"Katie says hello, and shut up," Jared said. "Just a minute. Since no one's in the office, let me put you on speaker phone so he gets out of my face. Okay. Now then, what type of cahoots did you have in mind?"

"Well, I'm looking for a mysterious wealthy heiress who's disappeared from off the internet radar. I need to find her if I can. That means snooping in places we probably shouldn't go and won't be welcome."

"A wealthy heiress you say? Then by all means, I'm in."

"I like the 'snooping into places we shouldn't go' part," Justin called out. "Tell me though, why do you need to find her? Is this some sort of bizarre contest where the eccentric heiress gives you half her fortune if you find her?"

"No, nothing quite so exciting, I'm afraid. I'm helping a friend, that's all."

"Ah," said Jared. "The shadowy unnamed 'friend' rears his ugly head. This intrigues me. Does your heiress have a name?"

"Rachel Jameson," she said.

Justin gasped. "Are you talking about *the* Jamesons over in Brazoria?"

"Yes, as a matter of fact, I am. Have you heard of them?"

Jared snorted. "Everyone's heard of them, Katie. At least everyone this side of Texas."

"Dude! If that's who you're after, then I'm definitely in. I could use a very large loan. When do we get started?" Justin asked.

"As soon as possible. I don't know what your immediate plans are, but my plane lands there at three-thirty. I thought I could take a tax—"

"If you know what's good for you, you will not finish that sentence," Jared warned. "We'll pick you up. The Jameson compound is in West Columbia. That isn't really all that far as the crow flies. Should only take us an hour or so to get there from the airport—especially if we let Justin drive. We'll let him get the ticket."

"Not going to happen. I'll just tell them I'm you," Justin volleyed back.

Katie laughed. "No, no. We don't have to go this afternoon. I mean, you have your construction business that needs attention, I'm sure. In addition, it's Friday, for goodness sake. You must have dates or some—"

"Nothing that can't be rearranged, right, Justin?" Jared asked.

"Absolutely. The town of cahoots sounds a lot more fun than anything I have planned this evening. Besides, for all the ghost stories told around campfires, I've had a hankering to see that creepy old mansion up close and personal. Now's as good a time as any."

Katie raised a hand to her throat. "Creepy? As in abandoned rather than lived in creepy?"

"That's the rumor," Jared said. "I guess we'll find out if she's hiding in there soon enough though, right?"

"Okay. I, uh, also want to stop at the Columbia Cemetery if that's all right with you guys."

"Even creepier. Let's do it," Justin said. "I'll bring along a camera and see if we can catch some ghosts while we're at it. Maybe that one guy will put us on his TV show and make us famous."

Her cousins' enthusiasm made her laugh. "All right, I'll see you both this afternoon and stop with all the creepy nonsense. You're creeping me out."

****

All throughout the flight Katie wondered what William would think of her spontaneous decision. On one hand she wished he had stopped in to see her before she left, but he didn't. The other hand told her she got off lucky. Although she hadn't seen him for three weeks, and missed him so terribly, she now hoped he stayed away until she got back. After all, she did promise she'd be home when he returned.

A weird mix of excitement and apprehension churned deep inside her belly as she got off the plane. She didn't know if she'd pass out or throw up. The feeling increased as she climbed into the vehicle with her tall, handsome cousins. With their tanned faces, deep blue eyes, and dark blond hair, she didn't find it any wonder the ladies flocked to them in droves.

She strapped herself into her seatbelt and leaned back against the backseat cushion. "Should we get a flat tire along the way, you will stop and fix it this time,

131

won't you? I mean, we're not in that big of a hurry."

The twins gazed at each other with mouths agape before Jared shifted his attention back to her. He cleared his throat. "Care to explain that offhand remark?"

"What's to explain? Did you or did you not tell me that during your last trip to see me you made silly spectacles out of yourselves while bumping along on the rim to the airport?"

Justin turned his head to the side as he narrowed his eyes. "What airport?"

"I don't know. That one in the podunk town you told me about while spouting your ridiculous story. What?"

Justin gazed at her as if she had suddenly sprouted two heads. "You actually heard us?"

Katie huffed out a breath. "I'm not deaf. Why wouldn't I have—" She stopped short. Now she thought on it, she had been in a coma the last time they visited New Mexico.

Justin bobbed his head as he stomped on the clutch and turned the key. At once the tricked out king-cab, Dodge Ram pickup rumbled to life. "Interesting. Very. Interesting."

"I'll say," Jared agreed. "I've always heard people in a coma hear what's going on around them. Now we know they do."

"Therefore, I believe we can—and will—take full credit for her recovery," Justin added with his usual arrogant nonchalance.

Jared scratched at the stubble on his chin. "That all depends on whether or not we said something we shouldn't have. Did we?"

Even now her cousins could make her laugh, and laugh they did. All the way to West Columbia.

"Where to first?" Justin decreased his speed as they entered the city limits. "Creepy cemetery or creepy mansion?"

"How 'bout we get something to eat first," Jared said. "I'm starving."

"So what's new?" she asked. "You're always starving."

"True, but this time I really am starving," Jared replied. "I haven't eaten a thing since breakfast—well, not counting the two cinnamon rolls and a bag of chips. Oh, and the strawberry shake and bag of trail mix. But that's not even worth mentioning."

"Okay then," said Justin. "Pulling into the local diner."

Once they were seated, the waitress gave them plenty of time to look over the menu. All the while the shapely brunette eyed the twins with blatant appreciation. At last she sauntered over to their table. "What can I get for you today?"

Jared slid his menu off to the side. "I want the double-beef bacon burger and don't be stingy with the fries. I'll also have a Coke to drink. For dessert, I'll take a piece of that apple pie à la mode your poster claims you're so famous for. I want to see for myself if it's as good as you say. If it isn't, I just might take my temper tantrum, caused by my high expectations, out on your tip."

"Make that two with double the tip threat," Justin said. "However, if you give us extra cheese, that might make up for any tantrums we may or may not have."

She laughed as she gathered the menus from off the

table. "And you, miss?"

"I'll take the BLT, strawberry lemonade, and I'll try a piece of the apple pie as well—minus the tantrum. If necessary, I'll have mine in private so as not to smear my mascara in public."

The waitress gave the boys a flirtatious smile while ignoring her altogether. "All right, I'll be back in a few minutes with your order. My name is Gina, so if you need something, just yell."

Throughout the meal, her cousins yelled for her often. Gina didn't mind though. After all, it gave her ample opportunity to strut her stuff. Once they finished their dessert, Gina took their bill from out of her apron pocket. "Can I get you anything else before you leave?"

Jared tossed his napkin onto his plate and smiled. "Not unless you can tell us where we can find Rachel Jameson."

She laughed. "Dreaming of fame and fortune are we?"

"Hey, if it's on the table, I'll take either one. If not, a very large loan on the no repayment plan will do just as well."

She shook her head as she brought her laughter under control. "Well, I'm afraid I can't help you there. In fact, I can't remember the last time I heard anyone speak her name, much less know someone who could tell you where she is."

"That's all right, darlin'. I promise we won't take that one out on your tip." Justin winked as he tossed some bills on the table.

"Well here—" She grabbed a napkin and scribbled a number across it. "I'll ask some of the older locals for you. Later this evening you can give me a call if you'd like. Maybe someone around here knows something. I'm, uh, off at eight."

As they left the restaurant, Katie shook her head and tsked. "She may as well have asked you to meet her parents and set a wedding date."

Justin grinned. "I always did have a way with the ladies. Unfortunately, the older I get the more pronounced the trait becomes. Probably why I haven't married yet. There are so many of them out there, why choose one?"

Jared rolled his eyes. "Oh pul-eeze."

Justin turned toward his brother. "Hey, I didn't see her handing her phone number off to you, did you?"

"You weren't the one she 'accidently' brushed up against when we left either. Now isn't that right?"

Their back and forth banter lasted until they parked at the cemetery and exited the pickup.

"Now what?" Jared asked. "Sun's going to set pretty soon, so unless you want to dance in the dark we better get down to business."

Katie looked past the boys and settled her gaze on the immaculate lawn and rows of stones. "First, find the grave of Donald Martin. Second, see if we can find a caretaker. Oh, and if you want to take pictures of ghosts, now's your chance. I think they're supposed to show up as floating orbs, squiggly lights, or something stupid like that."

"Okay, I'll bite—who's Donald Martin?" asked Justin.

"A young man who died during the Vietnam War."

Jared propped his foot on the retaining wall, leaned over, and rested his arms on his leg. All the while he kept his gaze fastened to hers. "All right, Katie, I'll go ahead and ask the obvious. What does a dead Vietnam soldier and Rachel Jameson have in common?"

"At one time they were friends. I thought perhaps she might visit him here on occasion. If she does, perhaps a proprietor or caretaker knows where we can find her."

"Sound enough idea. But tell me, what are you going to do if you actually find her?" Jared asked. "What is the purpose of your visit really?"

"To ask her one very important question."

Jared stared at her. "One question. You've come all this way so you can ask one question."

"Yep. That should do it. Of course the answer could lead to other questions as well."

"Uh-huh—" Justin folded his arms against his chest and waited for her to speak.

She scrunched her shoulders together. "I'm sorry, guys, but that's all I can tell you. At least for now."

Jared raised a brow. "Really, Katie? I think your partners in crime should get the entire story, don't you, Justin?"

"Absolutely," he replied. "How can we cause our usual uproar in the good ol' town of cahoots if we don't even know why we're here in the first place?"

Katie bit down on her lip as she gazed back and forth between them. "Do you remember the last summer you spent in New Mexico before you moved to Texas? I think we were about eleven, maybe twelve years old or so?"

Jared grinned as he nudged an equally amused Justin. "How could we forget that? We had the time of our life."

"Then you'll surely recall that in the foolish and

mischievous behavior of youth—especially yours—you hot-wired the Millers' brand-spanking-new four-wheel-drive pickup. You and Justin took turns driving me all over town like you were competing in the Indy 500. To this day I count it a miracle neither of you got caught nor killed."

Her cousins laughed and with a nod, agreed with her.

"The way I recall it, you were so short back then that you peeked through the steering wheel, rather than above it while you drove. As a result when you coasted back into their driveway—on an almost empty gas tank I might add—you caught the side of their block wall fence. In so doing, you scraped off the paint on the passenger side of the vehicle. I think you may've even left a dent or two."

Jared pointed a finger at Justin. "He's the incompetent fool who did that."

"That part doesn't matter," she said. "What does matter is that as we stealthily crawled out of the cab and crept into the bushes, we swore each other to secrecy. Do you remember our little pact?"

They looked at each other and nodded. "On pain of death," Justin said.

"As you can see, I'm still alive. No matter how many times the story of the stolen, wrecked truck comes up in conversation, I still haven't told a soul that I know anything about it. Now if I can keep that secret under wraps after all this time, I think I can keep this secret as well."

"You know, she does have a point," Jared said.

Justin rubbed his hands together as he flashed a smile. "I love secrets. Especially my own. Now, where do we start? Should we split up or what?"

Katie's gaze fell on the tall monument to the left and center of the graveyard. "No, I think I know where I'm going. Well, at least the vicinity."

She led them across the grass. If not mistaken, that headstone, blurry at best in the photograph, sat somewhere behind Donnie's marker. She slowed her steps and as she approached it, she glanced at her cousins and drew a circle with her hand. "I think we'll find it somewhere in this area."

Mere seconds later, Jared dipped his head to his left. "Rachel Jameson's boyfriend is right here, Katie."

She did a double take. "I never said Donald was her boyfriend."

An annoying smirk emerged on his face. "You didn't have to—you had it written all over your face."

Justin chuckled as she dismissed them both with a wave of her hand. "Whatever. You can think whatever you want."

As she arrived at her cousin's side, Katie took in a deep breath. She knelt down in front of the stone and swept away the leaves that had fallen on top of it. Not a single flower graced his grave today. She wished now she would've thought to bring some. She traced the worn lettering of his name and the dates for birth and death. Did Rachel ever do that? Did she cry over his loss?

"Relative of yours?"

All three of them turned toward the owner of the gruff voice behind them. Katie stood up and as she brushed her hands off, she smiled. "Are you the caretaker here?"

He wagged his head from side to side. "One of a

handful anyway, and for about forty years now. As you might guess, I can tell you where everyone is buried if you need to find someone."

"After forty years, I suppose you could." For a moment, Katie dropped her gaze to the stone. "We're here for Donald Martin, though. He is a good friend of a friend of mine. We stopped by to pay our respects."

"That's nice. So many of the young men who died in Vietnam have been forgotten. Until you showed up he was one of them."

Her heart sank. "No one visits his grave? Ever?"

He shrugged. "Not unless you count the local veterans' association. They'll come and decorate the graves of all military personnel on appropriate holidays."

"No one else has ever come?"

"Excluding his parents when they were alive? Not that I've seen, ma'am. Of course, I'm not here twenty-four seven, so—" he let the rest of his sentence lead them wherever it might.

She swallowed her disappointment. "Then I'm glad we made the trip."

The caretaker gazed at the setting sun. "I'm sorry to cut your visit short, but unless you want your vehicle locked in overnight you'll have to move it."

"That's okay." Jared glanced at his watch. "We've got to get going anyway."

Once they were back in the truck, Katie sighed. "That didn't turn out as well as I'd hoped."

Justin put the gear-shift in reverse and rolled backward. "Maybe we'll have better luck at the spooky old mansion."

"If nothing else, it'll give us bragging rights around

the campfire," Jared said.

Katie held her phone aloft. "Do you know where you're going or do you need me to give you directions?"

"Nah, we've been by the place a time or two." Justin turned right as they left the cemetery. "By way of a secret entrance—which therefore everyone knows about—we also know how to get you onto the property without a whole lot of notice."

She gave him a sideways glance. "What do you mean?"

"Oh, come on, Katie," Jared said. "Surely you know we can't just go waltzing up to the front door by way of the front entrance. The iron gates are locked up tight. That means an alternative method is required."

"How would you know that? Earlier today you said you wanted an up close and personal look at the house. I took that to mean you'd never been there before."

"What the comment meant is that we didn't hop over the fence that separated the orchard from the main estate."

Justin snickered. "Let's just say the opportunity for that particular adventure escaped us at the time."

Katie sucked in a breath. "So you're telling me you trespassed on private property without a single concern as to whether or not you'd be arrested or shot?"

"Now that's harsh, Katie. Really harsh," Justin said. "We value our lives a little more than that. Allow me to put your mind at rest. We have some friends from this neck of the woods. Several years ago they invited us along while they—with permission—picked some fresh, luscious peaches from the Jameson orchard."

"Yeah, a lot of the locals do that. I mean, it's either

that or let them rot on the trees," Jared added. "I also might add the peach cobbler we had later that night made tramping through the weeds all worthwhile. You can trust me on that one."

"Who gave them permission?" she asked.

Jared shrugged. "I don't know. We didn't ask, nor did we care."

"Okay. Let's assume for a moment that someone connected to the estate gave them this permission. Would it be possible he or she, by way of your friends, could get us in touch with Rachel if we find she's not at the estate?"

"Nah, I didn't get that impression," he said. "I think it's more of an 'understanding' known by all of the locals if you get my drift."

"Oh brother. Let's hope that understanding extends to us then," she muttered underneath her breath.

Within minutes the magnificent red brick structure loomed ahead of them. Even in the dusk of early evening, she could see the pictures on the internet didn't do the place justice. No less than ten white, ornate pillars extended up to the second story gingerbread gables that surrounded the home. Lush ivy crawled up and around the four pillars in the middle. Wrap around porches graced both floors. She counted eight floor-to-ceiling windows on each story that faced the front of the property. One could assume that for decade upon decade those inside could've looked out over the immense lawn. From their vantage point they could enjoy the trees and flower-filled bushes which beautified the mansion. As she gazed at the arched double doors in the center, she imagined the happy Rachel in the yearbook inviting her king into her home.

She didn't envision the lights that suddenly lit up the porch though. Katie put a hand over her mouth as she pointed toward the doors. "I think someone's in there."

"That's a possibility, I suppose. But that happened last time we were here as well. I think they're on an automatic timer." Justin didn't stop in front of the place. Instead, he drove around the corner and to the end of the deserted street. Once the pavement ended, he made a u-turn and parked on the gravel off the side of the road. "There's a space big enough to squeeze through just beyond the hedge. Come on, I'll show you."

Katie's heart doubled its pace as they climbed out of the truck and entered the back portion of the property. She lowered her voice to a whisper. "How do we get to the house?"

Jared burst out laughing as he tugged on a lock of her hair. "Why are you whispering, little Katie? As you can see, there isn't a soul around."

She leaned in close, put a hand on his chest, and smiled. "Maybe there are more souls here than you think there are."

He grimaced. "Now that thought put a cold shiver down my spine."

"Oh, don't be such a pansy," Justin said. "There's no such thing as ghosts. Now come on, let's go see if we can find dear Rachel—or an acceptable substitute— at home. This is why we're here, after all."

No one said a word as they cut across the orchard behind the mansion. The lack of conversation called attention to the chorus of crickets, toads, nighthawks, and every other nocturnal creature that called this area home. All the while the stench of stagnant water permeated all around them. On top of that, a host of overgrown weeds grappled with Katie's jeans as they cut a trail to the gated fence.

Jared gave her a boost as she climbed up and over it. Seconds later the twins joined her. Together they gazed at the back of the house and the vast well-manicured lawn beyond it. The lavish courtyard off to the left must've played host to countless gatherings in the past. On the right hand side she could see the barn where Quinn surely met his death, and what looked like a fancy garden house of some kind.

She brushed off the back of her jeans. "I don't see any lights coming from inside the house. In addition, I don't see anything back here that even remotely resembles a caretaker's bungalow."

Justin shrugged. "Maybe Rachel, her groundskeeper, butler, or whoever, lives inside—down in the basement—along with the bats."

"Only one way to find out," said Justin. "Come on. Let's go around to the front and do something really brazen."

"Like what?" she asked.

He flashed a grin. "Ring the door bell."

The moment they stepped onto the porch and faced the door, her well-rehearsed speech fled her mind. Her heart pounded loud in her chest as she turned her gaze toward her cousins. "What should I say if someone actually answers?"

Jared chuckled. "Isn't that what you counted on? Didn't we come all of this way in the hope we'd find your mysterious heiress right here?"

She nodded. "Yes...yes, we did."

"Then just tell her why you're here," Justin said. "I'm sure when she knows you've come to ask her one very important question regarding good ol' Donald Martin, she'll invite you in with open arms."

Katie huffed out a breath. "I never once said my question had anything to do with Donnie. Why do you keep saying stuff like that?"

As both cousins laughed, Jared shook his head. "I want you to look us in the eye right now and tell us that it doesn't."

Justin put a hand on her shoulder as he fixed his gaze to hers. "Do keep in mind we're standing right next to you. Should someone open that door, you will have to speak. In turn, we will hear every word you say. Might as well come clean now. You'll be less embarrassed that way."

She bit back the witty retort that begged release. Instead she pushed Justin out of her way. With reluctant steps, she approached the bronze doorbell but stopped short of her destination.

"Yeah, that's what we thought." Jared laughed as he leaned against the brick wall and pressed the button for her.

The melodious chimes seemed loud enough to wake the dead. She listened for footsteps, but nothing interrupted the silence that followed. How long they stood there waiting she couldn't say. Longer than any reasonable person might, she supposed, since Jared took hold of her hand and tugged her close to his side.

"Either no one lives here, or no one deigns to answer," he said. "So—this is your show, Katie. What would you like us to do now?"

Justin's gaze darted back and forth between her

and Jared. "We could just break into the place and see if we can find a clue or two as to Rachel's current whereabouts. I mean, there's bound to be something in there."

"Or we could call Gina and see if she's had any luck," Jared said.

Katie couldn't respond to either suggestion. For just as the words left her cousin's mouth, the deadbolt as well as the latch clicked, one a split second behind the other. The doorknob made a rough shimmy to the right and then turned toward the left in like manner. For the life of her she couldn't tear her gaze away from that handle no matter how hard she tried. At once the air grew heavy as the door creaked, moaned, and stuttered its way open. The smile she had pasted on her face faded away. For no one stood in the doorway.

No one.

Instead of the person they all expected, nothing more than a dark, empty foyer invited them inside.

Chapter Twelve

None of them moved from where they had planted their feet. As they stared into the darkness, Jared took in a deep breath and gave it a slow release. "Most unexpected."

"Yes indeed." With the utmost in caution, Justin swept past them and stepped into the house. Jared grabbed hold of her hand, firmed his grip, and followed a step behind.

"Hello?" he called out. "Is anybody home? Look— I assure you, we're not here to disturb your peace, vandalize the place, or cause you trouble in any way. We're here to speak with Rachel Jameson on a matter of great importance and nothing more. Hello?"

No one responded.

Justin fumbled around for a light switch. He found one off to the right of the door and flipped it. In turn, he awakened one sluggish bulb in the crystal chandelier above them. The faceted candelabra globe offered no more than muted light. Once her eyes adjusted, Katie settled her gaze on the grand staircase in front of and to the left of the large foyer. She'd never seen anything like it. The intricate work of newel posts, balusters, and hand railings were something to behold. Exquisite crown molding and wainscoting set the tan and cream fleur-de-lis wallpaper off to absolute perfection. At the top of the stairway, a set of French doors with frosted glass reflected the dim light of the chandelier.

In that same moment, a shadow of movement behind those doors caught her attention. Another reflection from somewhere below? Shadows from windswept trees perhaps? Or must something altogether different claim responsibility for what she saw?

Jared gently nudged her, and she all but vaulted off the floor. "What?"

This time he didn't laugh over her whispered response. He cocked his head to the right. "Maybe we should take a look in there first."

She turned her gaze toward the formal drawing room. At the far end of the spacious room, a floor-to-ceiling bay window separated two grand pianos. White, diamond tufted Victorian furniture and tables rested on highly polished, wide plank wooden floors. Persian rugs with a peacock motif in hues of blue, green, and white accented the large room. A huge, white marble fireplace centered the wall to her left. The unique artwork on the mantel and side pillars would amaze anyone who saw them. So did the framed landscapes and portraits on the walls. She couldn't help but wonder what Donnie Martin thought when he stepped inside for the very first time. Did he feel out of place? Did he ever feel at home here?

Justin shook his head. "I don't think there's anything in there that would give us a clue as to Rachel's whereabouts. I mean there isn't a single tub of Cheese Whiz, bag of chips, peanuts, or pretzels on any of those tables—much less any mail tossed around the place. How boring is that?"

Jared bobbed his head. "I concur. So I wonder if there's an office or library in this ugly rat hole."

The off-handed comments, surely meant to lighten the mood, made her smile. "I don't know. If there is, do you think we'll find it on this floor?"

He turned and met her gaze. "With the luck we're having, we'll find it upstairs and in the last room we check. Of course, we won't know if I'm right until we explore each of the rooms down here."

Her stomach turned over at the very thought of climbing those steps. She took in a few deep breaths and prayed she wouldn't lose her dinner. "Let's hope we find something or someone down here."

Justin grinned as he gently chucked her chin. "Are you scared, little Katie?"

She pushed his hand away. "I'd rather use the term uncomfortable, if it's all the same to you. After all, we really shouldn't be in here."

"I don't see why not," Justin said. "If whoever didn't want us in here, whoever wouldn't have opened the bolted door and let us in."

"I think you mean 'whatever' opened the door, don't you?" Jared asked.

"One in the same, brother, one in the same."

As Justin moved down the hallway, they followed. The first door he opened led them into the elegant dining room. Once they searched every cabinet and cubbyhole, they wandered into and through a kitchen that would delight the fussiest chef. Along the way, they peeked inside closets and cupboard doors. Finally, they discovered the large conservatory. The magnificent room with marble floors took up the entire east wing of the house, that on any other day, she would've loved to explore. They found nothing out of place in the opulent home, nor did they find a single shred of paper that would help them locate Rachel.

Jared lifted a brow as he turned his gaze toward Justin. "Up the stairs?"

"Might as well," Justin replied. "After all, we don't want to leave a stone unturned and later wished we'd turned it, right?"

"Nope, not even if we have to visit the attic."

Katie gulped as they headed up the steps. Jared took the lead. Justin sandwiched her between them as he brought up the rear.

About half-way up, Jared swung out his arm and halted their progress. "Did you hear that?"

"Hear what?" Justin asked.

"Shh. Listen."

Katie held onto her breath as she turned her ear toward the landing. Again her heart took off. Seconds felt like minutes as she stood rooted to the spot. All the while she didn't hear anything out of the ordinary. Just as she opened her mouth, what sounded like a drone of garbled whispers wafted down the stairway. A series of intense chills raced up and down her spine. "What is that?"

"I'm not sure," Justin said.

"Do you think it's the wind coming down through all of the chimneys in the house?" she asked.

He shook his head. "No, the wind wouldn't sound like that. Not even if it wailed in every fireplace in this house. Besides, I don't recall it being particularly windy, do you?"

Jared narrowed his eyes. "Do you know what I think? I think someone's up there, and whoever it is just might have company."

"If that's the case, why wouldn't they just come

down and talk to us then?" she asked.

"Maybe our heiress has become a recluse and has a difficult time greeting her guests. On the other hand, perhaps she has a couple of bats in her belfry and wants to play hide and seek."

"That wouldn't be good," Justin murmured.

"You know what," she said, "maybe we should just go."

"No, not yet," Justin said. "We've come this far, let's at least go to the landing, knock on the door, and see what happens."

She took in a deep breath and let it go as she nodded. "I don't know if that's a good idea or not, but if it can lead us to Rachel—"

Katie held onto Jared as they climbed the rest of the stairs. Once they arrived at the top, he knocked at the door and stepped back. She stared at the handle with a strange mix of dread and anticipation. Despite the long wait, nothing happened. The doorknob didn't move. The whispers had also stopped and just as suddenly as they had come.

"I'm going in." Jared grabbed the knob and opened the doors. Once inside the hallway, he hit the switches on the wall. All the sconces on both sides of the area lit up.

Justin urged her reluctant feet forward. They crossed the threshold into the large hallway. She counted three doors on the right side, two on the left. At the end of the hall a window that matched the ones she saw out front, offered a spectacular view of the vast Jameson property. She also spied another hallway that extended in both directions. Paintings as well as multi-colored marble pedestals with a variety of unique sculptures on top of them, decorated the magnificent hall.

"Okay, 'Let's Make a Deal' fans, shall we see what's behind door number—" Jared clamped down on his mouth as all of the lights dimmed. At the same time, a flash of lightning lit up the window. A deafening rumble of thunder followed. An instant later, a torrent of rain pounded against the glass. Katie stared at the sight. Her mouth went dry as a wave of dizziness overcame her. Without conscious thought, she stepped back and bumped into Justin. In response, he wrapped his arms around her and held her tight in a protective embrace.

The last door on the left flung open. Katie's heart dropped into the pit of her stomach as Quinn Jameson strode out of the room. He headed straight for them. Anger marred the young man's features. He didn't look at them, rather it seemed he looked past them as if they weren't even there.

"No," he yelled over his shoulder. "I already told you, I'll no longer follow your orders like some sniveling coward without a mind of his own. Go ahead and cut me out of your precious will for all I care. Your money and your holdings mean nothing to me, old man. They never have. When will you ever learn that?"

"Get back here at once!" Gustavus flew out of the room right behind his son. His wrinkled face, twisted now with hatred and loathing, scared her half to death. He grabbed the back of Quinn's shirt and whirled him around so that his son faced him. His hands slid down the boy's arms as he held him in an iron grip. All the while, the devil himself couldn't have looked any more menacing. "Do not defy me, boy. You will do as you're told!"

Quinn pushed him away and as he backed up, he shook his head. "No. I won't. I'll no longer be your pawn or your reluctant cohort in the despicable game you've played. I refuse. Do you even halfway understand that?"

"You'll not destroy my reputation," Gustavus snarled.

Quinn lifted a brow. "Your reputation, Father? You lost that a long time ago, alongside your honor. At least with all those who should matter most."

Gustavus bellowed his rage. The old man drew back his hand and struck his son full across the face. Quinn tumbled backward. As the boy fell, the side of his head slammed against the sharp corner of the pedestal nearest them. He landed on the floor at their feet. With a bit of effort, Quinn rose up on an elbow and wiped at the blood now trickling down his face. The scene faded away into oblivion as father and son gazed into each other's eyes. The lightning, thunder, and rain disappeared as the hall lights returned to their former brightness.

For a time, no one said a word. No one moved from where they stood. They all just stared down the hallway.

"Dude!" Jared recovered first. He grinned from ear-to-ear and smacked Justin on the back. "Did you see that?"

Justin snorted. "Don't be stupid, man. We all saw it."

"So much for ghosts that don't exist, huh?"

The moment Jared made the comment, something clicked. Katie turned to face them. "Residual haunting."

Jared drew his brows together as he shook his head. "What?"

"Residual haunting. I heard about it on one of Mom's TV programs. It's...it's like a film from out of the past. The ghosts, in this case Quinn Jameson and his father, are not really there. Experts in the paranormal say it's an imprint on time, created by a high level of emotion or trauma. One that will play over and over again. Some say it repeats on the anniversary it took place. Others say it can replay far more often and even as much as daily. From what I saw, the scene definitely qualifies."

"How do you know who those people are?" Jared asked.

"I've seen pictures. Lots of them, in fact. However, I must admit, I didn't expect to see them coming out of that door as if they were alive and well. A door, by the way, that's still shut."

Justin stroked his chin as both cousins shifted their gaze to the door in question. "Maybe that's why we can't find dear Rachel, or anyone else for that matter, at home. If I had to witness something like that every day of my life, I'd move out too."

"And in less than a heartbeat." Jared moved a couple of steps forward. "I wonder if we'll find the old man's office or library behind that door."

Justin gave it a nod. "Let's go have a look-see."

Though her heart had yet to resume its normal pace, she followed her fearless cousins down the hall. Justin took hold of the handle and with a bit of effort, pushed the door open. In the same instant the most putrid air she'd ever encountered belched out at them. As she lifted a hand to cover her mouth and nose, a dark swirling mist at the back of the room stole her attention. The thing moved toward the center. Only then did the vile, misshapen mass transform into the ghost of Gustavus Jameson.

His entire being emitted hostility and malice. She couldn't blame the image on residual haunting. Not this time. The unearthly specter shook with unleashed fury as he gazed at each of them in turn. Fear, such as she never experienced before, took hold of her. She couldn't move. She couldn't scream.

"Get out!" He pointed at the door as he stormed toward them. The floor shook beneath their feet while the windows rattled. "Get out of my house!"

Jared grabbed her hand and headed for the stairway, with Justin at their heels. They didn't stop until they arrived at the fence behind the house. As Jared released her hand, he leaned over, placed his hands on his bent knees, and laughed.

Justin joined in his laughter. "What a rush. Wait 'til the guys hear this story."

Jared stood straight, took in a much needed breath, and shook his head. "They'll never believe us. Never."

Justin nodded. "Yeah, well, would you?"

"No, I guess not."

"Exactly. So moving right along—I think maybe it's time we get out of here. After we do that, we'll call Gina. Maybe she'll restore a bit of sanity to this very bizarre evening."

"You have her number with you?" Jared asked.

He patted his pockets. "No, I think I left it in the truck."

"Then shall we?" Jared turned toward her with his fingers twined together in invitation.

An invitation she immediately accepted. After they all had scaled the fence they made their way to the safety of the vehicle.

Once inside, Justin grabbed the napkin and took his cell phone from his pocket. "That's strange," he said. "I should have a full battery, but it's dead."

Jared handed him his. "Here, you can use mine."

As Justin pressed the button, he shook his head. "Would if I could, but I can't so I won't. Yours is dead too."

"Seriously?"

"Seriously."

"This just keeps getting weirder by the second. Katie? How about yours?"

Katie turned the black screen toward them. "Same."

"All right." Justin leaned forward and took hold of the key. "Let's get the heck out of here before we all die. We'll go back to the diner and ask them where we can find—"

Jared huffed out a breath. "Now what?"

"Won't start."

"You've got to be kidding me."

While they spoke, Katie, for the life of her, could not. She tried, many times over in an effort to get their attention. Yet she just couldn't gather enough air to make a sound. Finally, with what sounded like some sort of pitiful squeak, she pointed toward the side of the pickup.

There—just in front of the back passenger window—stood the glowing form of Quinn Jameson. He pinned the intensity of his gaze solely to hers as he beckoned her with a wave of his hand.

****

With a hand on his shoulder, William knelt at the young soldier's side. The kid covered his eyes with his hands as he sobbed. He could feel the intensity of his pain as if it were his own. "Hey, it's all right. Everything is going to be just fine, Shawn."

He shook his head. Anguish and despair radiated from his entire being. "No. No, it isn't, sir. Nothing will ever be fine again. Not ever."

William stood up, offered him his hand, and smiled. "Come on, Shawn, let's go for a walk and we'll talk about that, all right?"

Private Shawn Abernathy rose to his feet and saluted. "Yes, sir."

For a time, they walked in silence. William knew Shawn needed no more than that right now. All throughout the walk, the kid took a keen interest in his surroundings. "What is this place?"

William folded his arms against his chest as he halted their walk. He turned and gazed into his eyes. "What do you think it is?"

Shawn settled his gaze on the bountiful trees, lush vegetation, and the clear, resplendent river off to the right of their path. "I don't know. This isn't what I expected Hell to look like."

"Is that where you thought you'd find yourself after that ill-conceived stunt you pulled a short while ago?"

He firmed his jaw. "It's where I deserve to be."

"Why?"

"Because like the coward I am, I left my platoon and hid from enemy fire. I thought only of myself. My preservation. I didn't care a whit about theirs. In the meantime, they all died as they honorably and heroically carried out the mission our commanding officer entrusted to us. I should've died with them that day."

"Every soldier in the field of battle gets scared, Shawn. There's no shame in that—it happens to the best of us. What does matter is that from that day until your honorable release from the army, you served courageously."

Shawn finally turned and looked him in the eye. "You don't get it, do you? I should've died while I was in Afghanistan! I wanted to die. I did everything in my power to make it happen. Now if you call that courage—"

"What possible good would such a thing have accomplished?"

Shawn dropped his head and closed his eyes. "My death would've righted a wrong."

"And now?"

His head snapped up. "What do you mean?"

"You said you wanted to die in the service. You didn't. Under the current circumstances, do you feel you've accomplished your objective?"

The thought, it seemed, hadn't yet occurred to him. Given time, it would. While Shawn mulled it over, William waited.

At last the young soldier shook his head. "No, I suppose I didn't. Nonetheless, please understand—I couldn't take the pain or the horrendous images in my head any longer. Every day, every night, I could see the faces of each man in my platoon. In those dreams I could hear their screams…see their suffering. Those images haunted me. They wouldn't let me sleep."

William nodded. "I can understand those reasons. But tell me, have any of those things lessened now that you find yourself here, in this place?"

"No, I guess not."

"I didn't think so."

"Not much I can do about that now. What's done is done. I'll live with it, I guess."

William didn't answer. Instead, he escorted him all the way down to the end of a long path that forked off in two opposite directions. "I'll let you in a little secret, Shawn. You didn't die during your service in the army because you were watched over and protected every minute of every day. That protection would've been in full force even if you had remained with your platoon on that fateful day you spoke of. You were meant to survive."

Shawn's mouth dropped as he stared into his eyes. "Why?"

"Because you had some important things you still needed to accomplish."

"Me?" He shook his head. "Like what?"

"Like a wife—now a devastated woman contemplating what widowhood might look like for her—to love, protect, and cherish throughout all the days of her life. A son and future children that need the unique guidance of their dad as they maneuver through the difficult years ahead of them. Trust me, they will be difficult. There are people—veterans like yourself—that only you have the power to reach and to help in the years ahead. All this, because of your experiences in the army, not in spite of them."

He pondered that for a time. "I guess I screwed things up again, didn't I."

"Not unless you choose to stay here—in this place."

His eyes narrowed. "I can go back?"

"If you have the courage." William placed a hand on his shoulder. "The doctors haven't given up. They're still working on you even now when all seems lost. I must warn you though, the road ahead will not be an easy one. Your recovery will be difficult. In spite of all that, what do you say?"

Shawn took in the vast panorama that surrounded him. "This place sure is beautiful."

"Yes, it is."

"Peaceful, too."

"Very."

"But it isn't Heaven, is it?"

William shook his head. "No, it isn't."

He nodded. "I guess I can figure it all out later—at the proper time. So if it's all the same to you, sir, I'd like to go back and try it again."

"Admirable choice." He turned down the path that veered off to the right. In the same moment that William revealed the crystal portal to Shawn's view, Richard appeared at his side. "Shawn has elected to carry out the remainder of his mission, Private Barnett. Would you escort him back to where he belongs at the present time, please? Make sure he's all right before you leave."

A huge grin broke out on Richard's face as he gazed at Shawn. "I'd be honored, Sergeant Griffin. Shawn? You and I are going to step right through that portal. You'll see a brilliant light and feel a bit of a rush as we are transported back to the hospital. Once there you'll re-enter your body. Don't worry about the sudden heaviness of it when you do. The weight is normal and to be expected. Any questions?"

"You'll be with me all the way?" asked Shawn.

"All the way. I promise I won't leave until you're safely with your family once again."

Shawn turned toward William. "I don't suppose I'll remember any of this when I wake up, will I?"

William chuckled. "You'll remember all of it—down to the smallest detail."

"Good, I don't want to forget anything. Not ever. Thank you so much, sir." He gazed at Richard. "Okay, I'm ready to go if you are."

Shawn and Richard entered the portal and disappeared. His current duty ended, William placed his concentration on Katie. Her terror resonated within him as easily as did Shawn's pain. Something had happened.

At once he headed toward her light. He didn't expect to find her in Texas, alongside her cousins. The three of them had just entered one of the biggest barns he'd ever seen on earth. The why of it escaped him, but not for long. He appeared right in front of her and blocked the next step in her path.

Katie gasped as she stopped short. "William! What are you doing here?"

"I could ask you the same thing."

Jared turned around and searched her face. "William? Who in the Sam Hill is William? Did some other unholy entity follow us in here?"

She looked at her cousin and tsked. "No, I—uh—don't pay me any mind. I'm just a bit frazzled, that's all."

William noticed him then. The young spirit that

stood off to the side of the stairs turned and gazed into his eyes. He took a single step toward him as he communicated his intentions.

In the mere blink of an eye William understood Quinn Jameson's purpose. "It's all right, Katie. I see him now. Go ahead and follow. Don't be afraid. He just wants to share a memory with you, okay? Consider it a movie clip from his past."

Katie answered with a subtle dip of her head.

"I think we're all a little unsettled," Justin said as he turned his attention back to Quinn. "Let's see what he wants, get this done, and get out of here."

Katie and her cousins followed Quinn up the rough wooden steps leading to the loft. Once they were assembled on top, William took hold of her hand and gave it a gentle squeeze.

The sudden thud of heavy footsteps drew the trio's attention toward the stairs they had just climbed. Another image of Quinn Jameson breathed heavily as he took hold of the railing and pulled himself up and onto the landing. Katie and the twins looked back and forth between the ghostly Quinn who led them here, and the one that seemed real enough to touch.

Katie put a hand on Justin's arm. "Another movie."

"Yeah, I sort of figured that," the twins said simultaneously.

All three of them fixed their gaze on the unfolding scene. Quinn staggered toward the enormous tool box at the edge of the loft. Once he settled his back against the steel frame, he put his full weight behind it and pushed the box aside. He dropped to his knees and took in several deep breaths. After a short rest, he stuck his finger in a large knothole of a newly revealed floorboard and lifted it away from the frame.

Quinn squeezed his eyes shut and grimaced as he retrieved a leather pouch from within the hollow. While clutching the bag, he extracted the wallet from his back pocket and opened it. He withdrew a wrinkled piece of paper and shoved it deep inside the pouch. The task complete, he replaced both pouch and floorboard. He inched himself into a standing position, leaned into the tool box, and as he returned it to its proper place, he moaned. Then in a swirling mist, Quinn's distant memory dissipated from view.

Katie's hand trembled as she covered her mouth. Her eyes filled with sadness as she gazed at Quinn. In turn, he gave her a little smile and shook his head.

Only the secret he carried concerned him, not the manner of his death. William knew that. Quinn put a hand on top of the tool box.

"I think he wants us to move it," Jared said.

Justin nodded at the ghost. "Yep, so let's get it done, shall we?"

The cousins wrestled the heavy steel box away from the wall, just as Quinn showed them.

Katie stooped down and removed the floorboard. She set it aside and lifted the leather pouch from its nest. She spared William a glance, and then gazed at Quinn. "May I see what's inside?"

Quinn broadened his grin and nodded.

She untied the strings and opened the bag as William knelt beside her. With the greatest of care she removed the stack of musty letters from inside and looked them over, one by one. Each one had been addressed to Rachel. The sender? PFC Donald R. Martin. None of them had ever been opened.

While Katie examined the letters, Quinn told William he died before he could give them to Rachel. He said the greatest sorrow he carried—even in death—was that his beloved sister didn't know they existed.

Chapter Thirteen

Katie put the letters in order by date and then wiped the tears from her cheeks. She gazed at Quinn. "Are you the one that opened the front door and let us into your home?"

Quinn nodded.

"That's good. I would hate to think that for some twisted reason, it was your father." For a moment, she dropped her gaze to the stack of mail on her lap. "These letters should never have been here in the barn, Quinn. A valid reason for it escapes me. I can only assume that for the memories they stirred, Rachel didn't want them. Maybe they didn't arrive until after Don's death and you wanted to protect her from the pain. Still, you must've kept them all of these years for a reason. From what we just saw upstairs in the hallway, it's possible you never had the chance to give them to her yourself. If that's true, then perhaps you intended to give them to her before—well, before the events of that night prevented it. Am I even close to the truth of the matter?"

A small smile accompanied the side to side nod of his head.

He looked so young, and so very sad. Katie's heart went out to him."I promise you—I absolutely promise you—Rachel will get every single one of them if that's what you want. Is it?"

Quinn nodded.

"The thing is, I had hoped to find her here. Obviously, she's not. Do you have any idea where she is living now?"

He shook his head, shifted his gaze toward William, and kept it there for a time.

"Well if he doesn't know where she is, how does he expect us to find her?" Jared groused.

"I don't have a clue. If we're lucky, Gina might've found out something that'll help us," Justin replied. "Maybe the phones will work now we have the letters."

"Let's hope the truck will too. If not, we better start walking."

Just as Jared made the comment, the ghost of Quinn Jameson turned toward her and gave her a smile. He placed a hand against his heart, dipped his head, and faded away from sight.

Jared huffed out a breath. "I guess that—as they say—is that."

"Yep. Looks like we're on our own from here on out. At least I hope we are. I'm already sick and tired of ghosts, residual haunting, and any kind of haunting in general." Justin offered her his hand. "Come on, cousin. We've overstayed our welcome. Let's get out of here."

As she climbed to her feet, Katie discovered that William had also disappeared.

"Wait a minute. Do you guys smell that?" asked Justin.

For the dread in his voice, Katie stuck her nose in the air and took in a good whiff. Something had caught fire! She turned around and looked at the steps. A thick blanket of black smoke drifted upward toward the loft. Jared cussed up a storm as he grabbed her hand and yanked her toward their one and only exit.

"Try not to breathe in the vapors," he yelled. "Cover your mouth and nose with your shirt."

They raced down the steps and toward the open doors at the opposite end of the barn. Katie kept her gaze fastened on her feet as she held her breath. Flames roared and crackled somewhere behind them. For all the smoke, she couldn't locate the point of origin.

With an unexpected suddenness, Jared halted their escape. "Watch out!"

The heavy barn doors slammed shut with an ease that seemed impossible.

Justin hurled his body against them, but they didn't budge. Jared grabbed hold of a heavy two-by-four that sat on top of a work bench and used it for a battering ram. All the while the twins coughed, choked, and sputtered, but they didn't give up.

Katie clutched the precious letters tight against her body and sank to her knees. In that same moment, she saw him from the corner of her eye. She turned her head and faced him head on. Gustavus Jameson settled his repulsive gaze on her. As his gaze drilled into hers, he threw back his head and laughed. The sound of it was both ugly and evil.

Katie couldn't control the need for air any longer. She sucked in a breath. In so doing, her throat and lungs burned. She coughed, and the more she coughed, the worse it became. Her eyes watered. The heat and smoke affected the twins in the same way. How long would it take before death claimed them all?

Just then, William appeared at her side. He grasped her hand and raised her to her feet. He turned her toward him, cupped her face, and gazed into her eyes.

"None of this is real, Katie. You only think it is. The mind is a powerful thing. If you believe what you see, it can hurt you. This is what Gustavus wants." He fastened his gaze on the ghost. "Isn't that right, Jameson? You've had your fun. You can go ahead and slither back to the foul abyss from whence you came. We'll no longer tolerate your presence here."

In response to his words, Gustavus shook his fists and bellowed his rage.

"Leave now, or suffer the consequences of your defiance. A consequence that involves an inevitable appointment you and I both know you're not ready to face." Even though hatred emanated from his entire being, the ghost of Gustavus Jameson faded into nothingness. Katie blinked several times over. Her vision cleared. The cough disappeared. She no longer saw or smelled the smoke. The fire had also vanished without a trace. She grabbed Justin's arm. Still caught up in the vision, the twins hammered at the door.

"Justin! Jared! Turn around and look at me. This is only an illusion—just like those we've already seen. There isn't any fire and the doors are not locked. Gustavus just wants you to think that."

The boys whirled around. They blinked several times as her words sank in. They believed her. A sense of calm replaced the alarm of a moment ago.

Jared took in a deep breath, let it out, and nodded. "The old man ought to get a gig in Vegas. For a minute there, he had me convinced."

"Yeah—you know what? I've enjoyed this place about as much as I can stand. I mean creepy doesn't even begin to describe it anymore." Justin flung the two-by-four onto the ground. It landed with a bounce and a clatter.

"I'm with you, bro." Jared clapped him on the back and took Katie's hand. "I've more than worn out my welcome here."

In the moment she had after the boys boosted her over the fence, she gazed at William who had awaited her on the other side. "Where did you and Quinn go? Gustavus didn't do anything awful to him, did he?"

"Who are you talking to this time, Katie?" Justin planted his feet firmly on the ground and looked all about the area. "More spooks?"

"No—I'm thinking out loud again. Don't worry. I don't see any nasty ghosts or illusions. I'm just anxious to leave."

"I think we all are. So if Jared can get his tubby butt over the fence, we'll do just that."

Jared jumped down next to them and brushed off his hands. "Do you really want to walk down that path?"

Justin chuckled as he placed a hand over his heart. "I don't know what overcame me. Must've been the not so very real threat of death and destruction that loosened my tongue in such a dreadful, outspoken manner. In turn, I must also force an insincere apology."

"Not to mention your fear of reprisal if you don't?"

He nodded. "Yeah, that too."

While the boys volleyed insults back and forth, Katie sneaked a glance at William.

"We can talk later," he said. "I'll answer all of your questions then, okay?"

William remained at her side as they made their way back through the orchard and out to the street.

After she climbed into the truck, he settled himself beside her. He took hold of her hand and twined his fingers through hers. She didn't know how much she needed him until that moment. If she had already mastered the skill, she'd nestle herself against his chest. She'd beg him to hold her until all of the hideous experiences this evening disappeared.

The moment Justin got Gina on speaker phone, she turned her gaze toward William. "Can you stay with me or do you have to go?" she whispered.

A small grin accompanied a wink. "I won't leave you. I promise."

"So did you find out the whereabouts of Rachel Jameson?" Justin asked after he and Gina waded through the initial chitchat.

"Just that she's living somewhere in Alvin," Gina replied. "I'm sorry, but that's the best I could do."

Katie tapped Jared on the shoulder. "That's all we need. I think I know where she lives."

"Okay, thanks, Gina. You're a sweetheart," Justin said. "I'll catch up with you next time I'm in town and thank you properly for your help. Deal?"

Once he ended the call, he looked into the rearview mirror and captured Katie's gaze. "You say you know where she lives?"

"Well, not off the top of my head," she answered. "But I can find it again through the property records online. All I need is a computer."

Jared glanced at his watch. "It's getting late, so why don't we head home? Katie can find us an address tonight. We can head to Alvin in the morning after we get some sleep. Agreed?"

Justin started the vehicle and shifted it into gear.

"Sounds like a good plan to me."

All the way back to Houston they talked about the haunted Jameson mansion, Quinn, and Gustavus. They grilled her for every piece of information she had about the family. She couldn't expect any less. Still, it kept them from asking questions she'd rather they didn't ask.

Minutes after they arrived at her cousins' home, Jared handed her his laptop. She found again the address of the home Rachel owned in Alvin.

Justin entered it into his phone and then flashed a grin. "Let's hope she's there and the house isn't haunted, shall we?"

"Oh, but didn't you know?" she teased. "Sometimes ghosts follow their—"

"Stop right there and don't you dare say another word." Jared held a hand out toward her as he looked away. "I don't even want to know what ghosts do or do not do. I've had enough of that nonsense to last a lifetime. If I never see another haunted house, it will be much too soon."

Katie laughed. "Well, look at it this way. At least now you have some experience under your belt if you do."

For the remainder of the evening their conversation shifted to far safer topics and pleasant reminisces. As the clocked approached the midnight hour, they all headed off to bed. After she shut the door to the guest room, she turned around and all but bumped into William.

As he encircled her with his arms, he placed his hands against the casing, and held her captive. "Alone at last."

She leaned against the door, smothered her obnoxious butterflies, and nodded. "Um-hmm and that means you can answer all of my questions before you do another thing."

"Spoilsport." William winked as he dropped his arms and stepped back. "Okay, down to business then. To answer the first question you asked me, no, Gustavus didn't cause Quinn's sudden disappearance, nor did he hurt him. The old man doesn't have anywhere near that kind of power. Quinn left because, thanks to you, his work here is done. I simply escorted him from this realm into mine. Once there, his mother greeted him with open arms, so you needn't look so worried. He's well, and at long last, he's happy."

"Did he tell you about the letters?"

William nodded. "He did. As you might've guessed, Gustavus didn't approve of the relationship between Rachel and Don. He did everything he could think of and then some to keep them apart. At one point he even ordered Don out of the house and told him not to come back. That same night, Gustavus told Rachel she couldn't see Don anymore—that he'd lock her up if necessary. None of that stopped them though. The old man knew it, and it angered him beyond all normal reason. Quinn said he'd always ruled his home with an iron fist. Throughout their entire lives, he expected their unquestionable obedience. Even his wife had to tow the mark or suffer the consequences."

"Those horrible eyes of his are proof of that." She moved away from the door and sat down on the edge of the bed. "Why did he feel such a need to interfere? Why couldn't he have just left them alone?"

"That's something only he can answer. Anything

short of that is just a guess." William sat down beside her. "Quinn said the day Don got his draft notice, Gustavus hatched a simple plan. In phase one, Rachel could send off her letters to Don without interference, which she did. After a couple of months had passed, he went to the post office. There he offered a specific clerk a large sum of money. In exchange for that cash, he simply had to place a 'refused and return to sender' stamp on Rachel's letters to Don and mail them back to his daughter. He accepted the bribe and did the job."

"That's awful."

"Yes indeed. In phase two of his plan, he let Rachel receive two or three letters from Don. Then as more arrived, he ordered Quinn to get them from the mailbox and destroy them."

"Why did he involve Quinn? Why didn't he just get one of his servants do to his dirty work?"

"Because of the fondness the servants had for Rachel, Gustavus didn't trust them to carry out his orders. On the other hand, he believed Quinn would follow his orders just as he always had. Quinn couldn't do it though. Instead of destroying them, he hid them all away."

"In the loft of the barn."

"Yes. He knew his father would never lower himself to enter the barn, much less go up into the loft and move a heavy tool box. He didn't think the notion would even occur to him. That notion proved correct. Anyway, as time passed, Rachel voiced her worry over Don's well-being. She thought perhaps he'd been wounded or worse. At that point, a gleeful Gustavus sat her down. He handed her all the letters she had written that the mail clerk returned. In addition, he told her that for the sum of ten thousand dollars, her precious fiancé had eagerly severed the relationship. Therefore, she shouldn't expect to ever hear from him again. You can imagine what that did to Rachel."

"Oh, no." Tears stung her eyes as she thought of Rachel's devastation. "What kind of monster would do something like that to his daughter?"

"The worst kind."

She wiped at the tear that meandered down her face. "I'll not argue with you there. I don't see how she could've survived it."

"She didn't. At least not very well." William took hold of her hand and caressed the top of it with his thumb. "Rachel's deep sorrow and despair ate at Quinn. She didn't eat, she didn't sleep. Most of the time she stayed in her room. He worried for her health, both emotional as well as physical. Finally Quinn went to his father and confessed what he had done. He thought for sure his father would be relieved. For the love and well-being of his daughter Quinn thought he'd give her the stolen letters. He thought he'd offer her an apology for his actions just so he could see her smile again. Instead, Gustavus flew into a demented rage. He demanded the letters. Quinn refused to hand them over. Their argument turned into an ugly fight. That fight resulted in his death."

"Yes, I saw the ghastly movie from start to finish. We all did." Katie gulped. "Is that why he remained earthbound—because his father caused his death and he wants some kind of justice?"

"No. He doesn't care about any of that. Quinn stayed behind after his death so he could protect the letters. He vowed to stay in the house until they were in the hands of his sister even though by then Don had met his death in Vietnam. Countless times after Quinn died, he tried to tell Rachel the letters existed and where he had hidden them. He said she never heard him. No matter what he said or did, Quinn couldn't get through. He even tried dreams, which she promptly dismissed as just that. In the meantime, his father tore the house apart in search of them. Of course, he never found them and it drove him mad. That madness didn't end with his death. Anyway, you showed up at the door and Quinn heard you mention Don. He thought maybe he could enlist your help. See? You didn't let him down."

"I hope not." Her thoughts drifted toward Gustavus. "If I remember correctly, Jameson survived his son by not quite two years. Do I have that right?"

"You do."

"Why does Gustavus stay earthbound? Surely by now the letters are no longer important. After all, Don is already dead. That makes it impossible for Rachel to have any kind of future with Don now. Well, at least a normal one. So you see, his vile plan worked. He should be overjoyed."

"My impression when I saw him inside the barn is that he greatly fears a date with the devil."

"I bet. I would too, were I in his shoes."

William wiped away the tear that had dripped down and settled on her cheek. "I'm so sorry, Katie."

Confusion beset her. "For what?"

"For involving you in all of this. I shouldn't have asked your help. I should've found another way."

"Don't say that. Not ever." She shook her head and sniffed. "I'm not sorry at all. What happened at the Jameson estate is all part of the story that not only

Rachel should know, but so should Donnie."

"They will. I promise you they will."

****

From the comfortable recliner next to the bed, William remained at her side as promised. While he watched over her, he wondered what the morning would bring. Would they find Rachel at her home in Alvin? If they did, would she listen to what Katie had to say? He also wondered if it would matter even if she did. Rachel may've moved well beyond any feeling she once had for Don. They might even find a husband of many years at her side, just as Don feared. What then?

Katie drew in a deep breath and stretched her body from head to toe as her eyes fluttered open. She turned to her side and smiled. "Good morning, William."

"Good morning, my love." For the surprised look on her face, he chuckled. He claimed her hand as she inched her way into a seated position. "Too much for you? Would you prefer 'sweetheart,' 'darling,' 'cupcake' even?"

As she gazed at him, she opened her mouth and closed it. For a few precious seconds she did nothing more than gaze at him. All the while her eyes danced with a mixture of mischief and delight. "I suggest you stop before you get to 'Twinkie.' Cupcake will fall on deaf ears. I kind of think darling and sweetheart—although both most endearing to heart and soul—are a little overused, don't you?"

"My love it is then—it's my favorite out of the four anyway." He leaned down and gave her a kiss as she giggled,.

He meant to leave it at just the one, but he couldn't. The deep love he had for his woman bubbled to the surface and expressed itself in a series of kisses, each one far deeper than the last, each one expressing the various emotions she inspired. She responded with the same passion she always did. At last he allowed her a breath of much needed air. An adorable glow colored her cheeks. Wonder shone within those mesmerizing blue eyes of hers. They expressed the depth of her feelings for him, even if for now, she couldn't—or wouldn't—voice them. He could live with that. For now. The knock on the door prevented the next kiss he ached to give her.

Katie sighed. "I'm awake."

"Good thing, too," Jared shot back. "If you sleep much longer, you might as well stay in bed for the day."

"I mean, really," Justin hollered. "Did the Jameson ghosts and goblins take so much out of you that you can't get up at a decent hour?"

"Oh, give it a rest." Katie tossed her blankets off to the side and slipped out of bed. "It's not even eight o'clock for crying out loud."

"In the meantime, you're missing out on the delicious breakfast now on the table. If you don't hurry, Justin will have eaten it all."

"Would serve you right, too," Justin said.

"Oh, quit your whining, I'm coming."

Katie took some clothes from out of her backpack and went into the bathroom. A few minutes later she emerged. She looked quite luscious in a pair of faded blue jeans and a long-sleeved, powder blue t-shirt that somehow enhanced the color of her eyes.

Breakfast passed with the usual banter William expected from the trio, as did the ride to Alvin.

However, the moment they pulled up in front of the late nineteenth century Victorian home, the chatter stopped.

"Someone definitely lives there," Katie murmured.

Justin gazed at the pale yellow house as he mowed over the stubble on his chin. "What makes you think so?"

"Because the grounds are well-kept and the flower baskets hanging from the eaves are in full bloom," she said. "In addition to that, the furniture on the porch doesn't show the slightest sign of neglect."

"All right then, are you ready for whatever comes next?" Jared asked.

Katie lifted a shoulder as she took in a breath. "Whether I am or not, we're here and I have to go home tomorrow, so—"

Justin grabbed the door handle and tugged. "Okay, let's get it done."

Katie clutched the leather pouch as she exited the truck. William put a hand on her waist as they crossed the walkway and climbed the steps to the porch. Jared rang the doorbell and stepped back.

The woman that answered the door didn't in any way look like the pictures William had seen of Rachel. This lady looked about seventy-five years of age or so, had hazel eyes, and snow-white hair. He turned his gaze toward Katie who shot him a worried glance.

The woman wiped her hands on her apron as she looked them over. "May I help you?"

Katie moved forward. "Yes, please. I'm hoping we can speak with Rachel Jameson. Does she live here?"

The surprise in her eyes gave way to suspicion. "May I ask what this is all about?"

Katie looked down at the bag she held in her arms.

"A friend entrusted me with something that belongs to her. Something very important. I promised him I would make sure she gets it."

"I see. Well, I'd be happy to give it to her if you'd like."

Katie shook her head. "Please don't misunderstand, I don't have any doubt you would keep your word, but I must give it to her myself. I promise I won't take much of her time."

"Let her come in, Martha."

The soft voice came from somewhere behind Martha. Nonetheless, the emphasis on the word 'her' made it clear the twins were not invited inside. Katie looked at them and shrugged.

Jared glanced at Martha and then gave Katie his full attention. "Don't worry. We'll sit right there on that swing and wait for you to come out. So if for any reason you need us—"

Katie took hold of his hand and gave it a gentle press. "I know, and thank you. I won't be long."

Martha stepped back and ushered her inside. William accompanied her as she entered the living room.

An older version of the Rachel in the photograph sat in one of the two blue Victorian-style chairs turned slightly toward each other. She closed her book and put it on the small rosewood table that separated one chair from the other. Rachel waved a hand toward the empty one as Martha vacated the room. "Please sit down and make yourself comfortable, Miss—?"

Katie approached her with hand extended. Rachel readily accepted it.

"My name is Katie Adelton, Miss Jameson. Thank

you so much for seeing me."

"You've piqued my curiosity, Miss Adelton." She paused as she looked her over. "I know it isn't difficult to find out where one lives if one looks hard enough, the question is why. You said you had something that belongs to me. The trouble is—I don't recall losing anything of importance. I also can't imagine how a perfect stranger could get possession of it, even if I had. So would you care to enlighten me?"

As Katie sat down, she took in a deep breath and blew it out again. William could hear her heart pounding inside her chest as she dropped her gaze to the leather pouch. She toyed with the strings for a moment and then gazed into Rachel's eyes.

"I don't quite know where to begin. This will probably sound strange and maybe even unbelievable. Nonetheless, I'd like to ask you one very personal question before we get started if you don't mind."

Rachel clasped her hands together and laid them on her lap. "If I refuse, will you still tell me the reason for this visit?"

"Yes."

She nodded. "All right, fair enough. You may ask your question. However I reserve the right not to answer."

Katie gulped and nodded. "Of course. I know this must seem so bizarre, but—here goes. Did you ever marry?"

For a time Rachel didn't say anything at all. A host of emotions passed through her eyes though. William could see sorrow, regret, longing, and maybe even a touch of bitter resentment. Although the wait seemed long, especially for his restless lady, Rachel returned an almost indiscernible shake of her head.

"No, I didn't. That's all I'll say on the matter. Does that help you?"

"I hope so. These belong to you." Katie handed her the pouch. She leaned back against her chair as Rachel opened it and withdrew the stack of letters.

With the greatest of care she picked up each one of them in turn and examined them front to back. She paid special attention to the dates in which they were sent. Tears fell freely down her cheeks. Tears she didn't even notice. She closed her eyes while trembling fingers covered her mouth.

Katie fastened her dewy gaze to William. He covered her hand with his and gave her a wink as they awaited Rachel's response.

"Please, you must tell me—where did you find these?" she whispered.

"I didn't find them," Katie said. "Quinn gave them to me so I could give them to you."

Chapter Fourteen

"How long have you had them?"

"Since yesterday." Katie waited for some kind of reaction.

Rachel's gaze traveled away from hers and again dropped to the letters on her lap. She laid her hand on top of them and caressed the edges with her thumb. During the silent interval, Katie studied the lovely woman's delicate features. She could still see a fair amount of the prom queen Donnie loved so deeply. Yes, a few silver streaks had woven themselves throughout her dark brown hair. The faint lines around the corners of her eyes and mouth whispered that her youth had faded away. None of it distracted from her beauty. If Donnie could see her now, he wouldn't in any way be disappointed.

At length, Rachel again gazed into her eyes. The tears that remained on her face, she brushed away with a graceful hand. "You have my undivided attention, Katie."

"I know the claim must seem a strange one. I'm not sure if our positions were reversed I'd believe a single word you said. I might even wonder over your motives. Nonetheless, I'm not here to stir up painful memories or hurt you in any way. I'm here that I might set the record straight, and maybe, just maybe, provide a far happier ending to this tale."

Rachel's eyes narrowed as she turned her head to the side. "Are you clairvoyant? Is this something you do for a living?"

She shook her head. "Oh, heavens, no, not at all. I hope you don't think I'm some sort of charlatan, come to swindle you out of money or anything else. This is my one and only visit. I won't ask you for a thing while I'm here, nor will I disturb you again."

The silence that followed bordered on the uncomfortable. As Katie waited it out, she gazed at the simple beauty of the room. Although the Victorian-style furnishings were quite lovely, they didn't speak of her vast wealth. This home could belong to almost anyone.

At length Rachel nodded. "Your claim doesn't sound as strange as you might think. So please, I'd like to hear what you have to say."

Now the moment of truth had finally arrived, words escaped her. She hadn't prepared for anything beyond the question she had asked. Once again Katie looked at William for some kind of guidance. Right now she didn't know how she could possibly explain her involvement without giving him away.

William shrugged. "There's no getting around it, Katie. In order for her to understand why we've come, she'll at least need some of the details of your journey. Whether or not she'll believe what you share is something we'll take a chance on, all right?"

"Okay, here goes. My...um...my..." She stopped. Her what? Her ghost soldier? Phantom boyfriend? Her other worldly soul mate? They all sounded just as ridiculous as they did impossible. Katie raised a hand to her forehead and gave it a rub. "Oh, boy."

As Rachel leaned toward her, she breathed out a

touch of quiet laughter. "I'm sorry. I didn't intend to make this so hard for you."

Katie waved her concern aside. "No, it's not that it's hard. It's just that...well, you see I uh...have someone who is...who is very dear to me. William is a soldier. My soldier. He's not only handsome, he's also kindhearted and courageous—" Once again she stopped short. Why on earth did she say that? Katie felt like she babbled with no real purpose or destination. *Come on, get yourself together, girl.*

A touch of humor filled Rachel's eyes. "I think I can follow all of that without too much difficulty."

Katie turned her gaze toward William. Rachel had merely found amusement over her struggle. On the other hand, from the ear-to-ear grin on William's face, he thought the whole thing downright hilarious. That annoyed her to no end. *Really?*

She gritted her teeth. Fine then. "The thing is—my soldier died on Omaha Beach on June 6, 1944. What do you think of that?"

Rachel pursed her lips and nodded. "I'd say that's a little bit before your time. Unless, of course, you're very well preserved. Are you?"

"No. D-Day is well before my time, I assure you. But that doesn't mean he doesn't exist or that we don't speak to each other more often than you might think."

"Even though I find the prospect of that quite fascinating, I don't see what it has to do with—"

"William is very good friends with your Donnie Martin. Because of that friendship, William asked me to find you." *There.* She said it. "That search led me to your home in West Columbia and an encounter with your brother."

Rachel took in a ragged breath and slowly released it. "Why did this soldier of yours want to find me?"

"Ah, Rachel," she said. "Don't you get it? Your father never paid Don off. In fact, he never even sought him out. His letters to you are proof of that. Donnie loved you with his dying breath. He loves you still. The problem we have is that because of those letters you never answered, he thinks you're quite out of his grasp. Whether or not you are is a question only you can answer."

A new set of tears filled her eyes. "Have you spoken to Donnie about…about me?"

Katie shook her head. "No, I haven't, but William has. Because of what he said during that conversation, William and I began our search for you. We did this without Don's knowledge for several reasons. There is far more to this story than what I've told you so far."

Rachel nodded. "I can only imagine what you must've gone through in tracking me down. So I thank you for all of your efforts, Katie. I'm grateful for the letters regardless of how or where you got them. But if you don't mind, I need some time alone right now. Martha will see you out."

Katie's heart fell to the bottom of her stomach. A dismissal wasn't what she expected. They were far from any kind of hope or message they could give Don. She gazed at William. He shook his head.

"You must respect her choices, Katie," he said. "Keep in mind she has years of sorrow, bitterness, falsehoods, and betrayal she must wade through. That will take time. We can't hurry the process."

With more reluctance than she thought possible, Katie rose from her seat. She turned toward Rachel and smiled. "Of course. If nothing else, I hope the letters will bring you some comfort in the days ahead. I'm sure that's what Quinn intended."

Rachel didn't respond, but then Katie truly didn't think she would. The moment she stepped outside, the twins scrambled to their feet.

Jared offered her his arm as he escorted her down the steps. "All is well?"

She shrugged. "I suppose as well as can be expected. We came to give her the letters and now she has them."

"Did you get that one very important question answered?"

"Yes." She nodded and dropped her gaze. "Yes, I did."

"So you're saying you've accomplished everything you came here to do, right?"

They stopped at the bottom of the steps.

Jared turned toward her and fastened his gaze to hers. "No more haunted houses, gruesome ghosts, or rich heiresses? We're done with all that?"

"Yep, all done."

They resumed their journey down the walkway. "Good, because from here, we're heading off to Minute Maid Park where we will watch the Astros play an ordinary game of baseball with some ordinary friends of ours. We will stuff ourselves with ordinary hotdogs and get something ordinary to drink. Throughout the game, we will also yell ordinary insults at the umpire, whether or not they make stupid calls. You are required to take part in all of the above. Got that?"

"Got it."

"Good." Justin opened the back door to the pickup.

"We need some normal fun and recreation before you go home. You did notice I said normal, right?"

"Loud and clear."

"Excuse me, Miss Adelton?"

Katie turned. "Yes?"

Martha hurried toward her with a notepad and pen in hand. "Miss Jameson asked if you would be kind enough to give her your contact information, dear."

"I'd be happy to." Katie glanced at William and then wrote down her name, address, email, and phone number. "There you go. Please tell her she can get a hold of me anytime she wants and for any reason she might have."

"Thank you, I'll let her know."

The small hope she now carried made the baseball game with her cousins and all their raucous friends far more enjoyable. As did the dinner that followed, when their group took almost every available seat in the restaurant.

They followed up with a movie. All the while, William held her hand and whispered various comments that made her laugh in the most inappropriate places. After the movie ended, he leaned over and gave her a gentle kiss. He told her he was sorry, but that he had to go. With a promise to see her soon, he disappeared.

Did duty call or did it have something to do with Donnie? If so, what could William say at this moment in time that would make him feel any better?

****

The questions nagged her throughout the night. They remained a steadfast companion as she ate her breakfast. She pondered over them as her cousins took her back to the airport. Yet all throughout, she kept up with their uproarious play, just as she always had.

Jared gave her a silly grin as they all stopped short of the security check point. "Well this is it I guess—at least until next time anyway. So thank you, Katie. I can't think of the last time I had so much fun and adventure over a weekend."

"Yeah, that goes for me too." Justin bobbed his head in agreement. "This is one for the grandkids. One day, we'll tell them all about our awesome experience while they bounce on our knees with wide-eyed wonder. Monsters underneath the bed and in the closets will be a piece of cake after that."

"In order for you to pass it down to your grandchildren, you should get married first and produce a child, don't you think?"

Jared and Justin looked at each other and shrugged. "Nah," they said in unison.

She never could figure out how they did that. Did they have some sort of secret look or hand signal? If they did, she could never catch it.

Justin rubbed a hand against his chin. "I think we'll just go ahead and skip that part."

She raised a brow. "Which part? Marriage or the children?"

"Both," Jared replied. "We'll just borrow some nieces and nephews from time to time. We can pretend they're ours and destroy all sense of security when they go to bed at night."

"That, because it has become painfully obvious we can't nab any second-hand cousins from you," Justin said.

"And why is that? Is it because I am now and have

ever been your favorite? Therefore you wouldn't want to scare the tar out of my children with a tale you and I both know you'll blow all out of proportion?"

"Sweet sentiment, but no, that isn't the reason. We just don't see how you can have any children of your own when your boyfriend is a ghost. I mean—well—you know." Jared bounced his eyebrows and winked.

Justin cleared his throat in a most exaggerated manner but didn't say anything. He didn't have to. His expression said it all.

Could one blush, and at the same time have the color drain from one's face? Because that's what it felt like she just did. Her mouth dropped as her gaze drifted back and forth between them. "I have absolutely no idea what you're talking about."

The boys burst out laughing. In fact they laughed so hard she quite expected them to drop onto the floor and roll all over the airport. Instead Jared ruffled her hair, pulled her in tight against his side, and kissed the top of her head. "Don't worry. As always, your secret is safe with us."

"What secret? I mean, you're speaking complete and utter nonsense." Why, oh why did she even try? By those smirks they sported, they didn't buy a word she said.

Justin shook his head and tsked. "I know you don't know this, so I'll go ahead and tell you. The window behind Rachel's porch swing is very thin. Very. Thin. We could hear every word you said."

"Oh, and uh, don't forget all the conversations you were having within earshot. You remember those, don't you? The ones where you insisted you were speaking to yourself?" Jared gave her another smug little smile.

"Yeah, those. Top that off with those times you looked at someone in silent communication that we couldn't see. A dead giveaway, if I ever saw one."

"That's right. You also forget how well we know you. So I wouldn't deny it anymore, if I were you," Justin added. "Just makes you look rather foolish."

"All right then, I won't." She stood on her tiptoes and kissed them both on the cheek. "Thank you both for diving headlong into the wild and woolly town of cahoots with me. No one could've seen me through the events of our unexpected adventure any better than you did. I'll be forever grateful you remained at my side throughout the entire ordeal."

"Wouldn't have missed it. I can't remember the last time I had that much fun," Jared replied.

"Yes. Let's do it again soon," Justin said, "Like in another millennium or so."

She laughed. "Okay, you're on. Only next time, you'll have to visit me. I think I know a spooky road that leads to a spooky house we can investigate during the dead of night. The legends about that particular street will turn your hair white."

Jared grinned. "Sounds like great fun. Oh, and when you're ready, we'd like to know a little bit more about that soldier of yours. William will, after all, have to meet with our approval."

"All right. Maybe one day in the not too distant future, I'll tell you all about him."

"We'll hold you to that too," Justin said. "After all, you didn't do so well on your own last time around and we had to take matters into our own hands."

She shook her head. "Don't get me started on Chad or I'll miss my plane. Still, let me thank you for what you did at the restaurant and at that hayfield. The dweeb never bothered me again."

"Our pleasure." They tipped their hats in a cowboy salute before she headed for her gate.

Her smile didn't fade until she boarded the plane that took her back to New Mexico. All the way home she reviewed the experiences of the weekend. If nothing else, they had freed Quinn of his earthbound existence and finished what he couldn't do himself. Did William tell him they had found Rachel? Did he know they had given her the letters he gave his life to protect? She must've read them by now. What kind of difference, if any, did they make?

****

Rachel never strayed far from Katie's mind in the days that followed. She couldn't even dismiss her while she studied. Katie sighed and closed the cover on her psychology book. Breathing deeply, she filled her lungs with the musty odor of the old library's basement floor. Because of that aroma, most people avoided the area. She didn't mind it though. Katie liked the seclusion and quiet she could find down here.

"What is a gorgeous woman like you doing in a stuffy old place like this?" William now sat in the chair across from hers. He had his elbow on the table while his chin rested on top of his curled fingers.

No matter how hard she tried, Katie couldn't hide her joy. Her heart took flight. Her body tingled with the liquid warmth that pulsated throughout. Even though it had only been a few days, she had missed him far more than she thought she would. She leaned toward him and raised a brow. "Is that the best you've got? You may not know this, but that line is older than Methuselah and probably just as tired."

He chuckled. "That very well may be, but if I were to one up it, I might get myself in more trouble than I care to get into."

"Oh well, we can't have that now, can we?"

"We *shouldn't* have that, is a better fit." He winked. "Now, what do you say we quit this place and go for a horseback ride? The fall colors in the mountain forests and hills are nothing short of amazing."

Katie stood up and gathered her books. "I suppose I'll just have to see that for myself. So tell me, where did you park your horse, cowboy?"

As he rose to his feet he put a hand over his stomach and bowed. "Right next to yours, my love, right next to yours."

****

As they rode their horses side by side, she took in the beauty of the fall colors. They were indeed amazing. She enjoyed them as much as she did the chill in the air, for that meant the holidays were just around the corner. Underneath dark, cloudy skies, the threat of rain intensified the scent of dampened earth and autumn leaves discarded by the colorful trees. She loved this time of year. After all, it meant that she and William would have their first real Christmas together. She could hardly wait.

Their laughter died down a bit as they rounded the final curve, and headed for home. Her gaze lingered on him. He might not be a knight in the true sense of the word, but he was a warrior nonetheless. Even more enchanting, he rode that stallion her childish heart had always expected and rode him better than any knight ever could. Katie settled her gaze on his horse. "You know, I'm willing to bet that when you were a kid—and played cowboys with your friends—you didn't ride a broomstick. You rode a real, honest-to-goodness, hay-devouring, oat-munching, horse."

"Careful now. The last time you made a bet, you forked over twenty bucks of hard-earned money to your brother because you lost."

She leaned forward and patted Shahar on the neck. "You saw that one, did you?"

"Yep, I sure did. I must say I'm happy to see you're an honest woman who pays her debts."

She giggled. "I'm happy you're happy. Nonetheless, I'm sticking by the bet as stated. Double or nothing. Are you game?"

"Hmm. Currency isn't something we have where I'm from. So in place of the twenty bucks, what are the stakes in said bet?"

"Okay, in the place of cold, hard cash, how about one very special, out-of-the-ordinary request, for another very special, out-of-the-ordinary request?"

"Sounds intriguing. However, I'd like to alter the bet a little bit—just to make it fair on both sides."

"In what way?"

"In addition as to what I may or may not have ridden in my youth, let's include the horse I'm riding right now. What say you? Do you think I rode this very horse during my childhood games?"

Katie considered both the horse and the handsome rider who rode him without benefit of saddle or bridle. "You know what? It just occurred to me that I've never asked you the name of your horse."

"Are you stalling for time, Miss Adelton? If so, is it so you can see if my expression somehow gives the answer away?"

"No, I'm just curious, that's all."

"I'm not sure I buy that, but his name is Warrior."

"That's fitting." She smiled. "All right, then. From your devilish grin and that gleam in your eyes, I'd say this could go either way. So here goes. I think you know Warrior like the back of your hand. In my opinion, he anticipates every move you make and responds accordingly. Of course, since you died many decades ago, you've had ample time to establish such a relationship. Still, I think I'll go out on a limb here and say Warrior is the horse you loved all throughout your life. Therefore, he took part in all of your childhood games."

William chuckled as he leaned forward and stroked Warrior's neck. "I have to say I'm quite impressed. You're right. What you couldn't guess though, is that Warrior and I share a birthday. That's why at the tender age of six, my dad gave him to me as a birthday gift. But for the time I spent in the service, we were together every day. This old man outlived me by five years. When he crossed over into my realm, I saw him running toward me in the pasture. He looked like he did in his prime. He nuzzled me in greeting just as he always had during our mortality. In turn, I gave him the affection he had come to expect. All in all, I'd say we had a very sweet reunion."

She smiled as she envisioned the scene. "I'm sure you did."

"So what'll it be then?"

"What?"

"The special request you've just won."

"Oh, that. You know what? I think I'll just hold

onto my voucher for awhile if it's all the same to you. Do keep in mind though, I won't forget you owe it."

"You needn't worry. I won't forget." William leaned to his side and took her hand. "Now at the risk of casting a cloud over a most enjoyable day with my lady fair, may I ask her what's wrong?"

The question caught her off guard. "What makes you think anything is wrong?"

"Those eyes of yours. I've told you before there isn't a whole lot you can hide from me. So?"

She shrugged it off. "Nothing, really. I—just had a nightmare last night, that's all. Even after this magical day with you, the stupid thing crops up from time to time."

"What did you dream?"

"Just a bunch of mixed-up craziness that involved Quinn, Rachel, and Gustavus. I remember something about Gustavus directing his anger at the three of us. He said he would exact his vengeance when we least expected it or some other such nonsense. Things morphed in and out as dreams often do. Still, I just can't shake that evil look on Gustavus' face."

"Are you worried about them? Quinn and Rachel, I mean?"

"How can I not? I know Gustavus didn't kill his son in cold-blooded murder, but if not for the vicious blow to his head, Quinn would never have fallen into that pedestal. In turn, he wouldn't have died. Is that why his spirit is ugly and so filled with hatred right now?"

"I suppose that's possible."

"You said Quinn told you he thought his father would be happy that he had Rachel's letters. He thought

Gustavus would want to give them to her, just to see her smile again. Isn't that right?"

"Yes, he did say that."

"Then at one time Gustavus must've had at least some redeeming qualities for Quinn to say such a thing, don't you think? So if once upon a time he had even a shred of love for his daughter, why did he destroy her happiness?"

"I don't know, Katie. All kinds of reasons come to mind. One, he might not have liked Donnie. Two, he may've considered his background beneath the dignity of a Jameson. Gustavus also made a series of bad choices. Each one, worse than the other, could've destroyed whatever good he had left inside him. On the other hand, Gustavus may've simply thought she should marry someone equal to her in wealth and social class. Someone who would increase his fortune."

"That's stupid. Just because someone has a ton of money doesn't make them any better than anyone else. It only means they can buy things other people can't afford."

"I agree."

"What about Rachel? I'm sure by now she has read and reread every letter in that pouch. She knows Donnie didn't betray her. How is she dealing with all of this newfound knowledge?"

"I'm not sure, but I think you're about to find out."

Katie turned in the direction of his gaze. At once she reined her mount to a halt and stared. Parked in front of her house sat a late model, black Audi. Rachel Jameson—of all the unexpected people—opened the driver door. In a graceful move, she swung her legs to the side, and stepped out of the car.

Rachel dipped her head and offered a smile. She took her bag from off the seat and took a step toward her. "Hello, Katie. I apologize for not calling ahead, but I just didn't know if I had the nerve to show up at your door. Now that I have, do you mind if we go inside and talk for awhile?"

Chapter Fifteen

With nothing more than a whispered word, William sent Warrior back home.

Once he entered the house, he found his lady busy in the kitchen. She had just filled two mugs with hot chocolate and set them on a white porcelain tray alongside her homemade applesauce cookies.

"Have I missed anything?" he asked.

She shook her head as she added a few napkins to the plate and fussed with their arrangement. "Nope. I told her to make herself at home while I put together some refreshments. As you can see, I took my sweet time so I could wait for you."

He kissed her cheek. "You don't know how much I appreciate that."

"Well, for your sake as well as Don's, I think it's important you hear every word she says. After all, there might be something he should know, right?" She picked up the tray and turned toward the living room. "Are you ready?"

"Yep. Ready, willing, and eager." He followed her through the short hallway and into the living room.

She set the tray down on the tea table in front of the sofa. As she sat down next to Rachel, he settled into the chair beside Katie.

Rachel took a mug of the chocolate and raised it to her lips. She blew on it, took a couple sips, and lowered it to her lap. "This is good, thank you."

"You're welcome." Katie picked up the second cup and gave Rachel a smile. "Like I said when you first arrived, I'm so glad you've come. You've been in my thoughts more often than you might guess. I've wondered how you fared."

"I'm sorry that our last visit ended so abruptly. You must've thought me very rude, and quite ungrateful."

"No, not at all. I'm sure you didn't expect that a perfect stranger would invade your home and hand you a stack of letters from a man you once loved." She lifted a shoulder as she dipped her head to the side. "You might also have had a hard time believing I got them from Quinn."

"I'm sorry I gave you that impression." For a moment she dropped her gaze to her cup. "I know you can't know this, Katie, but Quinn died at one of the lowest points in my life. His death shattered my already broken heart. I didn't think I could tumble any further into the depths of sorrow than I did the day he died."

"Rachel, I know—"

Rachel held up a hand to stay her words. "Please, I need to get this out before I lose my nerve. I drove out here rather than take a plane so I could sort through my thoughts and share them with you without blathering like an idiot. Once I do that, we'll talk it all out, okay?"

Katie patted her hand and nodded. "Okay."

"Thank you." She took in a deep breath and let it go. "Two months and twelve days after my brother died, a friend called me. She had just learned that Donnie lost his life while fighting in Vietnam and thought I should know. That day I found out the sorrow could go far deeper. The pain could get far more intolerable. You see, despite what I thought I knew at the time, I still loved him. That love didn't go away just because I wished it would go away. After I made that particular discovery, I saw Quinn's spirit for the first time. I remember it so clearly. We had stormy weather that day. As I sat on my bed, and from my side bedroom window, I watched the rain. Somewhere along the way, a shadow kind of flickered in and out. Within that shadow, I glimpsed my brother from the corner of my eye. At once I turned toward him. Yet even as I did, I saw nothing more than the empty chair and my closed closet doors. I thought I had lost my mind.

"Time went on as time always does. As it did, I saw my brother far more often. I could see him for longer periods of time and in direct line of eyesight. Even when I blinked, he remained. At times he sat in the chair. Other times he lounged by one of the windows as he kept me company. We never spoke. I don't think either of us even tried. Yet whenever he looked at me I could see both love and sorrow in his gaze. His presence—whether a figment of my imagination or not—somehow gave me comfort when I needed it most. I didn't feel so all alone when he visited me." A small winsome smile curved the corners of her lips. "That's kind of pathetic, don't you think? That I would take comfort from a ghost?"

"No, I don't. I know about that kind of comfort."

"Perhaps you might at that. Anyway, that's the reason your claim didn't sound as farfetched as you might've thought. I think the one question that nagged at me the day you visited was why Quinn wouldn't have given me the letters himself. As I looked back, I could see ample opportunity during the time I lived at home. What's more, they would've been such a comfort to me back in the most difficult days of my life."

"I don't think we should tell Rachel that he tried," William said. "The knowledge wouldn't serve any real purpose at this point."

Katie cleared her throat. "Does that mean you didn't see him after you moved out of the house?"

"No, I didn't. I thought it strange too because I've often heard ghosts will follow someone from house to house—especially if they are emotionally connected to that person. I thought given the circumstances, Quinn would come with me. He didn't though, and I just didn't know why he would choose to remain there in that awful house."

"Perhaps he remained so he could watch over the letters and keep them safe."

Her eyes widened a bit. "I never considered that possibility, but I think you might be right at that. If nothing more, it makes sense as to why he would stay in a place so filled with bad memories."

"If you don't mind my asking, how long did you stay in the house?"

"Six months to the day after my father died, I moved out." Rachel took in a breath as she closed her eyes. "That day I saw something I wished I hadn't. Because of what I witnessed, I just couldn't stay in the house any longer. I got in my car and I left. I never went back."

"Would that be the scene in the upstairs hallway between Quinn and your father?"

Her eyes flew open. "You saw it too?"

"Yes, I'm afraid I did."

"I'm so sorry." Rachel gazed into her eyes for several moments. "That said, the truth of the matter is, you didn't have to see it. So the question is why? Why would you go so far as to break into the house when you obviously had an alternative address for me? What did you expect you'd find in an empty house?"

"Oh, we didn't break in. Really we didn't. We rang the bell in the hope someone would answer. Quinn opened the door and we—"

"He did?"

"Well, I didn't actually see him open the door. However, I did ask him later if he invited us in, and he indicated he had."

"I suppose that explains the reason the alarms never went off. I wondered about that." She shrugged. "Anyway, I'd like to know all the whys and wherefores of your search for me. If I understand all of this correctly, you didn't know about or get the letters until after you'd gone to the house."

Katie rubbed her fingers across her forehead. "This whole thing is so difficult for me to explain. I'm not sure where I should even begin."

Rachel smiled. "I know I cut you off when you first visited me. In fact, I didn't pay much attention to what you said once you handed me the letters. So how about we start over and take it from the beginning. Do you think we can do that?"

"The beginning—okay, I can do that." She traced the tip of her tongue across her bottom lip. "If I told you there are a great many spirits right this very minute who are deeply in love with mortals—and in turn the mortals love them back with an equal passion—would you believe me?"

Rachel raised her brows. "Well I don't know. That's something I've never considered."

Katie laughed. "I bet not. Neither did I. The thought would probably never cross the mind of a sane person. Nevertheless, I've been told there are many such relationships between mortals and spirits. William and I are one such couple."

Under any other circumstance, William might've shouted out a rousing hallelujah for the joy that filled his soul. Did Katie know what she just said? Without any forethought whatsoever, she admitted out loud that she loved him. She loved him!

"William has been part of my life for as far back as I can remember. I have no doubt in my mind of that for I sensed his presence whenever he was with me. Yet all the while I never once saw his spirit or heard the sound of his voice. I couldn't see or speak with him until I visited his grave in Normandy."

Rachel leaned toward her. "How very fascinating."

"Yes, it is. Since that day and over the course of time, I've learned a great many things about him. One of those things is that he takes care of various American soldiers in the moment they leave their mortality behind. They are all deeply wounded in one way or another. Either in the physical sense which caused their death, or they are wounded in mind, heart, and soul. As you can imagine, they develop close friendships with each other. Like I told you on the day we met, William has such a friendship with Don."

Katie told her about the day William had asked for her help, the why of it, and her subsequent search. She recounted everything that happened after she landed in Houston at both the cemetery and the Jameson estate.

She didn't leave a single detail out of her story, but for one. The encounters they had with the vile ghost of Gustavus, she kept to herself. After she finished her tale, she again turned her gaze toward William.

"You're giving an awful lot of attention to an empty chair, Katie. Unless of course, your soldier is sitting in it. Is he?"

"Busted." She laughed as she toyed with her necklace. "Yes. William is here and he's sitting in that chair. Does the thought make you uncomfortable?"

"No, quite the contrary actually. In a way I find difficult to explain, his friendship with Donnie makes me feel a little closer to *my* soldier. The fact he's here with you now makes that connection far greater."

"Is he your soldier, Rachel? I mean, despite what your father made you believe all those years ago—coupled with the passage of time—do you love him still?"

Rachel pulled a gold chain from out of her blouse and grasped the diamond ring that hung from it. "I've never stopped loving him, Katie. Not ever. Part of me never believed him capable of doing what my father said he did. The Donnie I knew and fell in love with would never have done such a thing. However, when his letters stopped, doubt crept in. You see, I couldn't reconcile the two."

"I'm sure that had to have been difficult. I know Quinn wanted so much to tell you all of this himself. He just didn't get the chance."

"He did, actually." Rachel dipped her hand inside her bag and removed a wrinkled piece of lined paper. "Did you see this when you opened the pouch and removed the letters?"

"No, I guess I didn't—" Katie stopped. "You know what? I think that might've been the last thing he put in the bag."

She unfolded it. "I found it at the bottom of the pouch, stuck between the layers of the seam. The note is from Quinn. The foolish boy didn't think I'd let him explain once he gave me the letters. He told me what happened and begged my forgiveness for the part he played in the deception. Can you believe that? I mean if anyone should beg for my forgiveness, it would be my father. Not that I expect such a request anytime soon."

Katie put a gentle hand on top of Rachel's. "I'm so sorry. I wish none of this would ever have happened."

A sad smile accompanied the slight shake of Rachel's head. "What's done is done. The one thing we can't change is the past. Right now though, I wonder if your William could do something for me."

Katie turned toward him.

He nodded. "She's but to ask. If it's something I can do, I'll get it done."

Once again Katie gave Rachel her full attention. "He'll give it his best shot. What do you have in mind?"

She held the note to her breast. "If it isn't too difficult, I'd like him to tell Quinn that nothing he did needs my forgiveness. He might also thank him for hanging around as long as he did. That he was such a comfort when I needed comfort the most. From my own experiences, I know that staying in that house couldn't have been easy. Finally, tell him I love him and I hope he's finally at peace."

****

William didn't wait a moment longer. At once he passed from Katie's realm and into his own. He headed straight for Don's house with the hope he'd find him there. Don opened the door and waved him inside.

"Well now, this is unexpected," he said. "To what do I owe the pleasure of your good company, William? Are we needed?"

"No, nothing like that at present. I'm here because there's something you should know." William sat down in the seat nearest the large picture window.

Don settled into the chair opposite him. "Sounds intriguing. Does it have anything to do with me personally, or is it someone or something else altogether?"

"I'd say it has everything to do with you. Well—you and Rachel."

"Rachel?" Don turned his head to the side. "I don't know what you mean."

"That's because you couldn't. So here's my confession. I meddled where I probably shouldn't have, but I can't say I'm sorry for it either. I'll also tell you that while I did this, I made Katie my accomplice."

"Okay, you have my attention, William."

William grinned. "And that's as it should be, I assure you. You see, after you told me about what happened between you and Rachel, I wondered if maybe I could find out what became of her. I thought if I found her happily married with the children and grandchildren you envisioned, I'd just leave it at that. The discovery would be my secret to keep. That's not what we found, though."

"What did you find?"

"More than you might think."

He rolled his eyes. "Enough, William. Just tell me straight out why you've come and what you want me to know."

"First, Katie is the one that made all of the discoveries. Without her meticulous research, I still wouldn't know anything. That research led her to the Jameson mansion, where, with the help of her cousins, she encountered Quinn's spirit."

Don's eyes widened as his mouth dropped. "Quinn's spirit? Hold up a minute! Are you telling me Quinn died?"

"Yes, he did—and accident though it was, it's a thing for which Gustavus must take full responsibility."

William told him the story of Katie's journey from start to finish without leaving out a single detail. He told him of the tragic consequences of the letters Don never received and those Rachel never saw. Once he finished the tale, his friend dropped his head, seemingly lost in his thoughts. William allowed him all the time he needed. At last Don looked up and gazed into his eyes.

"Thank you, William and thank Katie for me as well. I'm grateful for what you both did. Rachel knows the truth and she has the letters now. That brings me more comfort than you can imagine."

"I'm sure it does, but why don't you tell Rachel that yourself? I'm sure it would make her happy hearing that from you."

Don shook his head and chuckled. "Sounds good, but do you even know where she is right now?"

"As a matter of fact, I do. As we speak she's with Katie. When I left, they were enjoying some hot chocolate as well as each other's company."

Don bolted from his chair. "Why on earth didn't you say so when you first got here? Come on, let's go!"

William stood and held out a hand, palm out. "Hold your horses for a minute. I have one last thing you should know before we go."

"Get it out quick, William."

"Rachel wears the ring you gave her on a chain around her neck. I suspect she never takes it off, but that is neither here nor there. With ring in hand, she told Katie that despite what she accepted as truth, as told her by her father, she never once stopped loving you."

With that, Don grabbed him by the shoulder and all but dragged him out of his house.

William halted his steps just outside his door. "Wait a second. We need to make one stop before we go. I promise it'll be brief."

Don gazed at him as if he'd quite lost his mind. "Are you kidding? Can't whatever it is wait?"

He shook his head. "No, I'd rather it didn't. Rachel asked me to give Quinn a message. For her sake, we should do that first."

"All right. Let's hurry up and get it done."

****

Right after Rachel asked the favor, William left the room. Katie stuck her nose in the air and sniffed. "Well, it must not have been too difficult a task. William is already gone and without even a by-your-leave."

Rachel raised her fingers to her lips as she took in a breath. "I'm sorry. I didn't mean for him to leave right now."

"Don't worry, I'm sure he'll be back before you go since I insist you stay for dinner. I also invite you to stay the night, which invitation you must accept. After all, I have a very comfortable guest room that's never been used. I believe that should change. In the meantime, have a cookie or two. They are quite good if I do say so myself."

"Thank you and dinner would be lovely. We'll talk later about that guest room of yours." Rachel picked a cookie off the plate. "While I eat this, I'd like to hear a little bit more about William, if you don't mind sharing him with me."

"I don't mind. In fact, I might find it liberating. What would you like me to tell you?"

"Oh, I don't know. First, I think I'd like to know how he introduced himself to you when you visited Normandy. Your reaction to seeing him for the first time—I mean, were you scared? Did you know him right away as the presence you had always sensed?"

"No, I wasn't afraid, and yes, somehow I did know him as my special friend, though I can't explain how or why."

Katie didn't have any trouble at all telling her about that day in Normandy. In fact, it made her happy and somewhat relieved that someone else knew all of the details. *Better yet? That someone believes me.*

"Does anyone else know about him, or do you keep the relationship you have with him hidden from the world?"

"Because of what happened at your house in West Columbia, my cousins are the only ones who know he exists besides you right now. I haven't given them any of the details yet, though."

"Why not? You all seem so close."

"I'm not really sure. Maybe it's because I'm not quite ready to share him with anyone else yet. Or maybe somewhere down deep inside, I'm not sure anyone will believe—" She halted as William appeared just in front of her.

"I can see where that might be a concern. I've never told anyone but you that I saw Quinn after his death." Rachel seemed lost in her thoughts as she nibbled her cookie. Once she finished it, she brushed the crumbs from her hands and picked up her mug. "After what you've just told me, I wonder if it's too late for Donnie and me."

"No, my precious angel, it's never too late," said the unexpected voice.

Rachel all but dropped her cup as her eyes widened in surprise.

Katie stared at the spiritual form of Donald Raymond Martin, who looked just as mortal as William did. He approached his lady and knelt at her side. Katie gazed at William who gave her the most bewitching smile she'd ever seen. In response, her butterflies took off in some sort of uncontrollable, wild, whirling dervish. The heat of their dance filled every inch of her body. He moved to her side and took hold of her hand.

Tears filled Rachel's eyes as she gazed at her soldier. Don looked so very handsome in his army uniform. His picture in the yearbook didn't do him justice.

Rachel choked back a sob as she lifted her clasped hands to her mouth. "Donnie…"

He took her hands, drew them to his lips, and kissed them. "Hello, Rachel. I can't tell you how good it is to see you."

She pulled a single hand away from his grasp and combed her fingers through her hair as she dropped her gaze. "How can you say that? You're still so young and handsome…while I'm…I'm…"

"So very beautiful," he whispered. He tilted her chin upward until their gazes met. "In fact, you've never looked more beautiful to me than you do right now."

She wiped away the tears that cascaded down her cheeks. "Katie and I have talked about—well about everything that happened. I'm so sorry for what I must've put you through."

Don shook his head. "You have nothing to be sorry for, Rach. Neither of us is responsible for the lies or the misunderstanding between us. The beauty of it though, is that our love endured the agony of it. How many people can say that, huh?"

She sniffed. "I never stopped loving you, Donnie, not ever."

He cupped her face and as he leaned toward her, he smiled. "Nor I you."

As Don kissed Rachel, William tugged Katie to her feet. He cocked his head toward the kitchen. "What say you we give them a little bit of privacy?"

Katie nodded and together they slipped out of the room. Neither Donnie nor Rachel seemed to notice their exit and she smiled. "Should we go for a walk or something?"

"You'll get wet if we do. You may not have noticed, but there's a bit of rain coming down right now."

She slipped into her jacket and tugged the hood over her head. "That's okay. I've never been afraid of getting drenched in the rain."

"No, I guess you haven't at that." He opened the back door and let her pass.

Once outside she turned toward him. "Do you have

a destination in mind, or shall we just wander aimlessly while they get reacquainted with each other?"

The mischief in his eyes matched his grin. He took hold of her hand and drew her close to his side. "Rather than go for a walk, we could go inside your barn. We could rest against a nice, soft haystack and make out for awhile."

She laughed. "Well, if we're going to make out, I'd just as soon go next door and do it underneath the shelter of Johansson's cozy gazebo. I happen to know they're in California so they can meet their newest great-grandchild."

"Sounds fine to me. Lead the way."

Once they arrived at their destination, they sat down on the green cushioned bench. The soft patter of raindrops on the shingled roof created a serene melody. "So did you find Quinn?"

He chuckled. "Yes, I knew where I could find him. I wished you could've seen his joy as I related Rachel's message. He is completely at peace now."

"That's good to hear. You know, even after all of this time, I think Rachel misses him. She said earlier she wished he had moved with her to Alvin."

He looped his fingers through hers. "I think he'll visit her from time to time, especially now he knows she and Don are finally together—where they belong."

"He knows?"

"Well he knows Don and I were headed in your direction."

"That's perfect." Katie contemplated the sweet reunion going on inside her home between Rachel and Don. "I hope nothing will ever separate them again."

"I don't think that will be a concern. Out of

curiosity though, why would you even think it might?"

"Oh, I don't know. That horrid dream of mine, I guess. The awful thing plagues me still."

"A dream is all it was, Katie." William let go of her hand. He dropped his arm around her shoulders and cuddled her close to his side. "As much as he may hate his inability to control those around him, Gustavus just doesn't have the power to hurt anyone anymore. Trust me."

She nodded. "I know you're right. Really I do. I did see that for myself inside the Jameson barn."

"That's right, you did. Now that we've taken care of that, are there any other worries inside that gorgeous head of yours?"

"No worries. Although I would like to know about your chat with Don before you both appeared inside my living room. I bet his excitement knew no bounds."

"It didn't." William related the story just as it occurred. "However, if it hadn't been for the fact that I had no idea how long Rachel's visit with you would last, I might've drawn our story out a little longer than I did. You know, just to devil him a bit."

She sucked in a breath. "Now that's just mean."

"No, that's just fun."

"Well, I'm glad you restrained yourself." She ran her fingers through his hair. A thing she could now feel with ease. "They'll get to be together from now on, won't they? Just like us?"

He cupped her face and kissed her lips. "Yes indeed, my love. Just like us."

For a moment he did nothing more than gaze into her eyes. There was so much emotion within their magnificent steel gray depths. Katie could see the deep love he had for her. She saw admiration, joy, and even a bit of pride. But why? She hadn't done anything to deserve all that. "What?"

"You're an amazing woman, Katie Simone Adelton."

Heat rose to her cheeks. "Ah heck, what does a ghost know about such things anyway?"

"More than you might guess."

He kissed her again then, and followed up with another. She stopped counting after that. As always she lost herself in the enchantment of his kisses. Time and thought ceased as once again, exquisite, dizzying emotion overruled all else.

Finally, she leaned away. As she caught a much needed breath, she gazed into his eyes. "I love you, William. I love you with my whole heart and soul."

The joy that filled his eyes in that moment made her wish she had told him far earlier.

"As I love you—and with a love far deeper than you could ever possibly imagine—forever and always."

Chapter Sixteen

Katie turned the key in the lock and opened her door. With a bag loaded with gifts, and keys in hand, she stepped over the threshold. For a moment she stood there and enjoyed the sight her living room presented. Her perfectly decorated Christmas tree sat in front of the large picture window. The colorful bulbs provided a dazzling display of light in the otherwise darkened room. A festive garland with big red bows and glittering pine cones trimmed the fireplace mantel, setting off a pair of lovely golden candlesticks with red cinnamon-scented candles. She'd light them in a minute. Right now though, the miniature Christmas village, covered with sparkling snow on top of the piano, filled her with a touch of joyous nostalgia, as did her grandmother's delicate porcelain nativity set on her antique sideboard. Both had been part of Christmas for as far back as she had memory. Katie took a moment to appreciate the scene. In about a week or so, despite her reluctance, she'd put them all away.

She looked down at the bag full of opened presents she held in her hand. Next year the porcelain angel Austin and Lucina sent her from Germany would replace the star at the top of the tree. She'd find a prominent place in her jewelry armoire for her gorgeous sapphire necklace and earring set her parents gave her. Though meant as a private joke, she had fallen in love with the oval painting of a haunted mansion from her twin cousins. The mansion bore an uncanny resemblance to the Jameson estate. She couldn't wait to hang it on the wall.

Amid the other gifts inside the bag, the one from Rachel was a favorite. She had given her a stone replica of the beautiful quote found at the Normandy American Cemetery and Memorial, "Think not only upon their passing. Remember the glory of their spirit." She couldn't think of a thing that fit William any better than that. Beneath the quote, she had engraved William's initials and service number on the little golden plaque at the bottom. In turn, Katie had taken Don and Rachel's picture from the yearbook, and had the photo colorized on canvas. She encased it within a sculpted black and mahogany frame that set it off beautifully. The gift turned out better than expected. Rachel had said she loved it. Katie could see from her delighted expression that she meant what she said.

In a few short hours, the sun would set on her most favorite holiday of the year. The thought made her a little sad. However, without a doubt, the highlight of this very special Christmas season hadn't happened yet. The thought brought a smile to her face for the newest memory it promised.

She walked over to her tree and set the huge bag underneath it. As she turned around, she stepped right into William's arms.

He gathered her close to his chest and gave her a roguish grin. "At last, fair maiden, I have you right where I want you. I'm afraid there is no escape."

"What makes you—in any way—think I want to escape my current cage?"

"Even better. I like my victims willing."

His toe-curling, spine-tingling kisses smothered her giggle and filled her with delectable warmth from head to toe. Once he allowed her a much needed breath, she looked into his eyes. "Oh, William, how I've missed you."

"Maybe then I do have you right where I want you. After all," he glanced over at her clock and raised a brow, "we've only been apart for nineteen hours and twenty-eight minutes."

"That's nineteen hours and twenty-eight minutes way too long," she countered.

"Hmm, me thinks my lady fair has become a tad spoiled here of late. What to do, oh, what to do."

"I'm afraid there isn't anything you can do about it now." She bit back a smile. "The way I see it, you have no one but yourself to thank for my present condition, Sergeant Griffin. I mean, you're the one who has made an appearance every single day for the past month or so. Isn't that right?"

"What can I say? When the opportunity presents itself, I find I just don't have the strength to stay away from you. All self control goes right out of the window and drifts into a parallel universe that's somewhere far, far away."

"I'm glad to hear that—and—you don't know how grateful I am you've had that opportunity."

"Me too." He kissed her once more. As he released her from his arms, he took hold of her hand and towed her toward the sofa. Once they were seated, he dropped his arm around her shoulder. "So did you enjoy your time with family and friends on this beautiful Christmas day?"

"Yes, I did. Jared and Justin were hysterical as usual—especially when they got my Uncle Jake going on some of his past escapades. Trust me, it didn't take them all that long to get him going either. We played all of our favorite board games and exchanged our gifts. Oh, and Mom cooked the best dinner you'd ever want—"

"With your help, of course," he cut in.

She rolled her eyes as she let go of a breath. "Mashing potatoes isn't really a specialty dish, William. Anyone can do it."

"Not, I hear, with the same flair as you do. Need I also mention the pumpkin pie that no one will eat unless you make it? What about your homemade orange-dipped rolls, hmm? I could add a bit more to that menu if you'd like. You forget how long I've been around."

"Okay, okay. Everyone enjoyed dinner, all right?"

He chuckled. "Without a doubt. What about Rachel? How did she take the insanity of your family gathering?"

"Far better than I expected she would." She smiled as she recalled the events of the day and her dear friend's reaction to it. "Everyone made her feel welcome and right at home. I'm so glad I talked her into coming. I truly expected a firm but polite refusal. Still, I think she had fun and it helped her pass the time until she and the boys could board their plane and head for home. She could hardly wait for Don's promised visit tonight, you know. That's all she talked about whenever we were alone. You should see the joy that fills her eyes now. The emptiness and despair are both gone."

"I can imagine." William grinned. "Just so you know, he's with her as we speak. With any amount of luck, we'll both have several hours of uninterrupted time with the beautiful women we love."

Her heart dropped. "You're not expecting otherwise, are you?"

"No, but as you know, that can change at any given moment."

"Well then just in case, let's not waste one precious second of the time we have, shall we?" She slid toward the edge of the cushion, turned, and gave him the smile she couldn't hold back any longer. "I have a surprise for you."

"You do?" He searched her eyes. "Sounds mysterious. So what, pray tell, is making those beautiful eyes of yours sparkle with such mischievous delight?"

"My Christmas present to you, of course." She bounded to her feet and headed for the candles. Once she had them lit, she turned and faced him. "I thought and thought about it. I mean, what gift does one get a ghost—excuse me—a spirit for Christmas? It's not like you need a watch for keeping track of time, or a scarf to ward off the chill of winter. I don't know if stuff like that is even allowed. So I could only come up with just one thing. I hope you like it."

Katie turned about and walked over to her computer. She clicked on the Christmas tree icon on her desktop. As the toe-tapping music began, she snapped her fingers to the beat of the music. "All right, soldier, get up and dance with me!"

Just as Mrs. Johansson had taught her, she kept her shoulders straight and level as her feet glided along the carpet toward the middle of the floor. At the same time she swayed back and forth while she beckoned him with a wave of her hand. William burst out laughing as he took her up on the invitation.

For the next hour and a half they danced to all of the songs—all ancient and at times quite irritating—on the playlist she created just for William. He not only knew them well, he sang many of them to her as they danced. Especially those that spoke of the forever kind of love they shared.

Though quite out of breath as the final song ended, Katie wished now she had added a few more. Maybe next time.

With a broad smile on his face, William stepped back and shook his head. "Where did you learn the jitterbug and why didn't I know about it?"

"A Christmas gift should be a surprise, shouldn't it?"

"Yes, I suppose it should. I loved it more than you could possibly guess, so thank you very much. I'll treasure the memory."

"You're very welcome. That's what I hoped for. Now, in answer to your question, Mrs. Johansson taught me the dance. The dear soul had such patience as she taught me the steps. I wished you could see how agile she still is. You'd never know she's in her eighties. I'm also surprised—in a delightful sort of way—that you never caught sight of us while I practiced." Katie turned her head to the side as she narrowed her eyes. "You didn't, did you?"

"You can trust that I didn't. Now I believe it's my turn to give my gift to you." He took hold of her hand and led her toward the kitchen. He stopped just under the archway and glanced up at the mistletoe she had hung there. "In case you didn't think I noticed—"

The moment William touched his lips to hers, her entire being filled with a love so pure, so wondrous, and so deep she thought her heart would surely burst. The emotion shattered all sense of time and space. At once Katie felt as though a million iridescent stars carried them into a majestic realm, both strange and at once familiar. Hand in hand she walked with William down a luminescent fairy path, so beautiful that it took away her breath. He led her toward a crystal blue pond, surrounded by unimaginable elegant flowers and lush vegetation of every kind in every hue. Near the pool Katie spied an intricate white bench which sat underneath a magnificent magnolia tree unlike any she'd ever seen before. Somehow she knew—she knew—that long, long ago, they claimed this spot as their own.

In fact, without any doubt whatsoever, she had lived this very moment with William once upon a long forgotten time ago. At that moment an assortment of emotions filled both heart and soul.

As they sat down, he brushed away the tears that trickled down her face. She gazed into his captivating eyes. "I'm sorry, I didn't mean to cry—it's just that this is all so unexpected."

"I know it is, and I'm so sorry. But when they asked for volunteers for the coming conflict, I just couldn't say no."

"No, you of all people couldn't. I know that. In fact, the honorable and courageous man I fell in love with probably pushed everyone else out of the way and stepped forward first." She paused. "In truth, I would've been disappointed if you hadn't."

"Then why the tears and the heartache? Our separation will be but a brief moment in time considering the eons ahead of us."

She dropped her gaze as she shook her head. "I don't know. Fear, I guess."

He tilted her chin upward as he looked deep into her eyes. "What are you afraid of?"

"That you won't be able to find me…that once you step into the mortal realm and give your life for the noble cause, I'll never see you again. I'll never see you again because…because you won't remember me."

A small grin accompanied the slight shake of his head. "Impossible. Such a thing could never happen."

"What makes you so sure? After all, our mortal lives will never touch. There will be nothing to spark the memory."

"Not so. There is nothing in any realm—at any possible notch in time—that could erase you from my heart, mind, or soul. You are rooted in there too far too deeply, my love. You are mine, as I am yours. That's something that cannot and will not ever be forgotten. After all is said and done in fulfillment of my destiny, I give you my solemn promise, I will find you again. I'll find you if even I must search the entire universe."

"Even if you do find me, how will I know you're there? How will I recognize you if I can't see you, or hear you, or…or touch you?"

He cuddled her against his chest as he brushed his fingers through her hair. "Somehow, and in some way, you'll know. Perhaps you'll simply feel my presence at your side. If such is the case, I'll add warmth to the sunshine of your days. With my mighty sword, I'll dispel all of your shadows. Should that be all you recognize, know that I will fight until the last barrier between us is torn down and destroyed, all right?"

She smiled. "So not even a crumb remains behind?"

"Not even so much as an infinitesimal speck."

"Do you promise?"

"On my word of honor, I so swear. Will that do?"

"That will do." The most glorious, once in a lifetime kiss followed his promise. In a way she couldn't explain, the power of that kiss forever melded their hearts and souls together. Of a certainty, nothing in existence could break that bond. Brightness beyond description radiated from within as she traveled forward through time and space. She arrived at the here and now of Christmas evening despite the desire to remain in the place William had taken her.

He took a half-step back and as he broke the kiss, his fingers traced the contours of her cheek and jaw. "That distant moment, my dearest love, is my Christmas gift to you."

Even though she needed it, she couldn't find room for a breath of air. She didn't have the words that could possibly convey how she felt right now either. "Oh, William, I...I didn't know. I—"

He put gentle fingers against her lips. "You needn't say anything, Katie. The wonder I see shining within the depths of those beautiful eyes of yours speaks louder than anything you could possibly say."

"Well that's good, because there are no words. There are no words—just—thank you for sharing that beautiful memory with me. I've never had a gift that has or ever could equal it." She settled her hand over her heart. "Your gift has made me feel incredibly loved and unbelievably cherished. I only hope I make you feel the same way in return."

In response to the heartfelt desire, William kissed her again. In fact, he kissed her many times over as the magical night moved toward the dawn. Along the way, they laughed, they talked, and even took a stroll underneath the stars. The walk ended when he noticed the shiver she had held at bay until now.

Soon after they returned to her living room, William stopped in the middle of a story about his final Christmas in his mortal state. He dropped his gaze and turned his head to the side.

She glanced in the same direction. "Is something wrong?"

He took hold of her hand and gave it a squeeze. "I'm afraid so. A soldier has just arrived."

Though her heart sank, she put a smile on her face. "Then you've got to go. I'm sure he needs you."

As they both stood, he took her into his arms. "This is not the way I envisioned the end of our Christmas day."

She shrugged as she pasted a smile on her face. "Could be worse you know."

"How so?"

"Well—let's see." She tapped her finger against her lips. "Our wondrous Christmas magic could've worn off at midnight. If it had, you'd now be looking for the maiden who lost the ridiculous glass slipper. A slipper, I might add, she should never have worn in the first place. In all likelihood she was thrilled to death when the bell sounded at midnight. The pain in her feet would've been excruciating by then. Anyway, I digress.

During your frantic search for me, you would never have looked twice at the tattered girl drenched from head to toe in foul-smelling pumpkin gunk. As a tragic result, our courtship would've come to an abrupt end as duty called you away from the search."

William chuckled and as he cupped her face with his hands, his lips hovered just above hers. "Not so. Unlike the stupid prince in the story, I would've recognized you without the idiotic slipper and despite the pumpkin gunk."

****

Katie fell asleep with his whispered "I love you," echoing in her ears, and his goodnight kisses still warm on her lips. A beautiful end to the most wonderful evening of her life. She would never, ever forget it.

"You aren't stupid enough to actually believe the garbage that tumbled out of his mouth tonight, are you?"

The hateful voice crept inside her mind long before his terrible image made an appearance there. Gustavus Jameson sneered as he gazed into her eyes. Her heart began to race.

"Go away, Gustavus. You're not welcome here."

He shrugged. "You weren't welcome in my home either. Still, you entered anyway."

"You may not have welcomed us, but Quinn did, and with arms wide open. Now leave."

"Why are you so insistent I go? Are you afraid of what I might say? Are you afraid you cannot withstand the truth?"

"Truth? You wouldn't know the truth if it stared you in the face. Go back to whatever slimy pit you came from. I'm in no mood for your hatred or your lies."

"As marvelous and fun as that sounds, I needn't utter a single falsehood. The truth will work far better than any lie I could possibly tell you."

"Go away, Gustavus. Go away right now. I don't want you here." Why, oh why couldn't she banish him when William found it so easy?

"Oh, I'll go if that's what you want, but not before I give you *my* Christmas gift."

"You can keep it. I don't want anything from you."

"That very well may be. Nonetheless, I insist, because after all, I'm sure you would like to see William attending his present obligation, wouldn't you? I promise it'll be great fun."

Before she could utter another word of protest, Gustavus disappeared from the dark corners of her mind. The swirling mist he left behind gave way to clarity. She could now see William strolling through a park filled with stately weeping willow trees. With a smile on his face, he brushed the long branches off to the side and stepped through them. That's when Katie saw the beautiful, golden-haired woman who waited there under the canopy. The moment she spied William, she laughed and joyously threw her arms around his shoulders. In turn, he wrapped his arms around her waist, picked her up, and twirled her around. As he set her down on the ground, their lips met in a loving, passionate kiss.

Katie's heart dropped deep into the pit of her stomach. A lump formed in her throat as she fought back the tears she would not have Gustavus see.

"Oh, William! I'm so happy to see you," the woman cooed.

William caressed the side of her face. "My beautiful Laura Lea. I couldn't wait another minute to hold you in my arms."

Tears stung Katie's eyes as she suddenly recalled the signature on the bottom of the letter in William's personal file. Laura Lea Erickson. So *this* was the close family friend? In all the conversations she had with William, he never once mentioned her name. Why didn't he? Why did he feel the need to keep her a secret?

"You were gone so long, I worried," Laura said.

William shrugged. "As you know, the Christmas season is always a difficult one for a lot of our servicemen. Many of them choose this day, of all days, to journey from their realm into ours. When duty calls, I must answer. You know this."

"Yes, and I'm so sorry. I had hoped this season would be different for us." She brushed her fingers through his hair. "Maybe, my darling, I can help you overcome some of the sadness I see in your eyes?"

As he kissed her again, the scene faded away. Before Katie could recover, another such scene assaulted her with a ferocity that thrust her deeper into the depths of despair. This time a different woman held William's attention. The lovely brunette gazed at him with the same love and passion as the first. The only difference? This woman appeared mortal, rather than immortal. She and William were holding hands across the table in what looked like a restaurant of some kind. From her state of dress, she'd say the scene took place several decades ago.

In the intimate setting, William caressed the top of her hand with his thumb. "We couldn't have had a better ending to another perfect day."

"I agree whole-heartedly. I'm so happy you could spend the entire day with me. I always miss you so much when you're gone."

"As I miss you." He gave her the special look that spoke of his devotion. The same look he had given Katie just hours ago and one he just now shared with Laura Lea. "Just so you know? You've cheered me up when I needed it most."

The pain not only echoed but intensified what she had endured when she saw Chad with Heather. Despite all will to the contrary, tears cascaded down her cheeks. She didn't know if she could take another second.

Gustavus threw back his head and let loose a bout of evil, vile laughter. "Aww, tears already? But I have more such scenes I've gathered for your enjoyment. Don't you want to see them? After all, I went to so much effort. Wouldn't you like even a glimpse of the other mortal women he used and discarded when age took a toll on their faces?"

Her body shook with silent sobs. She took in a deep, stuttered breath, yet she couldn't manage a single word in response. How often had she worried over that very thing?

"Well, perhaps you're in no mood, hmm? I can't say I blame you. I'm sure those scenes filled you with a great deal of despair and sorrow. Still, I thought you'd like to see just how faithful your boyfriend really is to all of his women. All of them."

His lengthy pause tortured her even further. Still she refused even the smallest uttered response.

"Of course, you of all people shouldn't be surprised, right? I mean, what does a woman like you really have to offer a man like him anyway? He'll tire of you soon enough. Just like your husband did, he'll move on to someone else. When he does, it will be with someone far more beautiful. Perhaps you should prepare yourself for that."

At that moment anger rose up and somehow surpassed her tremendous sorrow. Katie clamped down on her teeth. She squeezed her eyes shut and threw her hands over her ears. "GET OUT GET OUT GET OUT! NOW!"

Laughter exploded inside her mind until little by little it faded into nothingness. Throughout the remainder of the night, her tears fell. They fell until she didn't have a single tear left. Her shattered heart lay in a million broken pieces. She felt dead inside. She couldn't undo the damage Gustavus inflicted on her heart. No matter what she did, the awful, gut-wrenching scenes he presented played over and over inside her mind. So did his malicious words. They wouldn't let her sleep and they wouldn't let her forget. She even wondered over the scenes he wanted to show her and she refused to see.

Give William the benefit of the doubt. Gustavus is evil and vindictive. Though her heart whispered the words many times over, her mind countered: *Do I really want to take the chance?*

****

Days passed in solitude. Katie didn't know how many, nor did she care. She turned off her phone as well as her computer. Right now she couldn't talk to anyone—not even her family. She didn't have the heart or the will.

"Katie! I got here as quickly as I could. What in the

world is wrong?" The voice, filled with both panic and concern, broke into her thoughts.

She turned toward the sound of it. William strode toward her and took hold of her waist. She broke away from his grasp and stepped back. "Go away, William, please…just go away."

He moved toward her again and cupped her face with his hands. "What happened? Are you ill? When is the last time you've eaten?"

Again she moved away from him. "Does it matter?"

His eyes filled with confusion. "Of course it matters. I could feel something wrong, terribly wrong, but I couldn't get here until now."

"No, I suppose you couldn't. Not when *she* required so much of your time, right?"

"She?" He shook his head. "Katie, what are you talking about? You must know I've been working with—"

"A beautiful girl with a soft, lilting laugh and long, golden hair?"

He drew his brows together. "What?"

She closed her eyes against the pain of the memory. To her horror, tears overflowed the boundary and cascaded down her cheeks. "Please…please don't lie to me. Don't you know that's far more malicious than the truth could ever be?"

"There is no woman, Katie, golden-haired or otherwise."

She held up a hand. "I saw you with Laura Lea Erickson after you left me Christmas night. I saw you."

He took a half-step back as he searched her eyes. "How did you—"

"Does it matter how I found out about the two of you?" she cut in. "The fact is, I do. Though I'm sure you'd rather I didn't, right?"

"I don't know what it is you think you know. But whatever is going on inside that beautiful head of yours, you're not even close to the truth of the matter."

"Don't, William, please don't—"

He firmed his jaw. "Okay, let's go ahead and talk about this. Did I ever date Laura? Yes, once upon a long time ago, I did. She wasn't the only woman I dated either, there were many of them along the way. That's what single mortal men and women do, don't they? Did I ever fall in love with any of them? The answer to that question is yes. To some degree I did hold affection for a few. Despite that affection, I never once considered taking any of them to the altar. Do you know why? Because somewhere in my soul, I knew none of them were you."

She huffed out a breath. "And while you waited for me to make my grand entrance, you passed the time with other mortal women?"

"Stop, Katie. You're not making any sense. What makes you think I would do something like that?"

"Gustavus showed me."

Anger replaced the confusion in his eyes. "Surely you know Gustavus filled your head with lies, Katie. Tell me you know that."

Unable to speak, she shook her head and sniffed.

William took her into his arms. He held her fast as he gazed into her eyes.

Despite all attempts, she couldn't escape.

"Look at me, Katie. Look hard and see that what I say is true."

She did as he asked, but still said nothing in return.

"Just like the fire in the Jameson's barn, Gustavus created a deceitful fabrication just so he could cause you a great deal of pain. There is no truth in the scenes he created. Not then and not now, do you understand that?"

She took in a tattered breath and held on to it for dear life.

"I love you and only you. Trust the part of you that knows this. You know you have filled every part and particle of my heart. The profound love we have for each other has endured for eons of time, Katie. Nothing and no one can change that now—unless you let it."

Her fragile heart couldn't chance acceptance despite the sincerity—maybe even the truth—she saw in his eyes. She swallowed past the knot in her throat. "In Normandy, when we first met face-to-face, you said you'd stay out of my life if that's what I desired, isn't that right?" The words came out in a pitiful sort of whisper.

William dropped his hands and took a half-step back. He shook his head. "Don't do this, Katie. Please for the love of Heaven, don't do this to us."

His pain tore at her soul. Despite the agony, she couldn't give him what he wanted. She couldn't. "I need...I need you to...to go away. I can't. Please understand...and don't come back."

He dropped his gaze for a moment. His agony, his suffering, shot like a blazing arrow through her heart.

As he lifted his head and gazed into her eyes, she saw both acceptance and resignation mingled with his pain. "So be it."

Katie opened her mouth to take back her words.

Somehow she must take away the anguish and the sorrow she inflicted.

But she was too late. Far too late. William had already disappeared.

Chapter Seventeen

"You all right, Sarge?"

The question cut like the sharpest of swords through his soul. No. No, he wasn't all right. He may never be all right again. Nonetheless, he turned toward Richard Barnett and smiled as best he could. "Rest assured this isn't the worst moment of my life."

True enough. The worst moment happened the last time he saw Katie and she said—

"If you don't mind my saying so, you've looked pretty rough around the edges here of late," he said. "Is there a reason for that and is there anything I can do to help?"

William shrugged off his concern. "Worry not, all is well."

"You aren't having trouble with one of the newer guys, are you?"

"No, for the moment the men are all fine."

"Okay, not my business. Got it. See you next time." With a firm grasp, Richie shook his hand and took his leave.

At last, all of the soldiers at this gathering had left his home save one. The one that remained behind shouldn't surprise him. He looked Don in the eye and nodded. "I thought you'd be the first one out of here since Rachel is anxiously awaiting your arrival."

"She is." For a time he held his peace. All the

while, the man probed his eyes. "The unfortunate thing is I can't leave. At least I can't leave until you tell me whatever it is you don't want any of your friends to know."

"There isn't—"

"Before you finish that sentence, know that I know you're in pain. I can see it. I have seen it, even if others cannot, even if others do not, or if they would rather not pry because of it. On the other hand, I'll not leave here until I understand the reason for your grief—plain and simple."

"I appreciate your concern. Really, I do. However, there's not a thing you can do about my present circumstances. Go on now. Rachel is waiting for you."

Don eased himself back against the cushion and propped his foot on top his knee. "Yep, she sure is and so am I."

"You can't fix the pain. No one can. So go ahead and go—your lady waits. Take advantage of each moment you can. They are most precious."

"I'll not argue with that. Nonetheless, a while back you sought me out when I would rather you hadn't. My despair and my reluctance didn't stop you from digging out the details I wanted left alone. Though I didn't tell you at the time, nor have I spoken of it since, you helped me deal with the heartache more than you might've guessed. Now if it's all the same to you, I'll return the favor. What has happened between you and Katie?"

"What makes you think this has anything to do with Katie?"

"Because I recognize that look in your eyes. I also know you've not visited Katie for quite some time now even though you've had ample opportunity. In addition, Rachel knows something is terribly wrong with Katie as well. She says Katie avoids her whenever possible. When she does get through to her on the phone, Katie keeps their conversation way too short. Rachel says she has used a number of excuses for this. None of them hold up under scrutiny. Without question she knows something is wrong. Very wrong. We both do. So with all due respect, Sergeant Griffin, spill it. Know that I won't leave until you do."

William took a seat in the chair across from him. "Okay, if you insist on doing this, you're right. I haven't seen Katie for a while. You see, the last time we were together she asked me not to come back. Ever. I've obliged the request. Does that satisfy you well enough?"

"That doesn't make sense. She loves you."

"Perhaps at one time that might've been true. I'm not so sure anymore."

"Don't be ridiculous. The kind of love you have for each other doesn't disappear overnight and you know it."

"No, but it might die over time if one believes a vicious lie long enough."

Don dropped his leg and stomped his foot on the ground. "Enough already. What vicious lie? Tell me straight out what happened, William. Don't make me drag it out of you. I hate it when you do that."

He shrugged. "I don't know all of the details myself. All I can tell you with any certainty is that sometime after I left her on Christmas night, Gustavus paid her a visit by way of a dream. At least I think he used that method. He inferred that I had—and am having—dalliances with a least a couple of women. Maybe more. Who knows what spewed out of that twisted mind of his? The images he conjured left her more devastated than you can possibly imagine. I can tell you right now, Don, I've never, ever, seen her in such pain. No matter what I said or did, I couldn't fix the damage."

"Didn't you tell her the foul miscreant conjured another bald-faced lie in order to cause her pain? She should know by now just how good he is at that. Look what he did to me and Rachel."

"Of course I did. I reminded her of all that as well. I told her I loved her and only her. Not a thing I said got through to her though. Nothing I said mattered. Somehow Gustavus caught wind of her past insecurities and vulnerabilities. Maybe he heard her discuss them with someone or simply guessed. Who knows? Regardless of how he found out, he used them against her—against us."

"Oh, man. I can't believe the sadistic old weasel would sink that low. I'm telling you right now, Hell is too good a place for the likes of him."

"Maybe that's why he avoids it." William rubbed a hand against his chin. "Anyway, I should've seen it coming. In another dream Katie had shortly after her first visit with Rachel, he said he'd exact his vengeance. I didn't think much of it at the time. In fact, I told Katie the dream probably came from her worry and nothing more. Rather than dismiss it, I should've prepared her for such an event. If I had, this might not have happened."

"I'm so sorry, William. You know time has a way of healing things, though, don't you? We see that here all the time among the soldiers within our ranks. I'm sure once she's thought about it long enough, she'll realize that everything Gustavus said and did—"

"No, I don't think so. At least not for as long as Katie's mortal. I'm not so sure there's hope even come the day she's not."

"Don't say that. In fact, don't even think it for a single moment. You can't let Gustavus destroy you as well."

William turned his gaze toward the ceiling. "You didn't see her, Don. You didn't see the expression on Katie's face, or the anguish in her eyes. I don't know if anything can heal it now."

"Let me talk to Rachel. Maybe if she just drops in on her when she least expects it, she can talk some sense into her."

"No, please don't do that. In fact, promise me you won't tell her about any of this. She shouldn't suffer any more pain than what she already has at the hands of her father. If Rachel finds out, she'll take responsibility for it. You know that just as well as I do. That's a weight she shouldn't carry."

Don dropped his head for a moment as he gazed at the floor. "You might be right about that. Have you told Isaiah about any of this yet? Perhaps he can help us find a solution."

"No, I haven't talked to him. There isn't anything he can say that will change things. In fact, there isn't anything anyone can do. Just let it go, all right?"

After their conversation ended, William went to his study and sat down at his desk. He opened the drawer and retrieved his journal. For a while he gazed at the cover and found he didn't have the heart to flip it open.

Where he once found solace in writing down his feelings, the thought of doing so now caused even more pain. He tossed it back inside the drawer and headed outside to his garden. Countless flowers were in full bloom. One in particular caught his attention. He had never before seen one with such exquisite beauty. In his opinion, the rose looked as if it created itself especially for his beautiful Katie. Any other time, he might've taken it to her. Once given, he would take delight in the radiant smile she'd give him in return.

The thought grabbed hold. What if he did? What if he put it on the table next to her bed as she slept? Would she understand and accept the deep love the rose symbolized? Such a visit wouldn't really break his promise, would it? After all, he would make sure she didn't see him.

Scant moments later, with rose in hand, he crossed the boundary that separated her realm from his. As he knew he would, he found her fast asleep. Her lashes were still wet with the tears she had shed before she had fallen into a deep slumber. He knew Gustavus didn't cause them. With the very real threat of Hell hanging over his head, he knew the worm would never devil her again. So why did she cry? Did she mourn the loss of their relationship as much as he did? If so, could they find their way back to each other, even if that moment didn't happen until the end of her life?

Though perhaps quite foolish, he would cling to that hope with all of the strength he had left. He found he couldn't do otherwise no matter how hard he tried. William gazed at the rose in indecision. Perhaps he shouldn't leave it after all. But then again—

He placed the rose on her bedside table then sat

down on the edge of her bed. For a while he drank in the beauty of her face. He took comfort in being at her side, even if he didn't belong there. The thought nagged. Once again he recalled the last time he and Katie were together and the words she had said.

No, he didn't belong here anymore. She'd made that quite clear.

With a heavy heart, he took the rose and slid it off the table. He stood, leaned down, and kissed her full on the lips. "I am so sorry for what Gustavus did to you. If I could take you back in time and prevent the incident, I'd do it in a heartbeat. You know that, don't you?" he whispered. "Nonetheless, if somewhere deep down inside you can still hear me, know that you still own my heart and soul. They are yours without condition. I've always loved you, Katie. I will always love you and only you. Nothing can or will ever change it."

****

The persistent hammering on her front door awakened Katie. She sat up and rubbed the sleep from her eyes. She drew her knees upward and wrapped her arms around them. So tired. Fatigue consumed her. As she dropped her head and closed her eyes, the knock sounded again. Louder this time.

"Katie? Open the door this minute or I swear I'll knock it down!"

"I'm coming, Mom. I'm coming."

Despite her exhaustion she slid out of bed. She donned her robe as she headed for the door. The moment she opened it, Diane barged in. Though unnecessary, Katie swept a hand toward her sofa anyway. "Come on in and make yourself comfortable. Can I get you a cup of tea or something now that you woke me up on my one and only day off?"

"Stop. Just stop. I've had enough of this nonsense, Katie. I won't stand for it a second longer. Do you hear me?"

She covered her mouth and yawned. "Enough of what nonsense, Mom? I haven't got a clue what you're talking about?"

"Oh, yes you do. I want to know what's going on. I'm not leaving here until you tell me." She held up a hand as she narrowed her eyes and gave her a sideways glance. "Don't test me on this. I promise you'll lose the battle. I've been patient long enough. I know something is terribly wrong and I'm tired of waiting for you to tell me what it is."

A lump formed in Katie's throat as she shook her head. "Please, Mom, don't—"

"Don't what? Don't care about you? Don't see the sadness in your eyes? Don't see the weight you've lost? Don't ask for the cause? I did that once before. I will not make that mistake again."

She took in a shallow breath. "No, what I—"

"Does this deep sorrow you carry have something to do with that soldier of yours?"

Katie's mouth dropped as she stared at her mother. "Wha…what soldier? What are you talking about?"

A slight smile emerged. "I thought that would get your attention."

"I don't—"

"I've seen him you know." Diane lifted her brows. "Are you surprised?"

Her fingers traveled to her throat. "When did you see him? Where?"

"In the hospital while you were in your coma. In

fact, I saw him on several occasions over the weeks you spent there. He watched over you with a ferocity that would intimidate Attila the Hun himself, I'm sure. Still, I couldn't help but notice you slept far more peacefully whenever he stood at your side. I knew then you sensed his presence. You took a great deal of comfort in it. In fact, I think you took far more comfort in his presence than you did in ours. That alone told me you were very familiar with him, so you needn't deny it."

"Well, I won't then, but—"

"Good. Now we have that out of the way, we can move on."

"You weren't afraid of him?"

"Not in the least. Should I have been?" Her mother shook her head and tsked as she patted the cushion next to her. "Oh, for Heaven's sake. Stop staring at me like I have my head on backwards and come sit down."

The lump in Katie's throat grew as she sat down next to her. "Now, is he the problem? If so, you need to tell me what's going on between the two of you."

She squeezed her eyes shut. "Please, don't ask me—"

"Sorry. I can't do that. Besides, you need to get it all out. I promise you'll feel much better after you do."

She felt like a small child as tears welled up in her eyes and slid down her cheeks. At once Diane gathered her into her arms and held her tight. She choked on a sob. The hurt tumbled out alongside the words she couldn't hold back any longer. From start to finish she gave up every detail of her relationship with William, including what happened Christmas night. "Despite it all, I still love him so much, Mom." She sniffed as she wiped at the tears. "Although I've tried so very hard, I can't make that love go away. I can't."

"Of course you can't. You know you may not agree with me right now, but he loves you too, Katie. More than you can comprehend, I'd wager. Never doubt that for a second."

She shook her head. "No, he couldn't. You forget, I saw him with those—"

"No, I don't think you saw him with anyone else at all. You only saw a disgusting illusion and deep down you know it."

She paused as her mom's certainty eased the ache in her heart. "Whether I did or didn't doesn't matter. Not when the vision plays over and over inside my mind."

"Look, regardless of what false images that awful ghost might've put inside your head, William loves you."

"How could you possibly know that?"

"Because I've seen the way he looks at you. Let me tell you something, Katie. There are countless women out there who would give up everything they own and then some to have a man look at them the way he looks at you. You are everything to him and that's a beautiful thing to see."

She grabbed a tissue from the tissue box and blew her nose. "Oh, I don't know about that."

"Well I do know. Trust me. I wouldn't say these things if I had even the slightest doubt they were true. The last thing I'd do is give you false hope. This Gustavus Jameson character has fed you a barrel full of lies and the biggest one is Laura."

"But what if she was one of the women William said he loved?"

"So what? Come on, Katie. You dated a lot of boys too. You even married one of them. Do you really think while in mortality William wouldn't have led the same kind of life?"

"No, I guess not."

"If you let the certainty of your heart overcome those fragile emotions of yours, you'll know I'm right."

"What do you mean?"

Her mother cupped her chin, tilted it upward, and smiled. "Oh, come on, Katie. Who do you trust, William or this vile Gustavus character?"

"Even if all you said is true, it's too late. I sent him away, remember? I don't think he'll come back."

Diane bobbed her head from side to side. "I'm sure if you think really hard, you can find a solution for that mistake, hmm?"

"You didn't see the look on his face when I sent him away. I'm pretty sure he won't forgive me."

"Why not give him the chance to say so himself?"

****

In the hours that followed Diane's visit, Katie thought long and hard about everything she had said. Along the way she found a touch of humor in the fact her mom didn't care that she had fallen in love with a ghost. Not—she had said—when said ghost loved her far more deeply than any mortal ever could. Katie would give anything if she could truly believe herself worthy of that love. Even if William still loved her after what she did, how long would it be before he didn't? Just as Gustavus said, she would age.

Katie gazed down at the open book on her lap then closed it and put it back on the table next to her chair. A knock on her door drew her attention. *Who would stop by this late?* Without removing the chain, she opened it, and peeked through the crack. She gasped as Donald Martin flashed a grin. "Donnie!"

"Hello, Katie. I thought perhaps it would scare you half to death if I appeared inside your living room without notice. So I thought I would knock on your door instead. Sorry if I startled you. Do you mind if I come in?"

She gaped at the spirit for a moment before her presence of mind returned. At once she unchained the lock. She opened the door wide and let him pass through. Not—she supposed—that he needed it. "What are you doing here?"

His smile broadened. "Paying you a visit of course. That is what friends do after all, right? How have you been?"

"Uh, fine. I'm fine." She waved a hand toward the living room. "Please sit down."

Once Don took a seat, she sat down in the chair nearest him. As they gazed at each other she searched for something she could say that didn't make her sound like a total idiot.

His grin said he guessed as much. Donnie chuckled. "I can see you're a bit bewildered, maybe even a tad worried over my unexpected visit. You needn't be. I'm not here because the world is coming to an end or anything else catastrophic in nature."

"Whew! What a relief." She wiped a hand across her brow and smiled. "So why are you here? Wait. I didn't mean that to sound rude, it's just that I—"

He held up a hand. "You needn't explain, Katie. In all likelihood I'm the last person you expected to show up at your door this time of night. As to why I'm here?

Well, there are a couple of reasons. One, Rachel is very worried about you. That makes me worried as well. Therefore, for both our sakes, I thought I'd stop by and make sure you're all right."

She shook her head. "I know she's concerned. I've told her many times she needn't fret over me, though. I've told her how busy I am right now with school and work. You see, I've got some difficult tests coming up and I have to—"

"Yeah, she doesn't buy those excuses any more than I do."

Heat rose to her cheeks. "I don't know what you want me to say, Don."

"You don't have to say anything. William is right. You do have very expressive eyes. They say what you might not say aloud."

A small breath of laughter accompanied the slight shake of her head. "Really? What are they saying to you right now?"

"Right now, this very minute?" He tilted his head to the side as he studied her. "That you're dying to ask me at least one question and maybe more. Am I close?"

Katie's smile faded away as she gazed at her companion.

"Come on now, don't be afraid. You can ask me anything you wish. There now. I've laid a golden opportunity in your lap. I'd take it if I were you. After all, you may never get such an offer again."

Her heart picked up its pace. She did have questions. A ton of them actually. She swallowed hard as she gathered her courage.

"Even at her age, Rachel is still a very beautiful woman, don't you think?" The words fell out of her mouth before she could put her questions in the order she wanted.

He grinned. "Not quite the subject I expected, but yes. I think Rachel is the most beautiful woman God ever created."

"Will you still think so twenty, maybe even thirty years from now?"

For a moment Don didn't say anything. He simply gazed into her eyes. After a time, he nodded. "Is that what this is all about, Katie? Is the inevitable result time has on the mortal body the reason you sent William away?"

"Well, not entirely—but shouldn't that at least be a concern?" she countered.

"Not in the least. Let me tell you something. When I look at Rachel, I see the woman I love. I see her beautiful spirit and every facet of her being which that spirit encompasses. The shell of her mortal appearance cannot in any way mask the beauty that lies beneath it. Now, if you should ask, you'd hear a similar answer from all those who are at this time in love with a mortal."

"You speak as if there are a host of such couples. William did too. But are there really as many as you say?"

"There are far more of us than what you might think there are. I'll leave it at that." Amusement filled his eyes as he gazed into hers. "Perhaps one day we'll all get together and have a huge party somewhere. Maybe we could even reserve Disneyland for an evening. I hear they do that. If so, the Haunted Mansion would have nothing over on us, right? We could really give it a run for its money."

"Sounds like a lot of fun. I've always loved the Haunted Mansion you know. It's my favorite ride—" She dropped her gaze. "But I think you'll all have to go on without me."

Don didn't respond. When the silence became uncomfortable she looked up at him. His gaze penetrated every portion of her being.

"I suppose that brings us around to the second reason for my visit." He leaned toward her and clasped his hands loosely together. "I've yet to thank you for the part you played in bringing Rachel and I together. I'd like to do that now. Without you, we wouldn't be in the glorious place we are at this moment."

She shook her head. "You don't have to thank me, Donnie. I found it such an amazing pleasure to help you both."

"Still, what you endured for us couldn't have been easy. Of course William had a hand in it as well. Because of that, I just can't sit back and do nothing for the two of you. So—" Don took a thick book from out of the side pocket of his uniform pants. He gazed at it for a moment before he placed it in her hands.

The book looked like something straight out of an elaborate, spared-no-expense, top-of-the-line fantasy film. An intricate pattern of golden spirals, intertwined with beautiful silver leaves, bordered all four edges of the umber colored cover. She had never seen anything like it. The edges of each page were all trimmed in gold as well. "What is this?"

"William's journal."

Her mouth dropped. "His journal? Why? Did he ask you to bring it to me?"

"Why? Because I know without any doubt

whatsoever you should read it." He paused as he searched her eyes. "Since he's quite busy at the moment, he doesn't know I borrowed it. He certainly doesn't know I've brought it to you. At least for now we must keep it that way. I'll return for it in the morning and put it back where it belongs. If I'm lucky, he won't have missed it while you have it in your possession. As you can see, there are a fair number of pages there. So if you want to read them all, I suggest you get started now."

With that, Don winked and disappeared. Katie gazed at the cover for quite some time before she opened the book. She fanned through the beautiful white pages. They were filled with words written in golden ink in a definite masculine hand. Katie took in a deep breath and slowly released it as she turned the pages back to the beginning. She gazed at the opening line on the very first page. As she did so, tears filled her eyes.

My dear beautiful Katie Simone Adelton, at long last I have found you...

Chapter Eighteen

The tears spilled over and trickled down her cheeks, blurring the words. At the moment, reading was impossible. She brushed the tears away then blinked until the passages shot into focus. A sweet sensation of warmth and peace engulfed her. She no longer felt she shouldn't read William's private journal without his consent. Rather, she suddenly felt she must.

With the greatest of care, she cradled the open book against her breast. She inched all the way back against the headrest and settled deeper into the cushions. Katie drew her legs up on the sofa and tucked them beneath her as she gazed at the first letter in William's journal.

My dear beautiful Katie Simone Adelton,

At long last I have found you! This in fulfillment of a promise I made you in another time and in another place. I cannot express the joy that filled my soul as the light within your spirit in an absolute and irrevocable way, interlocked with mine. No matter how far one might look, I'm sure a more perfect fit could not exist between two people. I didn't know such elation existed until that moment in time.

The thing that brings me the most joy? Isaiah said one day—and maybe in the not too distant future—the light within you would recall mine. If not in full remembrance, then at least in part. I give you my solemn vow here and now, I'll work toward that goal with all the fervor of my being.

Katie closed her eyes. For a few minutes she relived the precious memory William shared with her underneath the mistletoe. All of the feelings she experienced Christmas night returned again and with an intensity that caught her off guard. Everything inside cried out for her soldier in the hope he would hear and respond. After what she said and did to him that same evening, could she even expect it? Probably not, but she could hope, couldn't she? She waited for several agonizing minutes.

He didn't hear her, nor did he come.

"Oh, William, what have I done to you—to us?" The question gnawed at her heart as she returned to the journal.

Page after page, William expressed his deep love for her in one way or another. His letters made her laugh. Some of them touched her heart so deeply she cried. At times they called up memories long forgotten. With not even half the pages read, the journal promised so much more. She glanced up at the clock. The hands moved toward the dawn. To finish before Donnie returned, she silenced her thoughts and turned over the page.

Dearest Katie,

The raging storm cancelled your trick-or-treat plans this Halloween. When your mom broke this news, you knitted your little fingers together. You dropped your gaze to the floor and bravely fought back the tears. Without a word of protest, you nodded. Nonetheless, you looked so devastated. That look must've tugged at your daddy's heart just as it tugged on mine. In a single instant Andrew turned the tide and saved Halloween for you. Without a word of explanation, he grabbed his keys and left the house. He returned a short while later with what he deemed "scary movies ill-suited for the faint of heart." Therefore, he said, perhaps you might want to leave the room? You bristled over the suggestion and gave him "the look." I laughed outright when you told him that he rather than you might want to leave the room when you played them.

While you sorted through the movies, he filled the largest bowl he could find with everyone's favorite candy. He also insisted you wear your costume because, said he, it wouldn't be Halloween without costumes. Everyone in the household joined in the fun as did the friends and neighbors he invited over. You were by far the most adorable little witch I have ever seen.

You know what though? Those movies worked their intended magic in a most unexpected way. By the time you toddled off to bed, you were scared half to death. You thought any number of monsters had hidden underneath your bed, inside your closet, or outside your window. Although you couldn't hear or see me, I promised you I would keep you safe. You gave me such a sweet smile when I said I would banish all evil monsters from your room. I vowed I would send them so far away, they'd never find their way back. That brief connection between us took me by surprise. I took hold of your little hand and held it until you fell into a deep, peaceful sleep. The interesting thing? You curled your fingers around mine in return. Dare I believe I am finally making progress?

Katie remembered the Halloween he spoke of. Because of those movies, every shadow in her bedroom had become something sinister. So did the windblown branches that terrified her beyond reason. All throughout the night they scratched at her window. That night she knew her dear friend—William—truly existed. If he hadn't, then without a doubt in her mind, the zombies, vampires, mummies, and werewolves would've torn her limb from limb. The memory as well as the conviction brought a smile to her face.

Dearest Katie,

At last you heard the song I so desperately wanted you to hear. That song spoke the words of my heart far better than any other I have heard to date. As I wished, the lyrics found their way deep inside you, just as they had within me. I believe it no less than a miracle the song had been included in a ghostly movie your mom loved. She bought the film and invited you to watch it with her during the lazy afternoon hours. With time on your hands, you accepted the invitation. I'm so glad you did.

As I sat next to you there on the sofa, "Unchained Melody" began to play in the background. At that delightful moment, I asked you to listen to the words— really listen—for they were mine. To my utmost delight, you did. You must've mulled them over because at the end of the movie, you asked Diane if she knew the name of the song. She did and gave you the name as well as the artist. You hurried off to the store and bought it. At the risk of driving your mama crazy, you played it countless times. So much so that before I left you that evening, you could sing every word. Did you hear me sing it with and to you? Could you feel even the smallest portion of the love I have for you as I did so?

She looked up from the letter. Is that why she loved the song so much? The thought sounded as reasonable as any other. Besides, that particular reason made her feel better. As she dropped her gaze on the right hand page, a familiar name caught her eye.

I suppose I knew deep down inside that one day some lucky guy would take you in his arms. That he, and not me, would give you your first real kiss. Though I knew it, I guess I didn't prepare myself well enough to see it happen. I think if I could've somehow stopped Paul Adamson without an obvious intrusion on my part, I would have. Someone may as well have kicked me in the gut for the way I felt as he pressed his lips against yours. My own fault though, because I could've spared myself the heartache if only I'd left you sooner. After all, I should've known he'd end your evening that way. What man in his right mind wouldn't have? How I wished I could have been that man.

Ah, Katie, now that he's awakened the woman inside the girl, will you ever remember me now? If you do, will it even matter? Will you choose someone who can hold you with warm tangible hands over someone who cannot? At some future date will the desire for a husband and children become more important than the love we have ever had for each other?

The letter tore at her heart. In a vague sort of way, William mentioned the men in her life the night he had kissed her for the first time. Yet she didn't understand—until this very moment—his deep distress and utter devastation because of them. She could only imagine what he must've felt as he witnessed the parade of boyfriends she'd had throughout her life.

What about her marriage to Chad? William suffered the same pain she did when Gustavus showed her the images of those women. She knew that now. The only difference? For the need of revenge a hateful, twisted entity created brutal lies so he could tear them apart.

The scenes that caused such torment never happened. William couldn't say the same thing. If only she'd known—

After she had accepted the high school ring of her first steady boyfriend, William's letters took a turn. If the duration in between them served as evidence, he didn't visit her as much as he had before. In fact, he didn't visit unless he sensed that she needed him in her moments of deep sorrow and despair. He never once failed her during those times despite the anguish she must've caused him in return. Nonetheless, she captured a glimpse of his sadness in the letters that spoke of her marriage to Chad. The only thing that overshadowed his pain? His overwhelming need to protect her in every way he could.

At last she arrived at the letter where he talked about their first meeting in Normandy. His obvious joy as the hero that conquered their obstinate wall leapt from off the pages. The images he painted of that event made her laugh as only he could. He wrote her a letter each time he visited her thereafter. The detail, as well as his comments, both delighted and amazed her.

All of that changed with the last entry in his journal. In this letter he spoke about the final time they were together. She could feel his agony, his desolation, and pain as easily as she had her own. How she hated being the reason for it. Why did she—even for one minute—believe Gustavus? Oh, how she wished she could take it all back. She shook her head as her gaze fell on the final thoughts recorded in his journal.

Ah, Katie, can you not in any way understand the love I have for you is pure, perfect, and unconditionally yours? There is nothing in your world or mine that could ever equal it or destroy it—least of all another woman. All you need do is take it.

Katie released a ragged breath as she closed William's journal. She slid down the length of the cushions and turned onto her side. All the while she held onto the book. Somehow it made her feel close to him. In a strange sort of way, it seemed he sat beside her. As she centered her thoughts on William, her eyelids grew heavier and heavier still. One thought occupied her mind as she drifted toward peaceful slumber. She had to find a way back to him—she just had to because she loved him more than she could ever express.

"Please, William," she silently whispered. "Please, please forgive me."

****

Muted sunlight awakened her. Yet full consciousness lagged far behind. As memory returned, she looked down and found her arms empty. At once she bolted upright and looked for William's journal. She didn't find it. Donnie must've returned and taken it, just as he said he would.

Dear Donnie. She wished she could've seen him so she could thank him for the gift. A gift that wouldn't serve any purpose unless she somehow fixed her mistake. Would William listen? Would he give her a second chance?

She chose the words she would say with the

greatest of care. While she showered, she practiced the speech over and over again. Rather than wear her jeans, she chose her blue, three-tiered Renaissance dress that William adored. He said he loved it because the color matched her eyes. She brushed the tangles from her hair and fussed with her makeup. Katie studied the results in her full-length mirror.

"All right then," she said aloud. "I suppose this is as good as it will get today. Moment of truth time."

Her heart picked up its pace as she entered her living room. She stood in the center and swallowed past the dryness in her throat. "William? Can you hear me? I need you. Please come and talk to me, it's really important. Please?"

For several minutes she stood there and waited for his arrival. He didn't come. When fatigue set in, she sat down on the sofa and waited a while longer. Why didn't he come as he once promised he would? All throughout the day she paced and she sat. More than once she flipped through a magazine she didn't read and tossed it. Along the way she wiped the tears whenever they fell, and they fell often. The wait—and the fact that William ignored her plea—took its toll on her battered heart. She didn't know what else to do.

Well past midnight and any of the hope she had carried, Katie entered her bedroom. She changed out of the dress and hung it up in the closet. As the lump in her throat grew ever larger, she slipped into her nightgown. She sat down on the edge of her bed.

As the first tears fell, she gazed heavenward. "Oh, William, you said if I called your name, you'd come...but you didn't. You didn't. Then again, how can I blame you?"

****

Katie slept very little that night. Despite her exhaustion, she left her bed just as the sun peeked over the horizon. She slipped into her favorite pair of jeans and her black flannel shirt. Both had seen far better days. No matter. What she looked like didn't make any difference now. After she brushed her teeth and hair, she headed outside. She didn't have a clue as to why. Perhaps she simply needed fresh air and ample space in which to mourn. As she gazed about the area, the path she had walked so many times with William beckoned. Without a second thought, she accepted the invitation.

A soft breeze and the song of morning birds accompanied Katie as she wandered down the pathway. The bareness of winter still lingered. Before long the trees would wake up, though. They would dress themselves in the vivid colors of spring. The wild grass and flowers would follow in vibrant display. Would she see the beauty of it now—or for the way she felt dead inside, would she only see the weeds?

From afar off, the Johanssons' dog caught sight of her. With his usual gusto, the basset hound bounded toward her. The moment he arrived at her side, the dog sat down in the hope of some love and affection. Katie never felt less like giving it. Nonetheless, Bobo's big, droopy eyes and a wild tail that created a small vortex of dust coaxed a response. Katie stooped down, scratched him behind his ears, and rubbed the soft fur along the sides of his neck. In turn, he gave her a lick and dropped his head against her body.

She eased him back onto his haunches and shook a playful finger at him. "You men are all alike. You capture a woman's heart with no more than that soulful look and then you have us eating out of your hands. I'm not at all sure that's—"

"You mean that's all it takes? Really? What about the flowers, chocolates, and the long list of ridiculous promises? All this time I believed if a man could just discover the correct combination to this most mystifying of all secrets, he'd have his lady's heart without condition."

Katie gasped and leapt to her feet. She whirled around and almost stumbled right through him. At once he grabbed her waist and steadied her feet.

"Hello, Katie."

"Oh, William! What are you doing here? I mean, I didn't think you were com—well, it's just that I love you so much and…and… No, wait. I know I'm saying this backwards. First, I must tell you how very sorry I…I know now I should never have let Gus—"

William's captivating kiss ended her mindless prattle. Not that she minded. She couldn't remember a word of her rehearsed speech anyway.

****

Katie's passionate response to his kiss acted as a balm to his soul. How he wished the kiss could go on forever. Despite all will to the contrary, he took a half-step back. Without relinquishing his hold as she caught a much needed breath, he gazed into her glistening eyes. He caught the first tear as it fell. "Why the tears, my love?"

She brushed them away and sniffed. "I waited for you all day yesterday and half of the night. You didn't come. I thought you'd at least come and tell me you didn't want me anymore. I'd given up hope for even that and I thought…I thought maybe you couldn't be bothered. Not that I would've blamed you because—"

He put a finger against her lips. "I told you I'd always come, even if it took a little more time than either of us might desire. Don't you remember?"

"Yes, you did say that. I guess for all the turmoil, I must've let that part slip my mind."

He gave her a wink. "Understandable. I won't hold it against you, I promise."

"It's just that I really, really wanted to see you— needed to see you."

"You don't know how much that warms my heart. I didn't know for sure what you wanted to say."

"Does that mean instead of ignoring me, you were with some soldiers before you came then?"

He took hold of her hand and turned her toward her house. As they strolled along the path, he nodded. "A suicide bomber took the lives of several of our special forces at an army base in Iraq. Perhaps you saw it on the news?"

"No, I didn't. I haven't watched TV for...for awhile."

"Well, as you might expect, all of them needed time and a bit of help as they worked through a wide range of emotions."

"I'm so sorry. They, as well as their families, must be devastated."

"They are. One of them had just found out his wife had given birth to their son. He had but one week before his scheduled leave."

She stopped and faced him. With the softest possible touch, she laid a hand against his cheek and caressed his face with her thumb. An incredible blend of love and concern filled the depths of her beautiful blue eyes. He reveled in it.

"I wished I could somehow take away some of the sorrow I see on your face. I just don't know how."

He took her hand and kissed it. "Didn't you know? You already have."

The barest hint of a smile curved her lips. "How might I have done so wondrous a thing?"

"As always, by mere presence alone. However, I must admit your heartfelt 'I love you' a moment ago helped more than you might guess. To be quite honest, I didn't think I'd ever hear you say it again. I mourned the loss."

She gulped. "Oh, William, I never once stopped loving you. In fact, I found out I couldn't stop no matter how hard I tried."

"You tried?"

"For a while, yes, I did. I thought if I did, it would stop the pain."

The desire, if even a passing one, made him wince. "May I ask what changed your mind?"

"The impossibility of it, for one. My mom had something to do with it as well."

"She did?"

"Um-hmm. She paid me an unexpected visit. No matter what I said, she wouldn't leave until I told her the reason for my sorrow. I ended up telling her everything that had happened between us since I met you in Normandy. I left nothing out. The story didn't surprise her in the least." Katie paused for a moment. "I hope you don't mind?"

"No, I don't mind at all."

"That's good, because she saw you, you know."

He gave her a sideways glance. "Did she?"

"Yep."

"Would that have been at the hospital while you were in your coma?"

Her mouth dropped. "You knew?"

"Well, not for certain. A couple of times it seemed she gazed right into my eyes. I wondered then if she could see me or if that exact mark just happened to be her point of focus."

"No, she saw you. Several times, in fact. Want to know something else?"

"I'm all ears."

"She's quite happy with our—um—unusual relationship. Furthermore, she told me if I looked hard enough, I could find a way to mend my mistake in sending you away. What do you think of that?"

"I think her wisdom isn't anything less than phenomenal." He gave her hand a gentle squeeze. "Now. You said she had something to do with it. Did anything or anyone else have a hand in this fine reunion of ours? If so, I'll need to thank them."

"I, uh, don't want you to get upset at him or at me, okay?"

"Okay."

"You promise?"

He chuckled. "Cross my heart and hope to die."

She took a deep breath. "Donnie brought me your journal in repayment, he said, for what we did for him and Rachel. I spent an entire night reading it."

He grinned. "How could I possibly get upset over that? They are your letters after all. Besides, you heard them all once before, even if you don't remember much about it."

The faraway look in her eyes accompanied a

wistful smile. "I wish I did. If I had only remembered them, I would never have let Gustavus use me like he did. I would never have doubted you and I most certainly would never have sent you away. I hope you believe me. More important, I hope you can forgive me and maybe get back to where we were before I messed things up?"

William shook his head as he pulled her in close with a single arm. Though he held her fast, he used a gentle touch as he caressed the side of her cheek and traced down along her jaw. From there he cupped her face as he took full possession of her lips. He hoped his kiss told her she hadn't done anything that needed his forgiveness. That he loved her more than he could express with words alone. If his kiss could speak, he hoped it said his love for her was both endless as well as timeless. In every way imaginable, he was hers and hers alone.

She must've got the message for she responded with a kiss of her own. Through it she gave without hesitation or reservation, the gift of her heart and soul. He could feel it as easily as he did the sun. She promised him every moment of forever and everything forever included. Though he already knew the answer, he spoke the question aloud as he ended the kiss—just so he could hear her say it. "Are you sure, Katie? Will I be enough for you in the years to come?"

"Yes, I'm sure. There is nothing in this life or in the life beyond that I want as much as I want you." Of a sudden, her eyes lit up. "No—wait. Maybe there is something else I want. If not more, then at least just as much, and you're just going to have to find a way to give it."

"Something else? Like what?"

"Like more time with you than what I've had so far. You might say that's impossible. But I think I just might have a solution to the problem—at least, I hope I do."

He assumed the most serious look he could manage. No easy feat there. Especially not when he wanted to shout his joy all the way to Heaven and back. "You do?"

"Yep."

"I see. Mind letting me in on the details?"

A touch of mischief filled her eyes as she cleared her throat in a most exaggerated manner. "There isn't much to it, really. I'm just calling in my voucher, Sergeant William Malloy Griffin. Lest you've forgotten, you lost a bet a while back. Therefore, you still owe me one very special, out-of-the-ordinary request. One you must present to General Thomas right away."

Chapter Nineteen

"This is quite the birthday bash, don't you think? I've never seen anything like it ever before. Then again, I bet no one else has for that matter either." Donnie's grin broadened as he gave Rachel a gentle nudge. Yet he never once broke eye contact with Katie. "Don't worry. Even though Rach deserves full credit for putting this shindig together, you can thank me for it later anyway."

For a moment, Katie gazed toward the couples who filled the backyard of Rachel's lovely beach home in Galveston. Some of them were engaged in conversation with each other. Others sat at the tables and enjoyed food from the various buffets suitable to their taste and form. At one time it might've surprised her to know that spirits ate. It didn't anymore. Many couples danced to the music provided by Jared and Justin who, in hilarious fashion, acted as deejays.

Rachel had insisted Katie's cousins come and take part in the festivities tonight. After all, she said, if not for Katie's cahoots partners, she and Don would not be together now. The twins took pleasure, as well as full credit, for that.

They took just as much delight in her and William's relationship once they met him. She hadn't known about his visit until afterward. The moment he left them that day, they called her. William had said that since he couldn't seek approval from her father right now, he thought he would ask them instead. The twins put him through the wringer of course, as only they could. William didn't take offense though. Jared said by the end of their discussion, they were all the best of friends. Justin told her they didn't think another man on this earth—or one beyond it for that matter—deserved her heart more than he did. Therefore, they said, they gave them their blessing. Their love and support meant more than she could say.

From all appearances, the mortals in attendance tonight found it delightful there were others in this world that were in love with—and loved in return by—spirits. Here they could celebrate it with those who were just like themselves. She found it such a beautiful thing to see.

She gazed first at Don and then at Rachel. "I think it's amazing. Thank you both so very much for the gift. I've enjoyed myself far more than you might guess."

"Our absolute pleasure." Rachel looked out over the crowd. "You know what though? This has been just as much fun for me and Don as it has been for you, I'm sure. Everyone I've talked to this evening says the same thing. So Don and I thought maybe we could throw this same kind of party every year. Imagine how many couples we might have ten years from now. What do you think?"

"I think it's a brilliant idea. Maybe by then we really would need a night at Disneyland reserved especially for us." She giggled as she gazed at Don. "Haunted mansion, here we come."

"Now that one I could go for," he said. "I didn't tell you this when we spoke of it before, but my uncle took me there once a very long time ago. Up until I met Rachel, I considered it the best day of my life. I knew then I had to go back someday. I never did."

Katie shrugged. "What stopped you? The way you all pop in and out, traveling to Disneyland whenever you feel like it should be a walk in the park."

Don took hold of Rachel's hand as he turned and gazed into her eyes. "Well you see, once upon a time I promised my sweetheart I'd take her there. Therefore, I didn't have the heart to go without her."

As Rachel leaned in close for Don's kiss, William approached them. Though his eyes were filled with amusement, he shook his head and tsked.

"Looks like I've arrived just in time to rescue my lady from this shameless spectacle." He turned toward her and offered her his hand. "Care to dance with me, my love?"

She laughed as she placed her hand on top of his— a thing she now could do with ease. "Yes, I'd love to dance with you."

The moment he led her toward the courtyard that now served as the dance floor, Jared picked up his microphone. "Here they come, ladies and gentlemen, our lovely birthday girl and the man who captured her heart. Let's celebrate that, what say you?"

To the sound of applause, Martha wheeled out a very large, three-tiered cake, glowing from top to bottom with candles. Katie drew in a breath as she looked at William. He winked in return. This she had not expected and would rather not have had, thank you very much.

"Yes indeed, here she comes," Jared said. "If you can't see her for the crowd, she's the one with the red face that almost matches her hair. The very one whose eyes are shooting daggers at me right now. Ouch. Geez, Katie, none of this is my fault. I'm just a guest."

Justin grabbed his mic off the table. "Ah, but isn't she adorable? How about we sing 'Happy Birthday' loud enough to wake the dead? Uh-oh, now I'm the one in trouble. That's okay, I can take a hit for the team every now and again. Hey, check it out everyone! Her escort is laughing because he knows I'm right. Careful, William, that might get you in trouble as well. You know what that means, right? If not, it means no kisses later on, bro."

Everyone laughed as William steered her toward the cake. As the crowd sang, she blew out the candles in one breath.

"Perfect! I hope you made a special wish, Katie, because I know William has. You see, he has requested a very special song for his very special lady. So while Martha cuts the cake for all you mortals out there, let's get to it, shall we?"

The cheers, whistles, and applause died down as—much to her delight—"Unchained Melody" wafted through the speakers.

William wrapped an arm around her waist and took hold of her hand. As they swayed to the tempo of the music he gazed into her eyes. "Have I told you that I love you and that you look exceptionally beautiful tonight?"

Katie had chosen a semi-formal turquoise-blue, off-the-shoulder dress and accented it with the sapphire jewelry her parents gave her for Christmas. With the way he looked at her right now, it made her happy she took extra time with her hair and makeup. She smiled.

"Thank you, kind sir. I love you too, and you look pretty good yourself."

He did look good too, dressed in a black, western-style suit, white shirt, and tie. As always, his flirty grin sent her blundering butterflies into some sort of out-of-control, topsy-turvy free-for-all. She hoped that would never change.

"Thank you kindly, ma'am." He gathered her a bit closer. "So tell me, are you enjoying your evening?"

"Yes, I am and not just because it's my birthday. Take a look at everyone here, William. They all look so happy. I'm so glad they can share this moment with other couples just like them."

"Me too—and to think you had a hand in creating some of the joy you see right here tonight."

"*We* had a hand in it," she corrected.

"Ah, but if not for your one very special, out-of-the-ordinary request, the work we have undertaken would never have happened."

"I'm still amazed General Thomas granted us permission. I actually didn't expect it. Apparently he is as kind and compassionate as the history books all say he is."

"I won't argue with the history books on that point. Besides, General Thomas thinks it's good for the morale of those who've struggled far too long. If you stop and consider it, it's kind of an extension of what your future plans are anyway. So why not help the veterans you can now? Regardless of the general's reasons, I'm not about to question our good fortune. We've had far more time together because of it.

She wouldn't question it either. If anything, she hoped their work would continue until she drew her last breath. Even then, it still would be fun to help soul mates find their way to each other.

After "Unchained Melody" ended, the twins followed up with "Love is a Many Splendored Thing" and "Twelfth of Never" as William had asked. He had sung those songs to her as they danced on Christmas evening. That part of her Christmas day she would always hold dear to her heart. What followed shortly thereafter could sink into the outer depths of oblivion for all she cared. As "Twelfth of Never" faded out, William led her toward the edge of the dance floor. From there, they slipped into the shadows.

"Want to take a little walk with me along the beach?" He gave her a roguish grin as he cocked his head toward the ocean. All the while his eyes danced with mischief. "I found a place that no one else has invaded as of yet tonight. In this place we could be all alone."

"Oh, I don't know about that," she teased. "Is such a place safe?"

He shook his head ever so slightly. "Can't guarantee it."

"Hmm. Well, it is my birthday. So far everything has been perfect. So I suppose I can afford a small risk."

"Might not be so small," he countered.

"Now you have me intrigued." She kicked off her shoes and abandoned them at the far edge of the lawn.

Hand in hand they strolled along the sandy beach without a word passing between them. Right now they weren't necessary. Not when they simply enjoyed each other's company.

After a time, Katie gazed up at the radiance of the

night sky. The full moon and stars appeared far more brilliant than what she had ever seen them before. The sound of the lazy ocean waves as they crashed onto the shore made for a wondrous melody. For her love of the ocean, Rachel chose this venue as part of her birthday gift. For the beautiful memories her friend created tonight, Katie could never thank her enough.

She took in a deep breath of the heady brine as she closed her eyes. "The night is so beautiful, don't you think?"

"Yes, it is." He halted her steps and turned her toward him. "I conjured it especially for you, don't you know."

She hid her smile. "You did?"

William chuckled. "Yes, but only if you think so. Still, I'll have you know the night is not half as beautiful as you are."

Before she could respond to the compliment, he cupped her face and joined his lips to hers. At once he dropped his hands and wrapped his arms around her waist. He cuddled her close to his chest. She could swear she felt every portion of his body as if he were mortal. The warmth between them amazed her. One wondrous kiss turned into two and then three. Her heart swelled with the love she had for her soldier.

He broke away long enough for her to catch her breath and then he kissed her again. "I have a gift for you, but I'm not sure I should give it."

"Why not?"

"Because it just might freak you out. On the other hand—"

She lifted her hand. "I promise you I won't get freaked out, so give it up already."

"What I have to show you isn't like the other visions I've shared. This one is a future event. Do you think you can you handle it?"

Katie wrapped her arms around his neck and laughed. "Why don't we both find out?"

He chuckled. "Why don't we just—"

****

As William leaned down and kissed her, a brilliant, incandescent light flooded her mind's eye. Within the light, a lovely pink and white bedroom shot into focus. Dainty floral wallpaper decorated the walls from floor to ceiling. On the wall to her left, she spied a large framed picture of William. She had never seen the photograph before. Someone must've taken the picture before he entered the service. He wore a pair of jeans and a two pocket shirt that she guessed may've been beige in color. He had a booted foot propped up on an old wooden fence. His crossed arms rested upon his knee. With his cowboy hat tilted upward, he sported a charming grin for the camera. Her heart fluttered as she gazed at the portrait.

On the right hand side of the room there were pictures of her family hanging in small clusters above her bureau. On top of the bureau sat many of her personal treasures. Some of them she knew well, some she had never seen before. Nonetheless, she knew without question they all meant a great deal to her.

She gazed out of the open French doors. A warm breeze played with the white, sheer curtains that hung from them. While they swung to and fro, Katie inhaled the rich scent of honeysuckle mixed with roses. She gazed out over the ocean from what had to be the second floor of the home. The beauty of the rolling waves that tumbled onto the shore had a soothing effect on her soul.

William appeared at her side then. As he approached her, he gave her that grin that never failed to awaken her kaleidoscope of butterflies. Before she could say a word, he offered her his hand. "Are you ready to go home, my love?"

Home? Did he mean—? Excitement filled her entire being as she placed her hand in his. "Oh, William, is it finally time to begin the forever part of our life together?"

His grin grew ever broader as he gazed into her eyes. "Yes, my love, it finally is."

She let go of a breath as tears filled her eyes. "I've been ready for that since the first day we met."

"Come on then, let's go. I have so much I want to show you."

She didn't give her mortal body so much as a passing glance. In the mere blink of an eye she passed through a dazzling crystal portal that must surely be made of the most brilliant starlight. Once on the other side of it, she and William walked down a luminescent fairy path. The same fairy path she'd seen in a vision on a Christmas evening so long ago. This time, William turned in the opposite direction of where their magnolia tree stood. There along the side of the pathway, she saw a beautiful park filled with trees and flowers. Her parents and grandparents were there awaiting her arrival, as were Rachel and Don. A host of friends and family who had gone on before were also in attendance. Each of them welcomed her with smiles and open arms.

After the short celebration ended, William once again claimed her hand. As they continued their stroll along the path, she gazed at the unbelievable beauty of the luxuriant meadows on either side of the walkway. Beautiful horses grazed in the meadow to the right. She could see Warrior and Miss Scot among them. As she searched for Shahar, her gorgeous Saddlebred pinto bolted from the middle of the group and ran up to greet her. She knew now what William meant by that sweet reunion he had with Warrior, for she had one now with the dearest horse she had ever had.

After she gave her mare the affection she craved, they continued their journey. Magnificent trees in countless varieties beautified the path. So did the unimaginable splendor of the flowers in every shape and hue. They seemed to have grown in wild abandon everywhere she looked. Their fragrance was indeed, something to die for.

William gave her a nudge. With a nod of his head, he directed her attention toward the opulent home up ahead. "That one is ours. Does it meet with your approval?"

Her mouth dropped as she gazed at the amber walkway that led to the doors of their home. The white marble facade surrounded a multitude of square paned windows that reflected the light. Ornate pillars, such as she had never seen before, circled the home.

"Oh, William. Never in my wildest dreams have I ever imagined anything so exquisite."

William stopped shy of the large double doors and opened them. At once he picked her up in his arms and carried her over the threshold. She felt like a bride with her groom. Without releasing her from his arms, he kissed her as he had never kissed her before. That kiss caused an unquenchable fire to burn deep within her soul. A fire that encompassed every aspect of the wild, fierce, passionate love they shared. A love that at the same time also spoke of gentle tenderness and deep commitment for and to each other. Another such kiss followed.

****

William broke the kiss and flashed a devilish grin. "I think we better stop this vision right here, before I get in trouble."

As the vision closed, she breathed out a sigh. She hated the scene to end. How she wished she could live in the moment forever.

With a gentle touch, he caressed the side of her face. "There you go, happy birthday, from me to you."

"Thank you so very, very much." She gazed into his eyes. "Will it truly be so?"

"I promise you when the day comes, you will love every moment of it—and then some."

"Please tell me. How long will I have to wait for that day to arrive?"

He chuckled. "I'm so sorry, my love. I can't tell you the exact time or place. If I should do such a horrendous thing, I might risk everything we have right now."

"Can you at least tell me the location of the house where I'll draw my last mortal breath?"

He shook his head. "Sorry. I'm sure you'll figure it out yourself someday."

"Then in fair exchange, I want the picture of you I saw on the wall."

"That I can arrange."

She nodded. "Okay, I can live with that. As long as we are together as we are now for the rest of my life, I won't mind the wait. Besides, we still have a lot of work to do, right?"

"Indeed we do, and once you return home, we'll get right to it. You see, Bartholomew has asked us for a little help."

She gasped in delight. "Bartholomew? Finally, after all of this time?"

"After all this time he found the one he's been searching for. She needs a little nudge in the right direction, though."

"Oh, I'm excited to get started. Where are we headed?"

"A little village called Cherry Valley in Otsego, New York."

"Sounds like my cup of tea. Can we begin the preliminaries tomorrow?"

"I don't see why not." He paused for a moment as he searched her eyes. "I won't regret giving you my birthday gift, will I? I mean, you're sure you won't mind waiting for our own happily ever after?"

"Not if you kiss me now, I won't."

He complied. Her butterflies soared higher than they had ever soared before. She let them go without a fuss.

Instead, the joy within her grew. No, she wouldn't mind the wait. Because in the meantime she knew with the passing of each day—just as they had since that wondrous day in Normandy—they'd fall deeper and deeper in love.

A word from the author...

Making an impossible love quite possible after all...

I am an author of paranormal and fantasy romance. I have (and have always had) a soft spot for fairy tales, the joy of falling in love, making an impossible love possible, and happily-ever-after endings. I love music, art, beautiful sunrises, sunsets, and thunderstorms.

When I'm not busy conjuring my latest novel, I spend time with the members of my very large and nutty family here in the lovely, arid deserts of southern Nevada. I also pursue my interests in family history, mythology, and history.

Visit me at www.dk-peterson.com

~*~

Other Debbie Peterson titles
available from The Wild Rose Press, Inc.:
Bound by Oath and Honour
Court of the Hawk
Spirit of the Knight
Spirit of the Rebellion
Spirit of the Revolution